IN THE MATTER OF MICHAEL VOGEL

by Drew Yanno

A PELLEGRINO PRESS Imprint

ISBN: 0615757588

To Suzanne, for everything

Rock City Evening Telegram
September 23, 1966
"Inquest to Look Into Boy's Death"

New York State Attorney General Richard A. Palumbo announced today that a judicial inquest will be held to look into the August 10th death of eight-year-old Michael Vogel.

The Honorable George R. Bartlett will preside over the hearings, which are scheduled to commence on November 7th down at the state capital. Evidence is expected in the form of witness testimony and written statements from all key parties involved.

The attorney general stated that the inquest is necessary because authorities have determined that it's likely that no one will ever go to trial for the boy's murder and that it may be the only way to get the facts surrounding the investigation into the public record.

SAM FISHER

They found Mikey's body at the bottom of the deep end of the swimming pool, right under the diving board. The pool director said all the washed-off Coppertone and baby oil made it hard to see that far down and that was why no one saw him when they cleared out the pool earlier in the day to look for him. I don't see how anyone could have believed that. I know I didn't. Then again, I don't think anybody thought somebody would actually kill an eight-year-old kid. We live in a small town where nobody ever kills anybody. Well, not very often anyway.

I didn't really know Mikey, except by name. Like I said, our town is real tiny. The front page of the phone book says we have 8,787 people living here, but that's from the 1960 census. It's six years later, so it's probably less now that all the factories have moved out. Being that small, everyone pretty much knows everyone else. If you don't know a kid, you probably know his brother or sister. That's the way it was with Mikey Vogel. His older sister Sylvia is in my class in the junior high school here in town. She doesn't hang around in the same group I do. She wears glasses and keeps her hair shorter than most other girls, and so my friends make fun of her sometimes. You know, normal boy stuff. I have to admit I never did much to stop them. That was just another reason I should have felt bad for her. Heck, she's someone I sat next to at assembly in the school auditorium for a whole year. I even gave her a Valentine for six straight years in grade school, although the

3

teachers made us do that. Mostly, though, I felt bad because I was pretty sure someone killed Mikey and I thought I knew why and there wasn't too much I could do about it.

You probably wonder why I didn't tell someone what I knew, maybe my parents or one of my friends. The cops even. Any one of them might have seemed like a good idea, I guess, but fear will do that. See, I was afraid I might be next on their list if it got out that maybe I knew something about Mikey, and if it ever did get out, I knew nobody would be able to save me. Not my parents. Not any of my friends. Not even the cops. So I just kept my mouth shut and hoped no one would ever find out what I knew.

Even if I thought someone could protect me, there was another problem. I didn't really know who "they" were. I knew where Mikey was the night before he died and I was pretty sure I knew what they were all doing out there when he showed up. I just couldn't tell who they were. It was pretty much impossible really. First of all, it was nighttime and that had something to do with it, but they had a fire going so I could see OK. The main thing was they were all naked and covered in paint from head to toe, even their faces. Actually, I couldn't even say that for sure since they all wore masks. Not like the Lone Ranger kind, these were all different and scary, like something you'd see in a horror movie or National Geographic. It was so scary that when I woke up the next morning, I wondered if maybe I dreamed the whole thing and never even was out there. Until they found Mikey at the bottom of the pool later that same night. I definitely knew it was real then.

I was there at the pool that day, too. Most every kid in town was, just like on any hot summer day. I saw Mikey there too, right after it opened. We didn't talk to each other or anything. Like I said, I didn't know him. Besides, I was pretty sure Mikey didn't see me out there by the railroad tracks the night before. It's a place they call the old hobo camp, and it's in the middle of nowhere about a mile outside of town. They had already grabbed him when

4

I got there, at the end of the path. The rest of them were still busy doing what they were doing, which was scary enough to see, so I just took off running back the way I came.

The whole time I was running, I was afraid maybe somebody saw me and might know who I was. If they did, then they'd probably be coming after me too. I wondered later if I might have been able to help Mikey if I stayed, but after he showed up dead, I figured that would have just made two of us.

I actually thought I might never see Mikey again after that, so I was pretty surprised when I saw him at the pool the next day. Part of me even thought that maybe what I saw the night before wasn't so bad and that maybe things like that went on all the time. After all, there was Mikey, alive and walking around like the night before never happened, but then a couple hours later the pool director made an announcement over the loudspeaker that Mikey Vogel should come to the front desk. I got a sick feeling then.

"Oh shit," I said out loud. I didn't mean to.

"What?" my friend Richie asked. "Did something happen to him? Did you see it?"

Richie is the kind of kid who loves bad things. Gun shots. Hurricanes. Car accidents. Which is kind of weird, seeing as his own brother died in a car accident when Richie was five and his mother left a couple months later and he's been living alone with his father since then, which is no picnic. Not when the guy drinks a quart of Jim Beam every night.

I'm sure Richie meant did something happen to Mikey there at the pool. Some sort of kid thing. A fistfight. A cut foot. The usual stuff that happens at the pool. He couldn't have had any idea of what I was thinking.

I just shook my head.

"What did you say 'shit' for then?" he asked.

"Cause a kid gets lost and they make everyone get out," I said.

"How do you know he's lost?" my other friend Keith asked.

"Maybe he's got a phone call or something."

"An eight year old?" I shot back.

He shrugged. Then the pool director did just what I said she would. The announcement came for everyone to get out of the pool. That's what they always do when some kid turns up missing. Normally, they find the kid down on the football field, throwing stones or fooling around behind the bleachers. No kid before this was actually ever lost. At worst, a kid might walk home without telling anybody and a phone call would solve the mystery. That's how it always was before, until that day anyway.

We all stood on the cement shivering while four of the lifeguards and the director Mrs. Wisnewski walked the entire pool, from the kiddie section at one end, all the way over to the deep end with the diving board, looking for Mikey in the water. Some of us tried to help by looking over the edge, but the lifeguards told us to stay back. They did two complete trips around the pool, the second one real slow. Then Mrs. Wisnewski sent two lifeguards up into the woods in back of the pool to see if Mikey might have gone up there. Sometimes high school kids go up there to make out or smoke cigarettes, and a lot of younger kids will follow them to see what they could see. I once watched a boy talk a girl out of her bathing suit, but my friend Keith laughed and they spotted us and we had to run for it.

The two lifeguards came back and whispered something to Mrs. Wisnewski. Then she nodded and went back into the locker area. Right after that, they said that the pool was closing. Normally, if they don't find a kid after they get everyone out of the pool, they just let us go back in, but if it's close to closing time, they just send us home. That's what they did that day. Two different lifeguards stood on each side of the door leading out, looking at us as we went by, just in case Mikey was playing some sort of joke. Like I said, in our town everyone knows everyone, so they knew what Mikey looked like.

Me and Richie and Keith were the last ones to leave. Richie has a big crush on this 19-year-old blonde lifeguard who he thinks is the prettiest girl in town. Of course, she would have puked if she knew he thought of her like that. When we were about to leave, Richie asked her if Mikey might have got sucked down the drain at the bottom of the deep end, seeing as Mikey was pretty skinny to begin with. She didn't answer him, but the other guard, Tom Nevins, told Richie to clam up and get moving.

My father heard later that the sheriff went around to Mikey's friends to talk to them at their houses that night. That's because Mikey never showed up at home. They were still talking to one kid when the sheriff got a call from Mrs. Wisnewski, saying that she had spotted Mikey's body at the bottom of the deep end. It was almost nine o'clock, and she said she went back to check the chlorine level since she didn't get to do it before she left like she usually did. When she turned on all the lights in the pool, she saw him down there under the diving board. At least that's what the paper said.

I would have thought that her spotting him so long after the pool closed would make them wonder how anybody could have missed seeing him before, but they stuck to the story of the Coppertone and baby oil. I know my father didn't buy it. He thought there was something fishy about it right away. My mother didn't agree. She thinks small towns are the safest place on the planet.

"You know how cloudy the lake gets by the shore in the summer," she told my father. "You can hardly see your own feet sometimes." Which is sort of true.

"I'd still be able to see a body through all that," he said. "Especially in an empty pool."

"You don't know that," she said. Then she looked at my little sister, who's just a year younger than Mikey. It was pretty obvious she was worried that he might scare my sister from ever going back to the pool. My mother wouldn't like that very much, not just for my sister, but because the pool was like a baby sitter for her and just about every other mother in town.

I didn't say a word when they were talking. I just kept my mouth shut. I know you're supposed to think your parents will protect you from everything, but Mikey had a father and mother and it sure didn't do him any good.

After dinner that night, I met Richie and Keith over at the junior high ball field where we play hardball just about every morning in the summer. There wasn't anyone there at night so we had the place to ourselves. We were at our usual spot a few yards behind home plate where there's a huge rock that about five people can sit on. Keith and Richie were talking about Mikey and what might have happened. Keith was the first one to say that maybe somebody killed him.

"Who would want to kill an eight-year-old?" Richie asked.

"You think he really drowned?" Keith asked.

"Of course," Richie said. "That's the only thing that makes sense. You think some perv dragged him off and killed him, then trudged all the way back to the pool and dumped him there?"

That's exactly what I thought, but I didn't say a word. Keith then turned to me. "What about you?" he asked. "What do you think happened?"

I guess that was my chance to tell them. Looking back, I probably should have. Maybe things would have turned out different, except I knew if I told them, it wouldn't be a secret for very long. Keith would probably tell his father who is a town selectman, not that Keith is a kiss-ass, but that's just the way it is. And Richie would tell somebody. Not the cops. He hates the cops, but another kid, for sure, and like I said, I was afraid they might come for me next. After all, those people with the masks and the paint all over their bodies could have been walking around the park that night like everybody else and no one would have any idea it was them. Even me.

SHERIFF DARYL MIGGS

I had questions right from the start, as soon as I saw the boy's body in the pool. There were things that just didn't sit right with me, beginning with the idea that no one saw him in there earlier. Donna's explanation about the depth of the pool there and the murky water didn't convince me of anything. However, I didn't see the point of getting everyone all worked up. Not until I had some evidence that something was amiss anyway. After all, it certainly looked like he had drowned there.

I didn't share my doubts with any of my men that night. We went to the pool right after Donna called saying she found the boy, and my top deputy Pat Brisby kept looking at me like he could read my mind, but he never said anything. At one point, I caught him staring at me and asked "What?"

"Nothing," he said finally, but I figured he was thinking the same as me. I wanted him not to say anything, knowing that if either one of us told Donna what we were thinking, it might cause a panic and maybe even hinder the investigation, should there be one. As I look back on it, I suppose that was still an open question at the time.

However, that question was answered the very next day, Thursday, when the medical examiner called and asked me to come over to the hospital. Brisby wanted to know if he could tag along and I told him I didn't see why not. So he and I were the only ones there when we got the confirmation on the cause of death.

Dr. Kirk is our medical examiner. He's been a doctor here in town since he completed his residency down in New York City some thirty years ago. I have never asked him why he came all the way upstate to treat measles and chicken pox and put stitches into kids' split open heads. I suppose he had his reasons, although I'd never ask him now. If he was like me, he'd have probably forgotten why he did anything back then anyway.

He greeted us both with a handshake when we met him in the cool dark basement of the hospital. Mikey Vogel was still stretched out on the metal examining table, although the doc had covered him up with a white sheet. The smell down there was an odd combination of ammonia and something sweet. I didn't want to even think about what that might be.

"He drowned alright," Dr. Kirk told us as we walked in.

Brisby and I exchanged a glance.

"Thing is," the doctor went on. "The water in his lungs wasn't chlorinated. It was fresh."

We stood there silent for a few seconds to chew on that.

"You could tell that?" I asked finally.

"Sure," he said. "It's easy enough, if you're looking for it. I hadn't thought to check right away, but they use so much chlorine in that pool I expected to get the smell when I opened him up and didn't."

I could see Brisby wince just slightly when the doctor said that. Brisby has a son the around the same age as the Vogel boy. So do I.

"I took some out and tested it," the doc said. "No chlorine. Then I looked at it under the microscope and could see the kind of organisms you'd only find in one of our creeks or rivers. None of which would survive chlorine."

"Are you sure about that?" I asked him. He had to know the ramifications of what he was telling me.

"I am," he said. "It's simple science, Daryl."

I nodded, knowing he'd say something like that. "Did you see any signs of a struggle?" I asked, although I was pretty sure I knew the answer, having looked at the boy when they pulled him out.

The doc shook his head. "His knee's scraped. But you'd have trouble finding a boy his age without one. That was about it."

I looked at the body covered by the sheet for half a minute or so, afraid to ask the next question, although I knew it had to be on everyone's mind.

"Any signs of molestation?" I asked him.

The doc let out a breath, like he'd been waiting to have this conversation, but then he surprised me and shook his head. "I didn't see anything," he said. "And I checked all the usual places, for all the usual things, if you know what I mean."

I did, but didn't say anything. Frankly, once he said the thing about the water, I was sure we'd be going down that path and I was relieved to learn that it didn't seem to be the case. I looked over at Brisby and could see the relief on his face as well. I turned back to the doc.

"Is there any way it could still be an accident?" I asked.

"I suppose," the doc said. "Although that's more your department than mine. I know this. He sure as hell didn't walk back to that pool and climb the fence and jump in with his lungs full of fresh water."

We all three shared a look then. To my recollection, that was the first time anyone said anything out loud about the boy being elsewhere and then returned to the pool. Hell, I had thought it. Others must have as well. However, until the doc said it then, it was only a theory. I suppose none of us wanted it to be a murder, but it was hard to think anything else after what the doc had just said, and so that left me with a tough choice to make.

"OK," I said. "Let's keep this between us for now. He drowned. There's not much doubt about that. So we stick to that."

"What about the 'accidental' part?" the doc asked. "Whenever

I put down a cause of death as drowning, I always put 'accidental' in front."

"As far as I can recall," I said, "we've never had an intentional one, isn't that right?"

He stared for a second. Then nodded.

"Then just put 'drowning'," I told him. "We'll keep it like that until someone presses us or we find out something else."

The doctor didn't look too thrilled with that, but he didn't say anything. We all shook hands again and Brisby and I left him there with Mikey.

I had never conducted a murder investigation in my time in the department. We did have a murder once, but the killer could barely wait to confess, which he did within an hour of the crime. I wasn't quite sure how to proceed with this one, but something in my gut told me not to go public with what the medical examiner had just told us. Clearly, someone had gone to great lengths to make it look like an accidental drowning, and I thought that announcing what we knew might alert the killer, assuming there had to be one. I told this to Brisby in the car and, frankly, had expected a different reaction from him. I thought he might tell me I was crazy, but he surprised me by saying that he thought it was the right way to go.

Whenever a kid dies, the first place you look for suspects is in the kid's house. Like I said, I had no experience with that kind of crime, but all the books I've read and all the talks I sat through down in the state capital say that. It only makes sense. Usually, it's one of the parents, for any number of reasons, most of them psychological. And if it isn't the mother or the father, then it's a sibling. Since Biblical times, siblings have hated each other for reasons no one can quite comprehend. It's just the way it is.

So that's who Brisby and I went to see, right after what Dr. Kirk told us. Before we got out of the car, I told Brisby to let me do all the talking and he agreed. I was very careful when I spoke to the boy's parents. I simply informed them that the medical examiner had confirmed the cause of death as drowning and that I needed to ask them some background questions for the police report.

I was relieved to be able to eliminate them as suspects almost immediately. Both the mother and the father had been at work that day. The father drove a truck, so I couldn't be a hundred percent certain he didn't swing by the vicinity of the pool that afternoon. Nevertheless, I thought that if he had, someone would remember a big white bread truck near the swimming pool. As for the mother, she worked at the shoe factory in town and was there all afternoon. I had to make an excuse with her boss to get a look at her time card the next day, just to be sure. I told him something about having to confirm when she got the call and when she left. If he was suspicious at all about my motive, he didn't let on. As I expected, the time card showed that she was there all day.

Which left us with the daughter, Mikey's only sibling, who was twelve going on thirteen. It didn't look to me like she had what it would take to kill someone, let alone her own brother, so I didn't want to put her and the family through any more trauma by asking her a lot of questions. Donna had told me that the boy's sister was the one who had informed her that the boy was missing and had asked Donna if she would page him for her. I asked the girl to tell me more about that. She said she was getting ready to go home and was supposed to bring Mikey with her and couldn't find him. I asked if she remembered seeing him there earlier. She said she did, but that she lost track of him over the course of the afternoon, which is exactly what the boy's friends had told me, although neither the girl nor his friends could give me an exact time when they last saw him.

I asked the girl if she saw anything unusual at the pool that day and she said no without hesitation. It didn't take much for me to conclude that she had nothing to do with it. Her grief was real. No kid could fake that. So I thanked the parents and expressed my condolences once more and left right after that.

Even though I wasn't ready to declare it a murder, I wouldn't have been doing my duty if I didn't think about other possible suspects. Once you rule out the family, you have to go to the usual types of people who might commit this kind of crime. Basically, we're talking child molesters who don't trust the kid to keep quiet. However, without any signs of abuse, that didn't seem likely here, unless Mikey put up a hell of a fight before the guy could even do his thing. Even then, there would be signs of a struggle, so I pretty much ruled that out. Besides, from what I've read, if that happens the perpetrator just does his business after he kills the child and, based on the lack of evidence, that didn't appear to be the case here either.

The next group of likely suspects is the more psychologically impaired. The sociopath who kills for kicks. However, the books all say that they almost always disfigure the body in some way, and Mikey was clean except for that scraped knee, so that seemed pretty unlikely too. That pretty much left us in that gray area of someone who might have known the boy, but wasn't a family member, and who might have had some personal reason for killing him, in which case it could be just about anyone.

When we got back to the station, Brisby said he thought that somebody from out of town must have done this.

"That's one line of thought," I said.

I guess there was something in my voice because he said, "You don't believe that?"

I told him that with no signs of molestation or disfigurement associated with a psycho, what would be the motive of a stranger?

"You seem pretty convinced on that," he said. "Him not being molested."

"I have to think he would have left some sort of sign," I said.

"What if it wasn't a 'he'?" he asked.

I was going to tell him about the low percentages of women

molesting kids, but kept silent instead. The truth was, he was right. At that point, it could have been anyone, man, woman or child. Anyone at all. And they could be walking around among us and we wouldn't have any idea.

YANCEY HAGER

I am amazed to this day that in a town this size no one saw me carrying the boy's body from the car to the pool. It's a mystery to me, and I have wondered many times over these last few weeks how things might have changed had someone spotted me. I guess I had the good fortune to be doing it under the cover of darkness, while the band concert was going on and most people were over on the other side of town. The rest were probably home watching Dick Van Dyke. Then again, I suppose you probably wouldn't consider it to be "good fortune", getting away with disposing of a dead body, a child no less. Unless you were the devil himself.

Which I am not. I wish to make that clear. I'm just a regular person with a regular job in a town full of both. John was against the idea of putting the boy in the pool. He wanted me to take him out in the country somewhere and bury him where no one would ever find him. I told him that it was not only a risky thing to, but that it would only keep the investigation going longer. I suggested to him that the pool would make more sense. He argued that everyone would become suspicious, not having seen the body in there earlier. I have to admit that, on that point, he was right, but so was I. They weren't able to prove anything from that alone. True, they eventually discovered what happened. They just didn't do so from finding the body.

In addition to what happened to the boy, which was both tragic and preventable in my opinion, I was also terribly disappointed that our activities out in that clearing beyond the tracks had been brought to a close and we were forced to cease all that. It made sense, but I was hoping otherwise, at least at the time. When I suggested to John that we could probably just move the location and start up again after everything died down, he said that we couldn't take the chance and that everyone else felt the same way. Of course, I had to trust him on that.

I suppose it was unlikely that we could ever keep what we were doing a secret in a town this small. My main concern had always been that someone in the group might tell someone who they shouldn't have. I never for a second thought that an eight-year-old boy would stumble upon us at that time of night, in that location, and discover what we were up to. It goes to show how unpredictable life can be.

Though we weren't supposed to converse with one another, I gathered from the urgent whispers that night that there was some debate about what to do about the boy, but John quickly quieted them, assuring everyone that he would handle it. I was both grateful and surprised by his measured response in allowing the boy to leave after a long and private conversation between the two of them. I had hoped that we would have let it end there and be done with it. After all, the boy was only eight. If he told someone, who would believe him? And if they did, how could they prove who was there? However, in retrospect, it was foolish of me to think that it was ever a viable option in John's mind or that of many of the others. The life-altering potential of exposure was simply too great.

And so began the series of events that took place the next day and for the three weeks that followed. And, of course, my part in it.

SAM

They kept the pool closed for the rest of the week. They didn't say when they were going to open it again. I guess they thought kids might be too scared to go there after what happened. I don't know if that was true. It was probably the parents more than the kids who felt that way. Except for me. It was the last place I wanted to be.

By Friday morning, I was pretty tired of going to the field to play hardball, and I didn't know where else I could go where I wouldn't be looking over my shoulder and wondering if they were watching me. Any other day in the summer, I would have been out the door by nine and on my bike. My mother knew something was up when I was still home at nine thirty. I told her I didn't feel like going anywhere. She gave me a look.

"Are you feeling sick?" she asked me.

"No," I told her. "I'm just tired of playing baseball."

She gave me another look for that one, and I didn't blame her. I might as well have asked to sign up for summer school.

"Is this about that Vogel boy?" she asked.

I shook my head. She set her purse down on the counter and sat at one of the kitchen chairs. I knew right away I was in for some sort of advice or lecture.

"Look Sam," she said. "It's very sad that Mikey drowned. But these things happen. It doesn't mean the same thing is going to happen to you. There's nothing to be afraid of."

You have no idea, I wanted to say. I guess I was being given a chance to get it all off my chest, but I knew if I told my mother what I saw and what I was doing out there, all hell would break loose and I didn't want that. Not without knowing I wasn't going to end up at the bottom of that pool if I did.

"I'm not a baby, ma," I told her. "It's got nothing to do with him."

She stared at me. I don't think she believed me. Then she told me she was going shopping over in Oliander and that I could go with her if I wanted.

A twelve-year-old boy going shopping with his mother is just about the worst thing there is. About the only thing worse would be taking dance lessons. So I told her no thanks.

"Then you should find something else to do," she said. "No TV. Why don't you go to the library? It wouldn't kill you to do a little reading this summer."

I told her maybe I would. She nodded and then she left.

I just sat down on the couch when the phone rang. It was Richie.

"I was right," he said.

"What're you talking about?" I asked.

"Mikey drowned," he said. "Keith's old man heard it from somebody down in town hall. And he wasn't buggered or anything. Just drowned."

I was happy to hear that Mikey wasn't molested, but I knew it didn't really prove anything. Of course, I didn't say that.

"No surprise," is all I said.

"Right," he said. "Nothing exciting ever happens around here. So what do you want to do today?"

"I don't feel like doing anything," I told him.

"Why not?" he said. He sounded just like my mother.

"I don't know," I said. "I just don't. I think I'm going to stay in today."

"Don't be a pussy," he said. "Let's go exploring. We can go up to Vorelyn Park and look for diamonds."

"No," I said.

"Why?" he asked. "What's the matter with that?"

"It's kid stuff," I told him. Which it was. "They're all quartz anyway. It's a waste of time."

"You're a waste," he said and hung up. Richie gets like that whenever he doesn't get his way, but I've learned to ignore it, and he always comes around later on.

Despite what my mother said, I turned on the TV and flipped the channels. We only get three and all that was on was a couple of game shows and an old I Love Lucy repeat. I shut it off and looked around. There was no way I could stay in all day, no matter how scared I was, so I went out and got on my bike and pedaled toward the library.

The town library is on Main Street, at one end of the main downtown area. It's an old brick building that's three stories high and has polished wood floors and radiators that are always turned up high in the winter. I was never there in the summer till that day. I usually only go down there if I have some special assignment at school and the encyclopedia we have at home doesn't have enough stuff on the topic. For some reason I always feel safe when I'm in there. I don't know why. I also like to read a lot and it's a good place for that. One time I was in there with Richie and he was goofing around almost the whole time until the librarian got fed up and threatened to call our parents. One of the problems with growing up in a small town is that everyone knows who your parents are, too. I never went back with Richie after that.

When I walked in that morning, it felt different. First off, all the windows were open, since there isn't any air conditioning in the place. Other than the librarian at the main desk, the only other person there was Cyrus Robbins who is sort of a tramp and always smells like liquor and cigars. All the kids call him Robin Hood cause of his last name. He doesn't rob the rich and give to the poor. He's poor himself, and I don't think he ever robbed anybody. He actually has a place to live, up on the road out of town toward Herford, but his house is really run down and looks like it could collapse any minute. That's probably why he always seems to be walking the streets. I guess he used to be a normal guy, but then he killed Richie's brother in that car accident and hasn't been the same since. It's hard to say how old he is since he never washes or shaves and he wears almost all the clothes he owns. It doesn't matter what season it is, he always has on a coat and three or four shirts and two pants at least. A lot of kids call him names or throw snowballs at him in the winter and that gets him pissed off, but I never have, so I don't think he has it in for me like he might for some of the other kids.

It's sort of surprising, but Richie doesn't hate Robin Hood for what he did. That's probably because Richie's father is just as much to blame as far as Richie is concerned. He was supposed to be home watching Richie and his brother while Richie's mom was working the night shift, but he went out drinking instead and Richie's brother snuck out. He was the same age I am now and it's weird to think a kid that age died, but he did. Then again, so did Mikey, and he was even younger.

Anyway, Robin Hood was reading a newspaper in the main reading room when I came in. He just looked up at me and then went back to reading the paper. Just to be safe, I decided to avoid him and go into the back.

I was trying to decide if I should ask the librarian if I could see a Playboy. Every guy in town knows that they have them right there in the library, only they keep them behind the desk, instead of with the regular magazines. There's a rumor that if you come up with a good enough excuse, they have to let you look at one. It's like a law or something. The hard part is coming up with a good reason. Richie claims he did it one time, but when I asked him what he told the librarian, he said he couldn't tell me, so I knew he made it up. The librarian behind the desk that day was giving me looks like she knew I was up to something, so I decided not to even try. Instead, I got the idea that maybe I could look up something about what I saw out there by the tracks that night and maybe figure out what was going on out there.

The problem was that I didn't know where to start. I mean, naked people with paint on their bodies and masks wasn't much to go on, so I walked around in the stacks looking at the books, hoping to get an idea. I got sidetracked one time when I saw some books about wagon trains, but I didn't spend too long with them. Finally, I worked my way up to the third floor to where the real old stuff is.

It looked like most of the books up there hadn't been checked out in about a hundred years. I walked down each row, looking at the titles. Most of them didn't make any sense to me. I was about to give up when I saw one that made me stop. It was only one word. "Pagans". I'm not exactly sure why that got my attention. I mean, I sort of knew what the word meant so maybe that was it. Whatever it was, there was something about the book that made me take it off the shelf.

I leafed through it and it turned out it was mostly about ancient Greeks and Romans and their gods and that kind of stuff. Lots of stories and names and things. But when I got to the middle part, there were a bunch of pictures. I don't know about other kids, but every time I pick up a book with pictures in it, I have to look at them. Doesn't matter what the book is about. I just want to see what the pictures are.

These were all drawings, not photos. Old stuff. The first few were of a bunch of old guys with beards and long hair. Nothing interesting. But when I got to the last one, I almost choked. It was a drawing of a bunch of men and women, all naked, out in a clearing, dancing around a huge fire. They didn't have any paint on them, but they were wearing animal skins and headdresses. It wasn't exactly what I saw a few nights before, but it was close enough to make me start shaking all over again right there in the library.

"Can I help you with that?"

It was the librarian from behind the desk. I wasn't sure of her name, but I had seen her in there a bunch of times before. I closed up the book before she could see what I was looking at.

"I'm OK," I told her.

She looked at me and then the book, which I was trying to hide the best I could.

"Are you going to check that out?" she asked. "I can do that for you if you have your card with you."

I just shook my head. Then she said, "Well, if you're not going to take it out, then be sure to put it back in the right place. People won't be able to find it if you put it on the wrong shelf."

I told her I would. We looked at one another for another couple of seconds, then she walked out.

I came down about five minutes later and headed out the main door. She was at the desk and watched me go past and out the door. I was wearing my sweatshirt even though it was almost eighty degrees out that morning. When I got outside and grabbed my bike, I could see through one of the open windows that she was helping somebody else check out a book and probably had forgotten all about me.

After that, I rode over to the field and played some hardball with Richie and some other guys until three o'clock which is when I had to go pick up my papers for my paper route. When I got on my bike to go downtown to the newspaper office, I looked in the saddlebag on the back to make sure the book was still there. I'm not even sure why I didn't just check it out like normal. I guess I didn't want that librarian to ask me why I was taking it out. I guess I didn't want my mother asking any questions either because

I rode home as fast as I could before picking up my papers and went up to my room and hid it in the back of my closet.

I was late with my papers that day, but nobody said anything.

MIGGS

I spent most of the day Friday at my desk trying to figure out what to do next. The easy thing would have been to just let everything die down for a bit. Wait for something else to come to light. Everything seemed to point to a murder, but we had no definitive proof of that. A drowning, by itself, didn't equal an unlawful killing under the law. Not without some indication of how it had occurred. It still could have been an accident. Lots of reasonable doubt there. Someone obviously had to transport the body to the pool. That could have been done by the murderer or an accessory after the fact, but I suppose it also could have been someone covering up an accident. There's a law on the books about improper handling of a corpse, which is a misdemeanor, but if I opened up an investigation to see who might have done such a thing, I'd just be letting everyone know that the boy hadn't drowned in the pool and that would just stir up a hornet's nest.

From what I could tell, most people accepted the preliminary conclusion of a drowning and the explanation about the murky water making the discovery of the body so difficult. There seemed to be no concern that there might be a killer on the loose somewhere or that it might happen again. It was certainly on my mind, but apparently not on the minds of many others. Of course, they didn't know about the fresh water in the boys lungs. We had managed to keep that quiet.

Or I should say, the coroner and I did. Brisby came into my

office that afternoon and informed me that he had a friend in the state police, a detective, who he thought could help us. He suggested that maybe we should bring in the staties and see what they thought, since we hadn't had a murder in town in years. I looked at him hard.

"You didn't happen to say anything to this friend of yours, did you?"

He hesitated, and I knew immediately that he had.

"I thought we agreed not to tell anyone about this?" I asked.

"I thought you meant the public," he told me. "This guy's in law enforcement. He won't say anything."

"You're damn right he won't," I said, and grabbed for the phone.

His name was Irwin, and he said he understood that it was my call about starting an investigation and who to bring in on it. I told him what the situation was and that if I got one more piece of strong evidence that a crime had been committed, something more than moving a body, I'd be sure to inform the state police.

"What if you don't find anything?" he asked.

"Then we'll have nothing to go on except a dead boy with some fresh water in his lungs."

He was quiet for a bit. "You don't want the killer to know that you know," he said. "Is that it?"

"If there is one, no," I admitted.

"Does the DA go along with your thinking here?" he asked.

"He's on vacation," I told him. "I'll tell him what I'm thinking when he gets back on Saturday."

To his credit, he didn't argue the point. He assured me that he wouldn't say anything. He then offered to go through his files on child molesters to see if he might be able to find something there that might help. I thanked him and hung up. Then I turned to Brisby and told him that I wasn't interested in any more surprises and that he better keep quiet from now on. He apologized and said he was just trying to help, which wasn't that hard to believe considering my past.

I drove back out to the pool that afternoon, not that I really expected to learn anything new. It was closed to the public, in compliance with my request, but Donna was there when I arrived. The outside door was open and so was the one to her office, so I just walked in and sat down. She tried to smile when she saw me, but she looked like she'd been through a couple of rough nights.

"It's the damnedest thing, isn't it?" she said.

"It sure is."

"I can't figure out what he was doing in the deep end," she said. "I asked my guards if anyone saw Mikey using the diving board, but they all said no."

"You have to be twelve to use it, right?" I asked.

She nodded. "And pass a swimming test. If he had gotten up on the board, one of the lifeguards would have noticed. If they didn't, the other kids would have said something. They're very aware of the rules."

"He could've swam under the rope from the other part," I said, knowing full well he had done no such thing.

"That's what my guards said, too," she said.

We were quiet for a time. "You don't think there might be something more to this, do you?" she asked.

I have to admit I was surprised by her question. "What do you mean?" I asked.

"There's been some talk," she said. "People wondering how we could have missed him earlier. That maybe he wasn't there then."

"There's always talk," I said. "I can only go on the evidence and all the evidence here points to a drowning. The doc did the medical exam yesterday and confirmed it." It was an accurate statement, but hardly the whole truth.

She nodded and looked for a second like she might cry. "I

know it's not my fault," she said, "but I can't help but feel responsible. There's nothing worse than thinking that a child might have died on your watch."

I know she didn't mean anything by it, but I suppose my expression said otherwise.

"Oh, Jesus, I'm sorry, Daryl. I shouldn't have said that."

I told her not to worry. No offense taken. I told her that was the reason why I was there, in fact. I wanted to see how she was holding up. She seemed to accept that. Then I told her to open up the pool again on Monday and do her best to get things back to normal.

She gave me a small smile and I left, feeling far worse than I did when I had arrived.

HAGER

You're not supposed to go back to the scene of the crime. Anyone who's watched even a single episode of Perry Mason knows that. Nevertheless, for some reason, I decided to hike up into the woods behind the pool that day. I had taken the afternoon off and, to be completely candid, I wanted to keep an eye on things. John didn't ask me to. I did that on my own. He would never have condoned it. I was thinking only about myself at that point.

I had read in the paper that they had closed it, so I didn't expect to see anyone. That wasn't why I was there. I'd had a feeling the night before that maybe the police might not be letting the public in on everything they knew. I had no specific reason to think that, just a simple bit of intuition. Over the years, I've learned not to ignore that kind of thing. I'd like to think it's how I've managed to survive, despite my leanings.

I saw the woman who supervises the pool arrive around one o'clock and unlock the main doors and go inside. She didn't come out into the pool area, so I thought perhaps she was just going to stay in her office all day. Maybe she brought a book or maybe she had some paperwork to do, although I don't know what kind of paperwork one could have as the supervisor of the pool.

Then again, as far as the public was aware, a child had drowned there three days before. It seemed to me that you would have to file a report on something like that. If not, then you should. Someone should have to account for what happened. I was just thinking that when she walked out into the main pool area and stopped next to the diving board. I was far up in the woods, tucked away among the trees, but I had my binoculars with me, which allowed me to see her quite clearly. I had brought them not only to watch the pool, but also because I wanted to have an excuse in case the sheriff had an idea to send someone up there to look around, just as I was doing. If so, I planned on telling them I was bird watching. They would believe that. I was quite confident that they would.

The woman stood motionless at the diving board for quite some time. She was looking down into the area of the pool where I had placed the boy. Then, rather abruptly, she took something out of her pocket and flipped it into the air above the water. With the glint from the sun I could tell it was a coin. Judging by the size and the metal, it was most likely a quarter. She watched as it broke the surface and then disappeared down below. She stared for a long time. Then, almost as if she sensed that she was being watched, she looked up and all around the whole pool area for a few seconds. There's a chain link fence that surrounds it, about eight feet in height. There's no barbed wire, but the top is still that open twisty part that you can get a shirt caught on or even tear up your skin. Perhaps she was wondering how someone could have climbed that fence carrying a child weighing thirty or forty pounds without leaving behind some clothing or some other sign of having done so. Then again, she may have just been looking around for no special reason.

Shortly after that, she went to the gate at the rear, near the kiddie pool. She grabbed the handle on the chain link door and pulled on it. It was obviously locked and didn't open. That seemed to satisfy her and she went right back inside after that.

It was then that I heard a car pull up down at the bottom of the long stairway that leads up to the pool from the athletic field below. I saw that it was a sheriff's car and ducked down in the branches of the low pines, even though it would have taken an eagle's eye to see me up there from where the car was parked, even if they knew I was there. The sheriff stepped out of the cruiser and never even gave a glance in my direction. He simply headed up the stairs toward the pool house.

I probably should have left right then, but I didn't. I was curious to see what he was up to. My heart began beating a little faster as I watched him walk through the door into the main entrance of the pool house. In my estimation, Daryl Miggs is no fool. He's amiable and seems dedicated to his job. Unlike a lot of other folks in this town, I never thought he was in over his head or lacked common sense. Quite the opposite. After all, everyone makes a mistake from time to time, and when that mistake comes from the heart, it's even more excusable in my estimation.

His arrival only seemed to confirm the feeling that I had the night before, when I couldn't sleep. If he was convinced that the boy had drowned in the pool, as I had hoped, why would he be back there three days later? The paper had reported that an autopsy had been performed, although the results weren't in. Still, I was confident of what they were going to say. The boy had drowned. Of that there could be little doubt.

It occurred to me then that perhaps he was going to arrest the woman at the pool, but I couldn't imagine what for. Negligence maybe, although I don't think that's a crime. Then it occurred to me that Miggs and the woman might be engaged in some sort of affair, but he didn't seem the type for that. I know I had never heard anything in town about his marriage being in trouble, and I doubt that he drank too much. Then again, it's always the quiet ones. Just look at me.

I was thinking that it might be wise for me to get out of there when he suddenly came out of the building and into the pool area. I expected the woman to come out right behind him, but she didn't. He even looked back, like he expected the same thing himself. Then he turned and walked the perimeter of the pool, the entire cement walking area, all the way around to the exact same spot where the woman had stood and thrown the coin just an hour or so earlier. Like her, he stared down into the water for some time.

That was the first indication I had that our plan hadn't gone quite as well as I had hoped.

SAM

My father doesn't work on Saturdays. Not at his job anyway. It's his day to do chores around the house. He calls it his second job, and he has my mother make up a list of things she wants him to do, and he does them. He makes like she's some sort of slave driver, but I actually think he likes it. I know he likes it better than his real job. He works in a stockroom over in a factory in Oliander. He hates that and complains about it all the time.

That Saturday one of the chores he had was to paint the fence, so he woke me up early and told me I had to start it while he did the lawn. I would have argued about it normally, but I was kind of glad to have something to do. I told Richie and Keith that I couldn't ride bikes with them because I had to help my father. To tell you the truth, I was avoiding them so I wouldn't have to talk about Mikey anymore.

When I was little, I always used to hang around my father when he did repairs and stuff. I loved to help him fix things. I actually liked it when our TV went on the blink. We'd open up the back and take out all the tubes and bring them down to the drugstore where they have this machine you can plug them into to tell if one of them is burned out. Then you can buy a new tube right there and go back and put it in and start watching the TV again the same night. If you timed it right, you wouldn't even miss your favorite show.

I also helped him do more boring stuff like paint. That was

33

why he trusted me to start the fence without him. He started me on painting when I was pretty young. Walls at first, where I couldn't mess up too much. Then later I got to do more stuff like window frames and door jambs. He used to tell me I could do a better job than him cause my hands were smaller, but I think he just said that to get me to help.

Anyway, that was back when we used to get along pretty good. That all changed this past May after I took the stupid Iowa Test at school. It's this long exam they give to everybody in seventh grade. It's on all different subjects and takes two days to do it. I guess it's supposed to tell how smart you are and what you're good at. I took it once before when I was younger and did OK I guess. This time, though, it must have said I was some sort of genius. As soon as my father saw the results, he started talking to my mother about sending me away to a boarding school downstate where he said I'd get a better education. "I don't want him ending up like me," he told her.

Of course, I told him I didn't want to go. I know my mother didn't want me to either, but she always lets my father make all the big decisions in our house. So he just went ahead and talked to the school and even sent them those test results and they said they'd take me and it wouldn't even cost a thing for me to go there. It was about the most miserable news of my life. My father and I hardly said a word to each other after that, unless we had to.

When he was finally done with the lawn that day, he came over to help me with the fence. We just worked on it for awhile without saying anything, until finally he asked me if there was something bothering me.

"You mean besides having to go to a school where I don't know anybody in some town I never heard of?" I asked.

He gave me a look that told me I better watch my step. "I thought we already talked about that," he said.

"I don't remember getting to say that much," I said.

He gave me another look. "That's because you're the kid and I'm the parent," he said. "Someday you'll thank me."

I was going to tell him that was never going to happen, that you don't thank somebody for taking you away from all your friends and everything you've ever known, especially when it's your own father, but I knew I'd be in trouble if I did, so I just clammed up.

"Your mother thinks something else is going on," he said. "Besides that. It doesn't have to do with drugs, does it?"

I wanted to laugh. Drugs are the biggest fear of all the parents in our town. They read the papers and watch TV and see what's going on in places like California and think drugs are going to take over. They even talk to us about it in school. I guess there must be somebody in town doing drugs, but nobody I know. Not even Richie. Not yet anyway.

"I'm not doing drugs," I told him. "It's just that summer's almost over, that's all." I didn't have to explain what that meant.

"Alright then," he said. "But if you ever do have a problem you know you can come to me. I won't get mad."

I wanted to laugh again, because we both knew that was never going to happen either, but I decided to just let it go and nodded.

Luckily, he didn't get a chance to say anymore because Richie and Keith came by on their bikes then. My father doesn't like those guys very much, especially Richie, but he probably figured I wouldn't be seeing them too much longer, so he said I could go and that he'd finish up by himself. Like I said, I didn't really want to see them, but at that point I felt like if I didn't, my father would really think something was wrong. Anyway, I got my bike out of the garage and went off with them up toward the town dump.

I figured we were just going up there to throw rocks at the rats, like we always do, but as soon as we pulled in, Richie skidded his bike to a stop and jumped off and stuck his finger in my chest.

"We're going out to Gehring's farm tonight," he said, all excited. "I don't care what you have to tell your parents. We're going."

I didn't say anything. I was afraid of what might come out next.

"C'mon," Richie said. "Don't be a pussy."

"What's out at Gehring's farm?" I asked.

"Nothing," Keith said. "We're not actually going to Gehring's farm. We're going out to the old hobo camp. It's just down the tracks from there."

I knew where it was. I sure as heck didn't need him to tell me. Like I said before, that was where I saw Mikey the night before he died. Mikey and all those naked people with the masks and the painted bodies. In the old days, the hobos who jumped trains used to go there to sleep and eat and hide from the train cops. It's kind of a natural opening, surrounded by trees, not too far from the tracks. They even built a huge stone pit where you could have a big fire. The best part for the hobos was that there were only two ways to get there and you could hear the cops coming and escape before they found you. The tractor road on Gehring's farm was one way. Everybody knows about the camp, but nobody ever goes there anymore, mostly since there aren't any hobos riding the trains these days and it's too hard for anybody else to get to. Plus, there really isn't any reason to. That was probably why those people were out there that night. I know it's why I was.

"Tell him what you heard," Richie said to Keith then.

Keith nodded. He's used to taking orders from Richie. I guess it doesn't bother him like it does me. "I heard my father talking to my mother in bed last night," he said.

"Lucky for us he still sleeps in their bed," Richie said. Keith gave him a shove. I didn't laugh.

"I got up to sneak some ice cream and was going back to my room when I heard them," he said. He gave Richie the finger. Richie just shrugged. I told Keith to go on.

"My father said he heard there was some sort of funny business going on out there."

"What kind of funny business?" I asked.

"Parties," he said. Richie gave him a shot to the arm.

"Not just parties," Richie said. Keith nodded.

"Sex stuff," Keith said. "Grown ups. Doing sex stuff right out at the old hobo camp."

I must have looked strange because Richie laughed.

"Uh-oh," he said. "Too much for those sensitive ears?"

"Shut up," I said. "I can take more than you can, that's for sure."

"Good," he said. "Because we're going out there tonight. We're going to have a look. Wouldn't it be cool if we saw somebody's parents out there going at it?"

"You won't," I told him. "It's all bullshit."

"How the hell would you know?" Richie asked.

I turned to Keith. "You sure you heard him say that? You could've been dreaming."

Keith frowned. "I was wide awake," he said. "I heard the whole thing."

"Where'd your old man hear it?" I asked.

"He didn't say," Keith said.

"What difference does it make?" Richie asked. "It's still worth going to see, isn't it?"

"Yeah," Keith said. "Besides, my old man wouldn't make up something like that. You know how he is. So what do you say?"

They were both staring at me, waiting for me to say something. I didn't know what to do. Normally, I'm ready to do any kind of crazy stuff like that and they knew it.

"What's wrong with you lately?" Richie asked. "First you didn't want to do anything yesterday and now this. Is it your time of the month or something?"

"I'm just saying if it's bullshit, we'd be riding out there and back for nothing." It sounded lame even to me.

"Big deal," Richie said. "What else were you going to do tonight? Wash your hair?"

"Yeah, what do you say?" Keith said. "Are you coming or not?"

They were both staring at me. Waiting.

"OK," I said. "I'll go."

And so we did.

MIGGS

Fritz Seiver has been district attorney in our county for the better part of twenty years. There's not enough crime here to make it a full-time job with a full-time salary, so he has his own private practice on the side. Of course, he can't take any criminal cases due to the obvious conflict of interest. He handles wills and estates mostly, along with the occasional divorce and negligence case. He also acts as the lawyer for folks buying or selling their house, some-times for both in the same transaction. That always seemed like another one of those conflicts to me, but as far as I could tell, no one ever complained. More importantly, I never heard anyone ac-cuse him of any kind of wrongdoing. As far as I'm concerned, Fritz has always been on the up and up.

He's no fool either. He went to Cornell, so I guess that makes him an Ivy Leaguer, although I never think of him that way and he never flaunts it. To me, he's just another guy in town doing his job. Since the folks keep electing him every four years - heck, half the time no one even runs against him - everyone in town seems to share my view of the guy. His wife is quite pleasant, too. I've never heard anyone say anything bad about her either. About the worst thing anyone ever says is that she might keep to herself a bit too much, but my wife likes her, and that's always been good enough for me.

Fritz was waiting for me on the big wrap-around front porch when I came over to see him Saturday afternoon, after he got back from his vacation. He met me with his usual firm handshake and offered me a seat on one of the wicker chairs there. I looked around and said, "Maybe we ought to talk inside." After a second, he nodded. Fritz's house is on one of the town's busier streets and people are always walking by and stopping to say hello if they see you out on the porch. I'm not saying they would have heard anything, but I was just being safe. That's why I walked over to his house instead of driving. I didn't want anyone to see a police car in his driveway. I didn't wear my uniform either. No sense sending a message that the town's top two lawmen were having a big pow-wow. They might get to thinking that there was more to the boy's death than we were letting on.

So we went inside to his study, and he closed the door so his wife wouldn't even be able to hear us. After telling me about all the fish he pulled out of Lake George the previous two weeks, we got down to brass tacks and I filled him in on what had happened the past few days, starting with Wednesday. Everything. Of course, I had called him at his cabin the night it happened, but I didn't say much then other than it looked like the boy had drowned. I wanted to wait until he got back to tell him what the coroner told me. That's why I was there.

When I finished, he just stared at his hands for a time. I could tell he was running through a few scenarios in his mind.

"Well," he said finally. "A crime has certainly been committed."

"Moving a dead body, right?" I asked.

"I hadn't thought of that," he said. "But that's probably one, too. No. I mean, someone obviously killed the boy."

I guess I was still hoping for an explanation that didn't add up to murder. He looked at me like he knew what I was thinking.

"Fresh water in his lungs means he didn't drown in the pool," he said. "That means he drowned somewhere else and someone brought him back to make it look that way."

"And moved a dead body," I repeated.

"Think about it," he said, ignoring my comment. "If Mikey died accidentally, then whoever moved him would have just called you to report it."

"Maybe they were afraid it would look like they had something to do with him drowning when they really didn't," I said. "They'd have plenty of reason not to call me then. I don't think that's out of the realm of possibilities."

He shrugged. "Then they could have just left him wherever they found him," he countered. "Let someone else call it in. Why risk getting caught trying to make it look like he drowned at the swimming pool?"

"They might have a reason," I said.

"Like what?" he asked.

I didn't have an answer for that. "So you're convinced that somebody killed the kid?" I said.

"Mikey," he corrected me. I felt my face flush. I forgot that Fritz, like most prosecutors, liked to attach names to victims. We're not so good about that in the sheriff's department.

"Right," I said. "But suppose we do find out who dumped the body. Would that be enough by itself to prove that he killed Mikey?"

"Depends on who you caught and what evidence we found on him," he said. "Or her."

"That's funny," I said. "Brisby said the same thing. You don't really think a woman did this, do you?"

"It's unlikely," he said. "But we can't rule anything out."

I nodded. "But just the fact that the body was moved by that person, without any other evidence, wouldn't be enough to convict someone of murder, would it?" I asked.

"I suppose not," he said. "Although I believe that if we find whoever moved him, the odds are we'll find some other evidence. It's not likely that there won't be any. In my experience, one thing always leads to another. And when it does, it won't be long before you have all you need to convict."

"Are you saying I should have let everyone know that we're looking for a killer?"

He thought about that for a time. Then shook his head. "No," he said. "You were right on that. Better to let the guy, or woman, think they're in the clear."

"So you don't disagree with how I handled this so far?" I asked.

He looked at me sort of surprised. "No. Not at all."

I nodded, relieved.

"Is that why you listed cause of death as drowning?" he asked. "Instead of accidental drowning?"

I nodded. "Doc wasn't too happy about it, but he went along with it."

He stood up. "Alright then," he said. "If you don't mind, I'm going to bring in the state police and have them work on this. Quietly, of course."

I stayed where I was in the chair. "That's part of the reason I came over," I told him. "I was hoping you would let me handle this. At least for now."

He looked surprised at that.

I stood then. "Look," I told him. "I know what you're thinking. But I am the sheriff of this town and it's my job to keep everyone safe. Now you can argue that I haven't always done my best at that and I would have trouble saying otherwise."

"I never felt that way," he reminded me.

"I know," I said. "And I've always appreciated that. I probably have no reason to ask this, but I want to catch whoever is responsible. Myself. Just give me a couple of weeks. I want to see what I can do while everyone thinks it's still an accident. Then you can do whatever you want."

Again, he appeared like he was lost in thought. Finally, he said,

"I guess there's no time factor involved. It's not like someone's on the run. And even if they are, it wouldn't matter whether it's you or the staties looking into it, since we wouldn't know who that person is who's doing the running."

"That's how I see it," I told him.

"How are you going to keep it quiet?" he asked.

"I haven't figured that part out yet," I told him. "I just hope I can."

He nodded. "A couple of weeks," he said. "Then we bring in the staties."

HAGER

As I said before, Daryl Miggs is no fool. Walking to the district attorney's house and not wearing his uniform was quite clever. I'm sure he was thinking he could keep anyone from discovering that they were working behind the scenes. He almost did, too, but the sign for the attorney's private practice told me who lived there. As fortune would have it, I happened to drive by and saw the sheriff leaving there at around two o'clock.

Once I did, I drove back around the block, then past Woodland Street where I saw him turn to head back downtown. I came around South Ann Street, up Main from the west and then turned up Woodland in time to see him before he got down to Main, where I was sure he was going to take a left and go on down to his office at town hall. If he was going back to his house, he would have never turned toward Woodland from the district attorney's house. The sheriff lives in the other direction. I took that as further proof that they were trying to keep their meeting private.

John didn't agree. We had met in the parking lot of the grocery store over in Oliander that afternoon where I told him what I had seen. He said it was probably nothing, that the sheriff probably had to fill in the district attorney about the drowning. Even if it was just an accident, he still had to file a report.

"What about him walking?" I asked.

John said he probably just wanted the exercise, since all he ever did was "sit on his fat ass".

"I wouldn't underestimate him," I warned him.

John stared at me. He has a way of looking at you that is downright chilling. It certainly doesn't encourage you to want to challenge him.

"I'm not saying he suspects anything," I said, although I thought he most certainly did. "All I'm saying is that it would be unwise to underestimate him."

John lost the scary look and even smiled then. It certainly didn't make me feel any better.

"This will all blow over soon if everyone keeps a cool head," he said. Even though he said "everyone", I knew he was almost certainly referring to me.

"What about the others?" I asked. "What do they say?"

"Why don't you let me worry about them," he told me. "You just watch yourself."

Then he patted me on the leg. It was no comfort, I can tell you that. He watched me open the car door and get out. I could feel his eyes still on me as I got back into my own car. If I had told him what I was planning on doing that night, he probably would have killed me right there. Of course, I didn't. I figured what he didn't know, wouldn't hurt him.

SAM

I told my parents we were going to the movies and then back to Keith's house afterward and that I'd sleep there. Keith told his parents the same thing, only that we were going back to my house. He and I sleep over at each other's houses most Saturdays in the summer so it was a good story. Most times my parents don't question me after a night out like that. They didn't the night I saw Mikey out at the old hobo camp, and if there ever was a time that they should have, it was then. I don't know what Richie told his father. Probably nothing. His father is always down at the VFW Post and never knows where Richie is. Or cares. He just lets him pretty much come and go as he pleases.

We rode our bikes as far as we could out of town and then stashed them in the bushes just off the dirt road turnoff from the state highway. No one would see them driving by and they would have to look pretty hard to find them if they went on that dirt road for any reason. The Gehrings' house is across the road and down a ways from the turnoff, so we didn't have to worry about them.

The dirt road is really just a sort of path for the tractor and all the other farm equipment the Gehrings use to farm the place. If you follow it the whole way, you get to the end of their property. On the right side, there are a bunch of turn-offs leading into the fields which are almost all corn rows. On the left is all railroad land, mostly woods, except for the tracks which curve in from the north. You have to walk down along the tracks for quite a ways

46

before you get to the hobo camp. The only other way to get there is from behind the houses down on Main Street at the western end of town. Their back yards go all the way to the fence that's supposed to keep kids off the railroad tracks. Everything on the other side of the fence is railroad property for a long way. You could probably get there from the north and west too, but it would mean walking miles through woods and stuff and that wouldn't be too easy.

"How far is it?" Richie asked when we started down the tracks.

"I don't know," Keith. "I think we just walk down until we see it."

"Well, I don't know about you," Richie said. "But I got plans for the next year."

"It's about a half mile down from here," I said before I could stop myself.

They both stopped to look at me.

"How would you know?" Richie asked me.

"Cause that's how far we rode out here from the end of town," I said. "If you can get there from West Main, behind those houses, then it's gotta be about a half mile."

"You think those people walked in from behind those houses?" Keith asked.

"No," Richie said. "They took a helicopter. Didn't you hear it?"

Keith walked away from him. He didn't fight back much with Richie, but I know he got sick of his teasing sometimes.

"Trust me," I said. "It's further down."

At that point, I was just thinking that we might as well go see it. I figured none of those people with the masks and paint would be crazy enough to go back out there after what happened with Mikey. Besides, it would give me a chance to look it over again.

"Alright," Richie said, pushing me ahead. "Let's follow Chingachgook here."

We started walking down the road again, and it was right about then that we heard a car coming from where we had just left our bikes.

MIGGS

Saturday nights are either quiet as Christmas Eve or as crazy as New Years. For the most part, I don't work weekends, particularly Saturday nights. If all hell breaks loose, then I might have to go in. After all, I am the sheriff. Most Saturdays, the biggest problem my guys might run into is a fistfight between two drunks or a minor car accident. In my experience, those usually involve drinking, too. If it wasn't for idiots consuming alcohol, I'd probably never have to answer my phone again, especially on Saturday nights. Then again, if it wasn't for idiots consuming alcohol, I might be able to sleep through the night.

Seven years ago, I wasn't home on one particular Saturday night. I was working, filling in for one of my guys who was out of town at his sister's wedding. I thought it was going to be just another one of those quiet Saturday nights I mentioned, but I was wrong. It was actually Sunday morning around two fifteen when I spotted a car weaving a bit as it headed down Main Street. I immediately recognized it as belonging to Cyrus Robbins. I stopped him and asked him to step out of the car, which he did. I didn't even bother to have him walk a straight line or recite the alphabet. He was obviously intoxicated. My eyes and nose gave me all the evidence I needed to bring him in, but I kind of liked Cyrus. In fact, I felt sorry for him. I knew he was going through some marital difficulties at the time and had been hitting the bottle pretty hard. Like I said, it was quiet that night. No one else was on the street, so I let him go with just a strict warning to go straight home, no stops. In retrospect, I should have known better. I should never have let him back in that car. At the very least, I should have followed him.

I got the call less than a half hour later. Robbins had struck a boy over on Elm Street which was not on the way back to his house. The kid was twelve years old and shouldn't have been out that late, but that didn't make his death any less my fault. The boy died before they could get him to the hospital and I arrested Robbins right there at the scene.

He served a year and a half in county for vehicular manslaughter. By the time he got out, his family was gone and so was he, in a manner of speaking. Some people in town were pretty hard on me for letting Cyrus drive away that night, but no harder than I was on myself. I could have kept the earlier stop quiet and it's highly unlikely that Robbins would have even remembered, and on the off chance he did, even more unlikely that anyone would have believed him over me. Nevertheless, I logged it in and told Fritz what happened and never gave a thought to doing it any other way. It was in all the papers and people called for my head for a time. It nearly cost me an election three years later. There have been many days when I wished it had.

Cyrus hasn't spoken to me since the trial. Whether that's because he blames me for his decline or is simply too far gone to care anymore is open to debate. Other than the boy's father, Robbins probably has the most reason to hate me. Maybe if I had hauled him in when I first stopped him, he would have straightened himself out and wouldn't be walking the streets every night with a fifth of whiskey under his belt. Maybe he'd still have a family. Maybe a lot of things.

By comparison, this particular Saturday night was different. For starters, I was home that night with my wife and kids and not out in a patrol car. My oldest daughter Kimberly is just about to enter eighth grade, still too young to be going out on dates. She might go downtown with her friends once in awhile, but that usually ends up not lasting very long, there not being too much for kids her age to do in this town after dark. That night, though, she was at home, reading in her room and listening to her record player.

Kimberly has never given me a lick of trouble, which is more than I can say for the oldest boy. He was always getting into something. It finally got so bad that I had to send him to military school over in Vermont. He fought it at first, but he's going to graduate next year and is set to attend the Coast Guard Academy. My wife wasn't keen on sending him away when I first suggested it, but she's pretty pleased with how it's turned out for him.

She has always worried more about Kimberly than I have. After all, she's a girl and when a girl gets in trouble, military school is neither an option nor a solution.

To add to her concerns, Kimberly has matured more than her friends in the past year or so, and looks much older than her years. As a result, my wife's forever on alert for signs of rebellion, which to my way of thinking means boys. Kimberly had been especially quiet that week, which was not good news for my wife. She has always taken that to mean that Kimberly is hiding something. However, with what happened to the Vogel boy a few days before, I just assumed that she was spooked, like any kid would be when they hear about one of their own dying. Kids don't expect kids to die. It's just not part of their world, and it throws them.

My other two kids, one of each, are both in grade school. They were both in bed by the time Eileen and I sat down to watch some television. I had my top patrolman Vic on the schedule for the night, figuring he could take care of anything that came up. He is reliable that way.

I had just gotten settled on the couch when the phone rang. I knew it was Vic before I even picked up.

"Sorry to bother you, chief," he said.

I went through the usual rigmarole about how he wasn't bothering me and that it was my job. Then I waited for him to fill me in.

"We got a call earlier tonight about some sort of disturbance out at Larry Gehring's farm," he said. "So I went to check it out."

"What kind of disturbance?" I asked him.

"That's just it," he said. "When I got out there, no one was there. I didn't see any sign of anything."

"Well, what did the caller say exactly?" I asked.

"He said he heard some people shouting out in the fields," he said finally. "Said it sounded like somebody was being chased."

"Chased?" I asked.

"Yeah," he said. He paused then. "Thing is chief, the caller sounded young."

"Young?" I asked. "How young?"

"I can't say for sure," he told me. "But no more than a teenager."

I thought about that for a second. "What about Larry?" I asked.

"I tried the house, but no one answered," he said.

He went quiet again.

"Why the hell are you bothering me with this, Vic?" I asked. "It sounds like a crank call."

"Yeah, that's what I thought, too," he said. "But I thought I should probably investigate a bit more and so I went a ways down the tracks just to be sure."

"And?"

"I found something," he said.

There was something about his tone of voice that made my stomach tighten. "What was it?" I asked.

"A kid's shoe," he said. "In the tall grass. Right near where you pull off the dirt road to walk down the tracks."

"What kind of shoe?" I asked, my stomach getting even tighter.

He paused before answering. "A sneaker," he said.
We both knew what that meant and why he had called.

HAGER

I almost didn't see those boys out there at first. Of course, what reason could there be for three kids that age to be that far out of town, near those railroad tracks at that hour on a Saturday night? Naturally, the worst explanation came to mind: that they had been out there before and had seen what we had been doing and were hoping to catch another show. I thought perhaps the dead boy might have been part of the same group, since no one to my knowledge had ever adequately determined what he was doing out there. However, I knew that couldn't be the case. The other kids would have said something to someone after the boy's body was discovered. No child would be able to keep something like that to himself.

When I parked my car, there was no indication that someone else might be out there. In retrospect, it's a good thing I did see them. Otherwise, they might have followed me and discovered who I was. If they went and told someone, I'd have to explain what I was doing out there, and I had no credible reason for being there. In all likelihood, I would have broken down and confessed and everything would have turned out differently.

Fortunately, once I came upon them and surprised them, they took off instantly. There was almost no chance that they could have gotten a good look at me in the dark. I was concerned that their shouts might cause the lights to come on at the nearby farm, but the house remained dark when I emerged from the road and got back to the car.

I had to make a decision then. Since they had run off, I probably could have gone back out to look for the boy's shoe, but I decided that it would be better to come back at some later time. There was no guarantee that they wouldn't go right to the police and tell them someone was out there. They may have even still been out there hiding somewhere, and I couldn't take that chance. So I drove straight home and sat in total darkness in my kitchen and finished off a half a pint of bourbon, which I don't even like.

I decided not to say anything to John about it. I knew that it wouldn't go over very well, seeing as I never told him about the missing shoe. I wasn't even sure where it was, having only a general idea of when I may have dropped it the night I brought the boy to the pool. All I did know was that it was likely still out there somewhere and I was going to have to find it before someone else did.

SAM

Once we got back to town, it was Keith's idea to call the cops, so we made him do it. We were at the phone booth down by the supermarket. It was closed and no one else was around. Keith hung up right after he told them about people shouting and running. I didn't think his story was good enough to make them go out there, but then we saw a cop car take off in that direction about five minutes later, so I knew it did the trick.

We all heard the guy coming up the dirt road at the same time, and without saying a word to each other, we jumped into the bushes on the side opposite the corn rows. We might have found out what the guy was up to if Keith hadn't sneezed. He's had hay fever ever since he was seven and being out in those fields just got to be too much I guess. When he sneezed, Richie and I just looked at each other, and I know we were both thinking the same thing. So we took off like a shot, with Keith right behind. I caught a glimpse of the guy as I was turning to go down the dirt road back toward the highway, but I wouldn't have been able to tell you who it was. It was too dark, and he was standing at the edge of where the corn rows start. He must have heard the sneeze and was probably wondering where it came from. We went by him so fast, he didn't even have time to react. I never saw a parked car anywhere, so I'm not sure where he came from.

We talked for an hour about how the guy could have gotten out there. I said maybe it was old man Gehring, since he wouldn't need a car to get to his own cornfield, but Richie said the guy didn't look anything like Gehring, who is pretty fat. He was right. The guy we saw was shorter and skinnier. I didn't see him for very long, but long enough. Keith said it could have been a hobo, but no one has seen one of them in about twenty years, I don't think.

After the phone call to the cops, we thought we should get away from the phone booth so we rode our bikes over to Eastern Park and sat under the bandstand. We weren't there a minute before Richie gave Keith a hard time about sneezing. He said that if Keith hadn't screwed things up, we might have found out what was going on out there. We might have even solved Mikey's murder.

"You're telling me you would have followed that guy out there?" Keith asked.

"Damn right," Richie said.

Keith looked at me then. "What about you?"

I thought about it for a couple seconds. Then I just shook my head. Keith turned back to Richie.

"I guess you would have had to go out there alone," he said. "My sneeze probably saved your life."

Richie knew Keith was right, so he just shrugged. Then Keith said he had to get home. Richie and I didn't want to leave yet. I guess we were still pretty worked up about what happened.

"What do you think that guy was doing out there all by himself?" Richie asked after awhile.

"Maybe he wasn't alone," I said. "Maybe he was meeting somebody."

"If there was anybody else out there, where were they parked?" he asked. "They didn't walk out there. Grownups don't walk anywhere."

"Maybe there were a whole bunch of people out there and they have a secret place to park," I said.

"Maybe," he said.

"I know one thing," I said. "If he was alone, he wasn't out there to have sex."

For once, Richie didn't have a wise remark. We sat silent for a bit more.

"Maybe it's a good thing he sneezed," he said finally.

"Yeah," I told him. Although I have always wondered what would have happened if he didn't.

MIGGS

After I hung up, I drove straight over to the Vogels. Vic was already there with the family, holding down the fort, and keeping them occupied. He knew what I knew which was that when this got out, the town would be up in arms. And it would get out. There was no doubt about that.

When we first got the call about the boy being missing that day, the pool had already been closed and everyone sent home. Donna followed procedure to a tee. Whenever a kid turns up missing, she and the lifeguards are supposed to clear the pool and look for the kid in the pool first. If they're convinced that the child isn't in there anywhere, they can let everyone back in. If it's late enough, she can send them all home, which is what she did. Before she closes up, she's supposed to notify the child's parents, if the kid hasn't been located before then. And if the kid doesn't show at home, it's up to the parents to notify us. Which had never happened prior to this. The only quibble I had with what she did is that she didn't check the locker room when she closed the pool to see if the boy's clothes were still in there. If they were, you would obviously have a different scenario than if they weren't. When I asked her about it later, she said she didn't think of it. She was sure that the boy had simply left on his own, even though no one could recall seeing him do so. It's hard to blame her there. Like I said, nothing like this had ever happened.

When the boy didn't show for supper, we got another call, this one from the family. That's when we began to look at it differently, and so I sent Vic out in the squad car to look for him. Still, I expected the boy to show up by nightfall, which is the latest that most runaway kids surface. I was surprised then when Donna called again later to tell me that she found him in the deep end of the pool.

While I was waiting for the ambulance attendants to pull the boy out of the water, I could see that he was only wearing his bathing suit, so I sent a couple of my guys into the boy's locker room to see if they could find his clothes. There aren't really any lockers in there, just individual shelves that the kids call cubbies. It's short for cubbyholes, I guess. Donna told me that the cubbies aren't assigned to any one kid, so my men had to check all of them.

When Brisby came out about five minutes later, he was carrying a pair of shorts, a t-shirt and one sneaker. I sent Vic right over to get Mikey's father who confirmed that the clothes and sneaker indeed belonged to his son. He didn't ask where the other sneaker was. I think he was too upset for it to even register. I then sent my men back to the locker room to turn it upside down to look for the other shoe. They didn't find it, so I asked Donna what she thought it might mean. She just shrugged and said that things get lost all the time. "They're kids," she reminded me. She said it was possible that one of the other boys might have taken it by mistake when they went in to get their stuff after she closed the pool.

Like I said, I wished she had checked the locker room earlier, before she came back and found the boy. I suppose I should have thought to tell her to when she first called. If the clothes were there then, we would have one scenario. If not, then we would have an entirely different one. I had asked Donna if it was possible that she could have missed seeing the boy earlier in the day, down there at the bottom of the deep end. She assured me that it was. "It gets murky down there from all the lotion and sweat," she said. "It takes awhile after they leave to filter everything out."

I remember thinking then that what she said made sense on some surface level, but there was still something about it that didn't sit right with me. I suppose it was that missing shoe. Why would another boy take one shoe? Who needs three? I suppose someone could have lost theirs and taken Mikey's instead. There are only a few different brands of sneakers. Lots of kids have the same kind and color.

I have to admit, as I pulled up to the Vogels house that night, I found myself hoping that the one Vic found out by the tracks wasn't Mikey's after all. Of course, that wouldn't necessarily make the boy's drowning any more innocent. Not with the fresh water in his lungs. In any event, it didn't matter. As soon as I walked in and saw both shoes sitting on the kitchen table in front of Mr. and Mrs. Vogel I knew they were a match.

"You still think it was an accident that my boy drown in that pool?" she asked.

She had gestured at the shoes. I reached down and picked them both up. Anyone could see that they were the same size, same color, with the same amount of wear.

"We don't necessarily know that his shoe being out there changes anything," I said. Of course, even I didn't believe that.

Mr. Vogel laughed. More of a snort actually. "How the hell would his shoe get all the way out there?" he asked me. "He was eight years old for Christ's sake. You think he walked out there and left it and then walked back to town and went swimming like nothing ever happened?"

"What do you think happened then?" I asked him, knowing as soon as I did that I was in for it.

"Someone took him out there!" he said. "Then they did God knows what to him and brought him back and put him in that pool! You ever think of that?!"

Of course I had. Just about every minute since the boy's body was found. That was the prevailing theory alright. The one that both I and the DA thought explained the fresh water in his lungs.

I was spared from answering his question when their daughter appeared in the doorway in her pajamas. She just looked at us for a second. Then she saw the sneakers on the table. I was trying to guess whether she had heard any of what we had been talking about when she spoke up.

"What's wrong?" she asked. "Is this about Mikey? Are those his?"

Mrs. Vogel went to her immediately and ushered her from the room. Then the phone started ringing and her husband and I stood there uncomfortably while the noise pierced the silence for several rings. Finally, Mr. Vogel went over and answered it.

I took that opportunity to tell Vic to go wake up the DA and tell him what was going on. I then turned back to see Mr. Vogel holding the phone out to me.

"It's for you," he said, as his wife came back in and gave me a dirty look, as if the idea of me using their phone was revolting to her.

"Hello?" I said into the phone.

"Chief." It was Brisby. "I spoke with Vic earlier. He said something about finding the kid's shoe. Is it his?"

"Not now," was all I said. Then I hung up and turned around to find the Vogels still standing there staring at me.

"What is it that you aren't telling us?" Mr. Vogel asked. "We have a right to know."

He was right, of course. I couldn't see the point in withholding anything any longer. The killer hadn't been lulled into showing himself, and certainly wouldn't make that mistake now. Not after Vic found that shoe. So I told the Vogels that there was just one other thing and that maybe they should sit down before I told them.

HAGER

I didn't hear about the shoe until I got to church the next morning. John must not have heard about it the night before or I'm sure I would have gotten a call. Or worse, a visit. He didn't go to my church, or any church that I am aware of, so I didn't have to face him there, but I knew my time was coming.

Everyone in the choir was talking about it. I pretended to be as gossipy as the others, occasionally interjecting a question or a comment, although I don't think I caused any particular attention to be focused my way. The gist of it was that the boy had obviously been killed somewhere else and brought back to the pool to make it appear that he drowned there earlier in the day. No one could agree on whether the boy had actually been out near those tracks, but that seemed to be the position of the majority in the choir. The minority suggested that the shoe could have ended up there any number of ways, although certainly by the killer, intentionally or unintentionally.

I was going to ask why they thought that finding his shoe out there meant that he hadn't drowned in the pool, but that appeared to be too risky a statement to make. The general feeling was that an eight-year-old would have no way of getting out to that place outside of town without the assistance of an adult, and would have no business being out there in the first place. Of course, that was my very same feeling that night when he wandered into our midst. Unfortunately for him, he had somehow managed to do so, even

63

though he was so young and it was nearly eleven o'clock at night. Meaning they were wrong, although it was little consolation to me and I wasn't about to correct them. To them it was simple: the deputy found his shoe and the boy's murder was revealed.

After a stop at the bakery, I returned home to find that a note from John had been slipped under my door. It instructed me to drive to Herford to meet him at the Custard Cup at two o'clock. The Custard Cup is a drive-in just outside the town, but they also have tables inside where people often bring their families on Friday nights. On the other hand, Sunday afternoon is a slow time. I assumed that he picked that time not so much to give me a chance to get back from church and drive all the way out there, but because there would be fewer people eating there at that time. He was right. He was waiting for me in the parking lot, and when we entered, there was only one other couple there, along with a boy, their son I assumed. We took a seat far across the room from them so as to be out of earshot. I promptly told John everything that happened the night before, including why I was out there.

"When were you going to tell me about this?" he asked.

"I was hoping never," I told him, honestly. "I was hoping to go out and retrieve it and dispose of it so that no one would ever know." I meant him, of course, and I think he knew that.

"What was it doing out there in the first place?" he asked.

I told him that when I carried the boy back to my car that night, I also had his shirt and shorts and shoes in my hands, albeit clumsily. We had agreed that it was important that the clothes be kept dry and returned to the locker room at the pool, but it was hard to carry them and the boy at the same time. "I must have dropped one of the shoes on the way," I admitted. "I didn't notice until I got back to the car."

"Why didn't you go look for it then?" he asked, unable to hide his anger.

"You told me to get him over to the pool right away," I reminded him.

He frowned. "Then you should have gone back out there the next day," he said.

"When Larry Gehring was out plowing?" I asked.

He stared. He knew I was right.

"What the hell were those kids doing out there anyway?" he asked finally.

"I don't know," I said, once again being honest. I didn't want to tell him my fear that they may have somehow discovered us.

We drank our milkshakes in silence for awhile.

"We have to find out who those kids are," he said.

"And do what?" I asked. "Put them in the pool, too?"

I don't know why I picked that moment to be so bold. I was afraid of what his reaction might be, although he would never have acted in that restaurant. I was surprised at how calmly he responded.

"No," he said. "We won't be doing that again anytime soon. I just want to know what we're up against." He stood up and dropped his napkin on the table. "Of course, if it comes down to it, I'll do whatever's necessary," he said.

With that, he walked outside to his car, leaving me to think what that might possibly mean.

SAM

I heard about Mikey's sneaker at the funeral Monday morning. My mother said they had to wait that long to bury him because they had to do an autopsy. I sort of knew what it was, but when she actually explained it, I almost chucked up my breakfast. She said they had to cut him open and look inside at all his organs and stuff to figure out why he died. She said the casket was open at the funeral home, so I guess his face and head must have been OK. I didn't have to go to the wake, so I didn't see that.

I had never been to a funeral before, but my parents thought it would be a good idea for me to go, since Mikey was also a kid. I guess they wanted me to learn about death, which was pretty dumb since I already had a pretty good idea about it. I think a lot of other parents must have felt the same way because there were a whole bunch of us kids there. Most of Mikey's class and the ones above. Keith was there with his parents, and I saw some other kids from my grade, too. Richie didn't go, but that was no surprise. He said he had already been to one of those and that was enough.

People didn't talk much in the church. You're not really supposed to, but they were all talking outside after the cars from the funeral procession took off to bring Mikey's body out to the cemetery. I didn't see Sylvia until she walked down the aisle behind the casket with her parents on the way out. She was crying really hard and wasn't looking at anyone. I was glad of that because I don't know what I would have done if she had seen me.

When we were driving home, my father was practically gloating about them finding Mikey's sneaker. He said it proved that he was right all along. I guess my mother wasn't too worried about him talking about it in front of me. Heck, they both knew there was no way they could keep me from knowing. Like I said, everyone in town was talking about it.

What I couldn't figure out was why no one was talking about the other thing. I figured after the news came out about the shoe, Keith's father would have to tell somebody what he heard about all those people out at the old hobo camp having sex with each other. I mean, the camp is pretty far down the tracks from where they found Mikey's sneaker, but anybody would have to make the connection. I thought he'd have to say something then. So I couldn't figure out why no one was talking about it.

I found out the reason why after lunch.

My mother came up to my room and told me that Keith was outside and wanted to see me. Normally, he just walks in the house and up to my room. We go in and out of each other's houses like we live there. Nobody cares. It's just the way it is. That day, though, he asked my mother to get me and said he'd wait outside.

I came out of the house expecting Richie to be there with him. When I saw that he was alone, I asked him what was up. He said we needed to go someplace else to talk.

We ended up over at the elementary school down the street from my house, which was deserted. I guess maybe the thing about Mikey's shoe had parents pretty scared and they didn't want their kids going to the playground like they normally would on a Monday afternoon in August.

Keith sat down on the edge of the sandbox. I sat down across from him. When I looked around, I figured out why he picked that place. Nobody was in sight, and if anyone did come, we'd see them long before they could hear us. He must have noticed that on the way over to my house.

"You heard about Mikey's sneaker, right?" I asked.

"Yeah," he said. "That's all anybody's talking about."

"So did your father tell the cops about the people out there?" I asked. "He did, right?"

Keith looked around again, then shook his head.

"Why not?" I asked.

"Because I lied," he said.

"What do you mean?" I asked. "Lied about what?"

He didn't answer right away and wouldn't look at me. "I lied about hearing it from my father."

It took a second before I understood. "You mean you didn't hear them talking in bed?"

He shook his head.

"Well how did you hear about it then?" I asked. I was starting to feel a little squirmy then.

"I saw it," he said. "With my own two eyes."

It felt like somebody punched me in the stomach. "When?" I asked him.

"About two weeks ago," he said. "It was at night like I said. I saw them myself."

"Holy shit," I said.

He looked me in the eye then. "Yeah," he said.

"Why didn't you say something?" I asked. I meant to me and Richie. Not his parents. But I did wonder about that too.

"I don't know," he said. "I was scared, I guess."

"What did you see exactly?" I asked him.

"Like I said before, people having sex," he said. "Right out in the open."

"How many?" I asked.

He shrugged. "I don't know. Maybe twenty. Men and women. Some with each other. The men, I mean. Women, too."

"Jesus," I said. Not just because of how strange it was, but because it was pretty much the same as I saw.

"What were you doing out there anyway?" I asked. It finally occurred to me that I hadn't thought about that yet.

He looked away again. "I was with someone," he said.

"Who?" I asked.

"Promise you won't tell anyone?" he asked. "Definitely not Richie. He doesn't know any of this."

"Sure," I said. "I promise."

"Kimberly," he said.

"Kimberly Miggs?" I asked, just to be sure. "What were you doing out there with Kimberly Miggs?"

"What do you think?" he asked.

"I don't know," I said. But I was lying. I knew.

"You know what everyone says about her, right?" he asked.

"You mean that she does stuff?"

He nodded again.

"You went out there with Kimberly Miggs?" I asked. "To do stuff?"

He looked at me now. "She said she liked me," he said.

"She likes everyone," I said.

"What's that supposed to mean?" he wanted to know.

"It means she doesn't care how old you are or what you look like," I told him. "If you give her some beer, she'll let you do stuff with her."

"She said she liked me," he said again.

"Well, what does she say about all this?" I asked. "Didn't she tell her father?"

He gave me a look. "What do you think?" he said.

He was right. There was no way she could tell her father what she was doing out there. "She made me promise not to say anything," he said. "That's why I didn't tell you."

"So why'd you change your mind?" I asked him. "Why did you want us to go out there the other night?"

"Because I thought it might have something to do with what

happened to Mikey," he said.

"You saw him out there, too?" I blurted it out before I had a chance to think and knew right away I blew it. He looked at me like I had two heads.

"What's that supposed to mean?" he asked.

I didn't answer right away and so he got up and came over to my side of the sand box and made me look at him.

"Are you saying you were out there, too?" he asked.

I told him yeah, just not at the same time as him. He asked me what I was doing out there. I just looked at him. I didn't want to say.

"You mean you and Kimberly?" he asked

I didn't answer. I mean, I didn't think I needed to.

"Holy shit," he said. "And Mikey was there, too?"

I nodded.

"What the hell was he doing there?"

I told him I didn't know. At least that part was true.

MIGGS

The town meeting was Fritz's idea. He felt we owed it to everyone after word got around about the shoe. We had no choice but to answer their questions, he said. I reminded him that we were both up for re-election in the fall. It wasn't meant as a warning. Just a fact. I opened the door a crack and looked out to the large room in town hall where the selectmen hold their monthly meetings. The place was packed, with many forced to stand. I closed the door again and went back to my desk. "I'm sure my opponent will be out there," I said, as I sat down.

"Who's that?" he asked, looking up.

"What difference does it make?" I said. "They'll be lining up to take me on after tonight."

"I'm sure the same goes for me," he said.

"Then why don't you let me take the fall for this," I told him. "You were away when it happened. I asked you to let me handle it. They won't hold that against you."

He smiled, although he looked anything but happy.

"What kind of DA would I be if I let the chief investigative officer in town convince me to do something I didn't already feel was the right thing to do?" he asked. "It was my decision. You didn't have to convince me of anything. And I'm going to tell them that."

As always, he was good on his word. He told the crowd just that. He even made it sound like it was his idea from the get-go.

The audience erupted at that. Lots of cries for his job and

mine. It got even worse when I informed them of the fresh water in the boy's lungs. I got about the same reaction from the Vogels when I told them that on Saturday night. I had also ordered them not to tell anyone else until I had a chance to and, to my surprise, they seemed to have obliged.

"You mean you knew that all along and opened the pool up again and let all our kids go back up there?" one woman asked.

"The boy didn't drown there," I reminded her. "It seems to me that might make it the safest place they could be."

There was a lot more grumbling after that. When we got them to finally listen again, we explained about not letting the perpetrator know we were looking for him, hoping he would slip up and reveal himself.

"How do you know it wasn't a woman?" asked one of the younger men.

Fortunately, the DA took that one, explaining how studies showed women to be far less capable of crimes against children, so much so that it was difficult to even find a recent example. It made him sound like he knew what he was doing.

"Well have you focused on anyone?" another man asked. I looked at Fritz and he nodded for me to take it.

"No one specifically, although the state police have offered their assistance. We're waiting on some information from them."

"What about the boy's family?" asked another mother, someone who I've known for years. I used to think she was a friend, but I wasn't about to take anything for granted at that point. A number of the people in the room began to boo her. I waved my arms to quiet them down, which took some time.

"We have absolutely no reason to think anyone in the boy's family could have done this," the DA told her. He hadn't even waited for me to decide who should talk first.

"I work with her and I can tell you she was at work all day," another woman said, and there were some concurring statements from some of the other people in the room.

"What about the father?" one of the men asked. It was Joe Peters. He works at the pneumatic plant over in Oliander and is an OK guy. A bit of a crank sometimes. I don't think he meant anything by it. He probably just wanted to sound important, like he had some kind of inside knowledge about crimes and criminals.

There was a brief round of objections, followed by a sudden and awkward silence. Then everyone turned at once to the back of the room and I saw why. Mr. Vogel had stepped into the aisle and was walking slowly toward the front where Joe Peters was sitting. It was so quiet that I could hear the clock ticking in the clerk's office across the hall, even though it's a good fifty feet away and the door was closed.

I didn't know what to expect and looked over at Brisby who was stationed near the side door to warn him to watch for an altercation. I think everyone was thinking the same thing, as Mr. Vogel made his way down the aisle until he got to the row where Peters was. He stopped there and turned toward him.

"What about me?" Mr. Vogel asked. His tone was even, neither angry nor threatening. But you could tell something was brewing just below the surface.

Peters froze, and the DA stepped forward as if he had something to say, but I held my hand out to stop him.

"Are you suggesting I killed my own son?" Mr. Vogel asked Peters. Again, Vogel maintained his composure, but I was prepared for anything to happen at that point.

Peters didn't respond. He looked to me as if to ask me to intervene, but I kept quiet. Part of me wanted to hear what he had to say and for him to pay for his remark.

"What kind of man would kill his own son?" someone asked then. It broke the tension and all eyes turned to another man who I knew only slightly. His name had escaped me at the time. He was two rows behind Peters and stood up. He didn't appear ready to fight, nor did it look like he would have stood much of a chance against Peters if he did.

"What father would ever do such a thing?" he asked, this time addressing all of us.

Everyone stared, but no one said a word. Finally, Mr. Vogel's brother-in-law hurried in from the back and took his arm. Mr. Vogel didn't struggle or fight him. He just let him turn him around and escort him out of the room. Peters didn't say another word and looked rather relieved that it was all over. The other man sat down then and was patted on the back by two or three folks seated near him. I know I was grateful that he had spoken up when he did. It diffused what otherwise could have been a troubling incident.

The meeting ended shortly after that. We told everyone we were closing the pool for the season, even though we still felt it was safe there, and despite the fact that there were still three weeks left until school started. We also advised them to keep close track of their children. I said that we would be as open as possible about the investigation going forward, but that we weren't promising anything, since circumstances might arise where we didn't want someone to know we were watching them or were on the verge of an arrest.

There were some nods and a few mumbled responses, then everyone started filing out. Hardly any looked at us as they did. When everyone was finally gone, I turned to Fritz to ask him what we should do next.

That's when the two boys walked in from the side door.

HAGER

I went to the town meeting that night, like I assume most people did, simply out of curiosity. I wasn't afraid of exposing myself. After all, if the police knew anything, they wouldn't be having a meeting with the townspeople. They'd be arresting someone. They all but said as much. As far as I could tell, they didn't know anything, other than the fact that the boy hadn't drowned in the pool. That was my fault. I never even thought about the chlorine in the water.

Aside from that, there were a lot of angry parents making a lot of noise. I nodded and pretended to look just as concerned, which wasn't difficult since I did have concerns. They just weren't the same as theirs.

I don't know what made me stand up to defend the boy's father. Guilt most likely. I suppose I simply wanted to protect the family, knowing that they had already suffered enough. I have to admit that it was a risky thing to do. I don't know what I would have done if the sheriff or the district attorney had asked me why I spoke up. I hadn't thought that far in advance. In retrospect, it was reckless, but it was also too late to do anything about it.

Fortunately, the other man came and took the boy's father away. By the time the meeting ended, I was feeling a bit more relieved than I did after learning about the discovery of the boy's sneaker. True, my plan to have it appear to be an accidental drowning had failed, and that put me in a vulnerable position. However, based upon what the sheriff had said, they didn't know where the boy was killed or who might be involved. The only thing that troubled me was the nod that the sheriff had given me as the meeting concluded. I'm sure it was meant to thank me, but I was disappointed not only for having called attention to myself, but having done so in front of the man who was the biggest threat to my survival.

I reported back to John at his house as soon as the meeting was over. He seemed somewhat less tense than he had the last time we met.

"Did they say anything about the boys from the other night?" he asked.

"Not a word," I told him. "I don't think they know about them."

He nodded. "But then they lied before," he said.

"I don't think they're lying," I said, as reassuringly as I could. "They told everyone that they got an anonymous call about someone being out near that farm. They never mentioned anything about any kids. In fact, they specifically said that the deputy who went out there didn't see anyone."

"But he saw that shoe, didn't he?" he said.

Even though I'm sure he wasn't expecting an answer to that, I nodded. I knew how much that had disturbed him.

"Well," he said finally, "there's no reason to go back out there now. None whatsoever, right?"

"That's right," I told him. "We can always find somewhere else to meet when things die down."

He shot me a look. "You're going to have to amuse yourself some other way now," he said. "I've got too much to lose and so do the others."

Apparently, he didn't think I did. I asked him if that's what he thought.

"It doesn't matter what I think," he said. "The matter's

closed."

So that was it. Our select group had met only twice. Only one time was it undisturbed. It was quite exciting and, I have to say, addicting. The masks, the paint, the fire, the dancing and, of course, all the rest. The second time was interrupted by the boy after we had barely gotten started. It was quite disappointing then to hear John call a stop to it, even with the events of the last few days.

I stood up to leave, thinking I better go before I said something else to make him angry.

"One other thing," he said. "Don't call me again or come out here. Not until this blows over anyway."

"But what if something else comes up?" I asked.

"Then I'll come to you," he said.

I'm sure he meant that to be reassuring. However, I knew I shouldn't take it that way.

SAM

Keith and I stayed out at the playground almost the whole afternoon. Luckily, Richie didn't know where we were, so we got to talk without him trying to decide things for us, like he always does. Mostly, we were trying to figure out what to do and whether we should tell the cops. That was later on, though. The first thing Keith wanted to know was why I thought Kimberly would ever go back out there with me after what they saw the week before. He said she was pretty scared the night she was with him, and she told him she was never going to go out there again.

So I told him I had a confession to make, too.

"She never showed," I said. "I waited for her for over an hour, but she never came."

"Why would she say she'd go out there with you and then not show?" he asked.

I told him I didn't know. He asked me if I had talked to her afterward. I told him I tried. I said I called her, but she wouldn't talk to me. That was a lie. I never called her, but I didn't know what else to say.

"Do you think she told her father?" Keith asked.

I told him I didn't think so, otherwise he would have come to talk to us by now.

He said we had go to the sheriff then and tell him what we saw. We had no choice.

I reminded him of why he never said anything in the first

place. He was out there trying to feel up the sheriff's own daughter after filling her up with liquor. How do you tell the sheriff something like that?

Keith said maybe we could just leave that part out.

"So what do we tell him we were doing out there?" I asked.

"We could say we were out there stealing corn," he said.

I told him that sounded stupid. Nobody would believe that. Besides, the cornfields were pretty far away from the old hobo camp.

"We could just say we were out there to drink," he said. "Just you and me. Leave Kimberly out of it."

I told him my parents would kill me if they ever heard that. He said that considering what happened to Mikey, they probably wouldn't be too worried about me drinking. He was pretty sure his folks wouldn't.

"Yeah but then I'd be a liar on top of it," I told him. "I didn't tell them I was going out there that night. So then I'd be telling them that I drank and lied. They wouldn't let me go out again until I was twenty."

"Well, we're going to have to come up with something or we can't say anything then," he said.

That's when I got the idea or at least the beginning of it. "What if we don't say we were out there?" I asked him. He looked confused at that.

"What if we say we saw Mikey out on the road near Gehring's farm that night?" I said.

"How does that help us?" he wanted to know.

"We could say he told us about the naked people and stuff."

"Aren't they going to wonder why we didn't say anything right away, after Mikey was killed?" he asked.

"We could say we were scared," I said. "Or we could say we didn't believe him."

"They'll ask if anyone was with him," he said. "What do we say

79

to that?"

"We'll just say he was walking back by himself."

That sounded pretty dumb, even as I said it. We both knew they'd never believe that. We sat there quiet for awhile. Then he got excited like he just thought of something.

"What if we don't even mention Mikey?" he asked.

"What do you mean?" I said.

"What if we just say we heard that there was some stuff going on out there at the camp?" he said. "We could say it was something we overheard somewhere. That's why we didn't come forward before."

I was about to tell him that didn't make much sense, but then it seemed to me like it just might work. This town loves gossip. Everybody is always talking about stuff. Adults and kids. "We could say that since it was so close to the same place where they found Mikey's shoe, we thought it might be important," I told him.

"Yeah," he said. "That way we wouldn't have any connection to it at all, except for just hearing some gossip."

"Right," I said. "Our parents can't get too mad at us for that. We could even say we thought it was a bunch of bullshit when we heard it, but then when they found Mikey's shoe out there we changed our minds."

"Yeah," he said. "Like we just wanted to be helpful."

I thought that sounded pretty good. In fact, if I thought of it the day they found Mikey, I might have told that story myself back then.

"So what do you say?" he asked.

"Yeah," I told him. "Let's do it."

So that's how we ended up going to the meeting that night.

MIGGS

Kids are funny. As soon as the boys finished telling us their story, I knew that they weren't being honest. Frankly, I wouldn't be much of a police officer if I thought otherwise. Boys that age always think they're pretty smart and have every base covered when they make something up, that is until someone asks a question that they've never even considered. Which they always do, whether it's a parent or teacher or cop.

"Where did you hear that?" I asked them. I tried to use a casual tone. I didn't want them to clam up.

The look on their faces told me they hadn't thought it through. Not very well anyway. The only question then was why they were telling us anything at all. At that point, I pretty much convinced myself that they were probably making the whole thing up to get involved in what was the biggest story in town in years. Certainly, in their lifetime.

"I don't remember," said the one kid. I knew him to be the son of Nathan Somerset, the town selectman. I'm no fan of Somerset. There isn't anything specific about him that I have a problem with. I just think he's too much of a politician, which is pretty much saying he is not to be believed. His son looked to me to be headed down the same path.

"Well," I said, "That's quite a juicy bit of information. Naked adults? Masks? Having sex? I can't imagine you'd ever be able to forget where you heard that."

They exchanged a look again. For a long uncomfortable time, they sat there silent. I knew they couldn't have said anything to their parents or I'd be talking to them instead. I considered using the threat of asking where their parents were, but I wanted to save that for just the right time. Fritz looked on the whole time, but it seemed to be understood that I would be doing all the questioning. I looked back and forth between the two kids, patiently waiting for a response.

The other boy spoke first. He's the son of George Fisher who I didn't know all that well. George has always seemed like an OK guy. A little sour maybe, like he's got a permanent raincloud hanging over his head or something. His son had never been in trouble as far as I knew, and I remember him being a pretty good ballplayer in Little League. "I didn't actually hear it," the Fisher boy said. "Keith did."

That earned him a scowl from the young Somerset kid. He looked at me. It was apparent that he knew he was on the hot seat. I could practically see his mind working. The other boy saved him, though, probably realizing the predicament he had just put him in.

"It was when you were out at the Custard Cup the other day, remember?" he told his friend.

The Somerset kid's expression changed right away.

"Yeah," he said. "Me and my parents were out there on Sunday. The Custard Cup. I heard a guy say something to another guy there."

I nodded. Fritz suddenly looked interested. "And who were these guys?" I asked.

He said he didn't know their names, although he had seen one of them before.

"Where?" I asked.

He took a couple of seconds before he answered. "He was that guy who was here tonight," he said.

That took me by surprise, I must say. I looked at Fritz who

gave me a slight nod as if to tell me to keep pressing.

"Which guy?" I asked.

There was no pause. "The one who stood up for Mikey's father," the Somerset kid said.

Like I said, kids are funny. Either he was actually telling the truth or he was being pretty clever linking that fellow to his made-up story. Whatever way it went, I knew I wasn't going to be able to ignore their story then.

"Do either of your parents know you're here?" I asked them.

They both shook their head at the same time.

"Why's that?" Fritz asked. It was an odd time for him to speak up, and it seemed to scare them a bit. As usual, Fritz had good timing.

They shared another look before the Fisher kid answered. "Like you said, it's sex," he told me, emphasizing that last word. "I'm not talking to my parents about that."

He said it like I'd understand the discomfort that he would feel discussing that topic with his mother or father or both. And I have to admit I did. After all, I had two sons, one who had already been that age and would have never told me anything remotely having to do with that topic. The younger one didn't even want to know about the birds and bees, let alone adults outside somewhere having sex.

"You understand I may have to say something to them now, right?" I asked. They both looked panicked again, but the inevitability of that had to have settled on them. They both nodded grimly.

"Is there anything else you aren't telling us?" the DA asked then.

They exchanged looks again and shook their heads vigorously.

Fritz didn't quite accept that and went on to ask several more questions, seeking some specifics about what the fellow at the meeting may or may not have said in front of the Somerset kid at that drive-in.

Once again, he clammed up pretty good. He had no specifics, he said. Just what he already told us.

"I'm a little curious about something," Fritz said to him. "Wouldn't your parents have heard the same thing?"

The kid shook his head.

"Why not?" Fritz asked. His friend looked almost as curious to hear his answer as I was.

"I threw the trash in the trash barrel when we were done eating," he said. "It was right next to those guys. My parents were all the way across the room."

Like I said, the kid was probably on his way to becoming one hell of a politician. If he was lying, he was pretty damn good. I didn't think there was any point in keeping them there any longer, so I told them to head on home. I knew I was going to have to go out and talk to that fellow and ask him about what the boy just told us. And when he told me that he had no idea what I was talking about, as I expected he would, I would have to go over to the Somerset house and warn that kid in front of his parents about interfering with a murder investigation.

HAGER

It was the night after that town meeting when the doorbell rang. I was getting ready to go to the band concert and had just gotten out of the tub and was still drying myself. The sound of bell made the hair on the back of my neck stand up. No one had ever come to my door in the eighteen months I had lived there, except for my landlord and the paper boy, and the latter comes exactly at one o'clock on Saturday afternoon to collect, even in a snowstorm. He never changes the day or time. He's quite reliable that way. That's one of the reasons I liked him so much. He would never have a reason to come to my door on a Wednesday night.

I yelled out that I'd be right there and threw some clothes on. I thought about moving the suitcase from under my bed, but I didn't know where else I could put it in such a short time. I tried to stall by calling out two more times before I actually opened the door.

The sight of the sheriff and his deputy standing there startled me. I made a conscious effort to slow my breathing and paste a smile on my face. It probably appeared disingenuous, but they didn't react to it. In fact, the sheriff surprised me by returning the smile.

"Mister Hager?" he asked.

"Yes," I said. "Yancey Hager. That's right." I said it cheerfully, like he got the right answer on some sort of quiz show. We all stood there awkwardly for a couple of seconds.

"Sorry to bother you," he said finally, "but I was wondering if we could talk to you. We have a couple of questions we'd like to ask."

I nodded before I said anything. Then I said something that I realized later was probably the wisest thing I could have said. "Does this have to do with me and that boy's father the other night?" I asked.

Immediately, I could detect the sheriff relax a bit. He appeared almost sheepish, which told me that they weren't there to arrest me. Of that, I was quite sure.

"Do you mind if we come in?" he asked. "It might be better if we talk inside." He looked around as if to suggest that we wouldn't want the other tenants to hear.

I told them of course and led them into the kitchen where the sheriff and I sat at the table, while the other fellow stood in the doorway. That made me a little nervous, I must admit. I felt his eyes on the back of my head the entire time. The sheriff didn't introduce him and he never gave me his name, but the tag on his shirt read "Brisby".

"I didn't mean to cause any trouble," I told the sheriff. "Those words just came out. You know, with everyone talking about the boy's mother and father. I feel so sorry for that family."

The sheriff nodded, as if he did as well. "You don't have any information that would specifically exonerate the father, do you?" he asked.

I tried to look as contrite as possible. "No," I said. "Of course not. I guess I was only trying to ease his pain. I imagine he has suffered more than enough."

Once again, the sheriff nodded. I turned slightly to look at the other fellow who remained where he was.

"Well," the sheriff said. "That's actually not what we came here about."

"Oh," I said. Once again, I tried to hide my concern behind a smile.

"Did you happen to have lunch with someone out at the Custard Cup in Herford on Sunday?" he asked.

My heart immediately began to race, although I think I somehow managed to keep my composure.

"Why?" I asked, as innocently as I could.

"We'll ask the questions here," the other man said. The sheriff shot him a look, before he turned back to me.

"I'll tell you in a minute," the sheriff said, "but first I need to know if you were there."

My mind went into a sort of frenzy. Their appearance at my door and the direct question about the diner told me that someone had to have told them I was there. How else would they know to ask? It was probably one of the wait-staff or perhaps the cook. It might have even been that other couple who was there. As far as I could recall, those were the only possibilities. Whoever it had been, someone could identify me. So my first inclination, which was to deny being there, didn't seem prudent. Then again, I knew that if I admitted I was there, they would want to know who I was with. Whoever saw me must have seen John. If they identified me, they could probably identify him too, so it would be risky on my part to deny being there or to deny that John was there as well. In that brief moment, I was forced to make a choice. In effect, to take a gamble. So that's what I did.

"Yes," I said. "I ate lunch there on Sunday. I had a hamburger and a vanilla milk shake."

Once again, out of the corner of my eye, I saw the deputy look at the sheriff, then back at me. "Were you alone?" the sheriff asked, ignoring him.

There it was. Just like I thought. The question was rather clever. Did he already know about John being there and was only testing me? Or did he not know who my companion was? Did the person who told him I was there forget about John? Or did they see him but couldn't identify him? I thought about how John might react if he found out I had told them about him. I didn't have to think too long about that.

"Yes," I said. "I'm not very proud of it, but I often eat alone on Sundays. Not of my own choosing. I have no family."

I waited for the sheriff to confront me. To tell me that whoever saw me saw John as well. Instead, he nodded, which surprised me once more. "I take it you don't talk to yourself then?" he asked.

It was another comment that seemed like it could be a trap. Unlike the previous one, I felt I had no exposure in answering it. "Generally no," I said, trying to sound as sarcastic as I could without offending him.

The sheriff smiled and stood up. "That's about what I figured," he said.

"Can I ask what this is about?" I asked him.

The two men exchanged looks. "Someone said they saw you there," the sheriff told me.

"And why would that be of importance to the police?" I asked. "Was there a robbery?"

"No," he said. "Nothing like that. This person thought they overheard you and your friend talking about something. Something that may be of importance."

"My friend?" I asked. It just came out. I didn't even think about it. That's probably what made it sound so convincing. Once again, I had taken a chance and for the second time it had paid off.

The sheriff nodded. "Let's just say we don't hold a lot of stock in what we were told," he said. "You seem to have confirmed it for us."

I let out a breath that I hoped wasn't audible. The sheriff held out his hand, which I shook. "I'm glad I finally got to meet you," he said. "You're relatively new here, right?"

"I've been here about a year and a half," I told him. "I'm sorry I couldn't be of more help."

He smiled and headed for the door. The deputy followed, but

ignored me.

"If we need anything else, we may be back," the sheriff told me when he reached the door. "Though I doubt it will come to that."

I told him that would be fine. He nodded and they both left.

I closed the door and went and made myself a stiff drink. Although I appeared to have dodged a bullet, there was no escaping the fact that someone who was at the diner that day saw me and had reason to go to the police about it. How they knew my name was unclear. I could not explain how they didn't also see John, but it seemed to me that they didn't, so I decided in that moment not to tell him about what had just transpired. I knew what his reaction would be if I did, and it would not be pleasant. I knew also that I was going to have to think of a story to tell the sheriff if he ever did return, having discovered the truth.

SAM

I was up in my room listening to the Yankee game on the radio when I heard the doorbell ring. I just thought it was one of my sister's friends coming over to play with her, but then I remembered that she wasn't home. Right after the funeral that Monday, my father drove her up north to stay with our aunt for awhile. That was a surprise to me. My sister likes going up there and was happy to go, but I couldn't remember them talking about it before that day. After they left, I asked my mother if it had something to do with Mikey and she said no, that she and my father talked about sending her up there even before all the stuff with Mikey happened. I didn't believe that for a minute. I think they just wanted her to be somewhere safe until they caught whoever it was who killed Mikey. There was no telling how long that was going to take, so that got me wondering if she'd be back before I left for that school. She can be kind of a pain in the neck sometimes, but she is my sister and I didn't like the idea of not seeing her again until Thanksgiving.

It was a few minutes later and I had almost forgotten about someone being at the door when my father came up to my room and asked me to come downstairs. He looked dead serious and didn't even wait for me or tell me who it was. I knew I was really in for it then, so I shut off the radio and ran to catch up with him.

When I was halfway down the stairs, I could see the black boots of one of the cops, who turned out to be the sheriff. He was sitting on our couch. Another cop was standing near the door. It was that Brisby guy, a deputy, who's always a real prick to kids my age. After what the sheriff told me and Keith at the town hall that night, I guess I shouldn't have been too surprised to see them there. I guess since they didn't come to see us right away, I thought we might be in the clear.

They were all staring at me when I got to the bottom of the stairs. I just froze when I got there.

My father said that the sheriff told him all about our talk after the town meeting. He didn't look too happy and asked me why I didn't say anything to him about it.

I told him the same thing I said to the sheriff that night - it had to do with sex, so I didn't feel too good talking to him about it.

"So you went to the police instead?" my father asked.

"We just thought it was one of those crazy rumors," I told him. "You know. But then they found Mikey's sneaker out near where that stuff supposedly happened, so we figured maybe we should say something."

My father stared at me. I could tell he was trying to decide if I was telling the truth. "But you had to know I was going to find out eventually," he said.

It was a good point. I didn't say anything, though. He didn't like that too much.

"Is it alright if I talk to him now?" the sheriff asked my father. "Now that you know what it's about?"

My mother looked at my father and I could see they were both thinking about something. My father asked the sheriff if I was in some sort of trouble. The sheriff didn't say anything right away. That scared the crap out of me.

"Not unless he's done something else we don't know about," he said finally. "He's not in trouble for coming to see us and telling us what he heard, if that's what you're wondering."

"Maybe we should call Zachariah," my mother told my father.

Zachariah Pickens is a lawyer here in town. I've heard my parents talk about him every once in awhile. Personally, I never met the guy in my life, but I've seen him around. If you live here, you can't miss him. He has wild white hair and big bushy eyebrows and his suits are always wrinkled. His office is just a block off Main Street, not too far from the candy store all us kids go to. His kids are all out of college, so I'd never see him in all the places where a kid might see somebody their parents know. I was guessing he must be our lawyer.

"If you'd feel more comfortable having him here, I can wait," the sheriff told them.

My father said he thought that was a good idea and that he was going to call him just to be safe. I didn't know if that meant he was worried that I had done something wrong or if he was worried that the cops might do something wrong.

Either way, I felt a little better that the lawyer was coming because Keith and I made up that whole thing about that guy at the town hall saying stuff at the Custard Cup. The only reason we told the sheriff it was him was because we just saw him standing up for Mikey's father at the meeting. When he did, Keith turned to me and said that he had just seen that guy on Sunday when he was out eating with his parents. I told him that I knew him, too. He was on my paper route. I guess because we were just talking about him and the Custard Cup a few minutes earlier, it was on my mind when the sheriff asked us about where we heard about those people out at the hobo camp. The whole thing was my fault. The sheriff had me so scared I couldn't think of anything else, so I just blurted it out. Keith only went along with it because he didn't have any choice. He told me afterwards that he said it was Mr. Hager because he and the other guy were the only other people in the place when he and his parents were there.

It was pretty awkward with us all sitting around in the living room waiting for the lawyer to show up. My mother brought out some lemonade and cookies and my father and the sheriff tried to make small talk about Little League. The sheriff still coaches one of the teams, even though he doesn't have a kid playing. Meanwhile, my father hasn't been to a single one of my games, but acted like he knew all about it.

Finally, after about a half an hour, Mr. Pickens showed up. He was still wearing his suit, so I guess he hadn't changed after work yet. Not many people in town wear suits to work. I have to admit, it made him look pretty important, even with the wrinkles. I think I knew then how serious things were.

The first thing Mr. Pickens said was that he wanted to talk to me and my parents alone, without the police in the room, so we all went into the kitchen and shut the door. That never happens. I didn't even know you could shut it. The lawyer asked me all about what Keith and I said to the sheriff that night after the meeting.

I told him exactly what we said, as best I could remember. He stared at me the whole time I was talking. When I was done, he just nodded. Then he asked me where we really heard about "all that business going on out there by the tracks."

That really threw me for a loop. It was like he was trying to trip me up. I told him again about Keith and the diner in Herford. I didn't tell him the real story, of course. Just what we told the cops.

He nodded again, although I'm not sure he was buying any of it. "Alright then," he said. "Let's go out there and see what they want. But I want you look at me before you answer any of their questions. I might not want you to answer, depending on what they ask. Do you understand?"

I told him I did. So we went back out and sat down with the sheriff again. He looked at Mr. Pickens who told him it was OK, that he could ask whatever he came there to ask.

"What exactly did your friend tell you when he came back from the diner on Sunday?" he asked. I looked at the lawyer, but he didn't say anything, so I turned back to the sheriff.

"He just said he heard some guys talking about people out at the old hobo camp near Gehring's farm," I said.

"People?" he asked. "What kind of people?"

"Grownups," I said. "Not kids."

"What about those people?" he asked.

"That they were all wearing masks," I said.

"Anything else?" he asked.

"Yeah," I told him. "He said they were all naked and had paint all over their bodies."

I purposely didn't look at my parents. I was sure they were pretty mad by then.

"And what were they doing?" the sheriff asked me then.

I looked at the lawyer. He didn't say anything so I turned back to the sheriff. "Sex stuff," I said. "With each other. Out in the open."

"That's it?" the sheriff asked.

I looked at the lawyer again. He nodded. So I turned back to the sheriff and said, "I guess so."

"He didn't hear them say anything else, like who these people were?" the sheriff asked.

Again, the lawyer nodded like I should answer. I wish he hadn't, since I didn't know what to say to that. I was afraid that the sheriff had already talked to Keith. If he did and Keith told him something different, then we'd definitely be in trouble. I didn't know what else to do so I decided to tell the truth, although it wasn't really the truth.

"No," I said.

The sheriff nodded and looked at Brisby, then the lawyer, then my parents. "I spoke with the man the Somerset boy said he heard it from. He confirmed that he was at the diner that day, but he said he was alone. So unless he was talking to himself, it's unlikely that the Somerset boy heard anything at all."

As if he was reading my mind, my father asked the sheriff if he had talked to Keith yet.

"I did," he said. He didn't say anything else, which scared me a little. Then he took his hat from next to him on the sofa and put it on his lap like he was getting ready to leave. He turned to me and asked, "Is there anything else you want to tell me?"

I never saw an old guy move so fast. Mr. Pickens shot up and stood in front of me and told me not to answer. He then reminded the sheriff that I never said that I heard anything myself and that if he had any other questions he ought to go back and talk to Keith and his family.

The sheriff just smiled. It was kind of weird. I guess he probably knows Mr. Pickens pretty good. It sure didn't look like he was surprised by what Mr. Pickens said.

The sheriff stood up then and said he didn't believe what Keith said down at the town hall and didn't believe him when he told the same story at his house. He told the lawyer he didn't think Keith heard anything at all and that he and I probably made this all up as some sort of prank or maybe to make ourselves look important.

"Is that right?" he asked me.

Once again, Mr. Pickens told me not to say anything. He then asked the sheriff if he was accusing me of making a false statement.

The sheriff shook his head. "In light of everything that's going on, I don't think that would be very productive," he said. Then he turned to my parents and said, "You might want to have a talk with Sam about making up stories and telling them to the police. Next time we might not be so understanding."

He and that Brisby guy then walked to the door with my father right behind them. The sheriff said thanks to my mother and was just going out the door when my father asked, "What if that other guy's lying?"

The sheriff stopped and looked at him. "Who? You mean the

guy at the diner?"

My father nodded. "I know Keith Somerset and I know my own son even better," he said. "Maybe he's the one who's lying."

The sheriff smiled. "Why on earth would he do that?" he asked.

My mother went to the door and took my father by the arm. She nodded at the sheriff and said thanks. Then she pulled my father back inside and shut the door.

MIGGS

The meeting with Hager went about as I expected. I came away believing that he had never said anything like what those boys described. I went with Brisby the next night to see both boys and came away even more convinced that they had made up the whole story. In all, it seemed like a big waste of my time.

When Brisby and I got back to the station, Vic told me that Mr. and Mrs. Vogel were waiting for me in my office. I looked at Brisby and indicated that he should leave me alone with them. He nodded and went back out to his own office down the hall. I was about to enter mine when Vic stopped me.

"We got a call from somebody saying they found a hole in the ground in the woods up above Vorelyn Park," he said.

"A hole?" I asked. "What kind of hole?"

He shrugged. "Don't know," he said. "They didn't say. Just a hole, I think."

I thought about it for a few seconds, trying to figure out why Vic would be bothering me with that information. "Did somebody fall in it?" I asked. "Did anybody get hurt?"

"Not that I know of," he said. "I'm just telling you what they said. I think everybody's just trying to help. They think anything they see could be a clue. You know how it is."

I nodded. I did. "Right," I said. "Except that it's all the way across town from the swimming pool and nowhere near where you found the kid's sneaker. So I wouldn't have the slightest idea why they would think it would have anything to do with anything. It's probably just kids fooling around."

Like I said before, kids are funny, although sometimes adults are even funnier.

I went into my office and shook hands with Mr. Vogel while Mrs. Vogel remained seated and averted her eyes. I sat down behind my desk and started by apologizing to Mr. Vogel about the outburst at the meeting. I told him that I had talked to Joe Peters, the man who asked the question about him, and that he admitted that he had gotten caught up in the moment and didn't mean to make an accusation. I didn't tell him about speaking with Yancey Hager. It didn't seem relevant at the time.

"Still don't make it right," Vogel said. I agreed with him. I told him I just wanted him to know that no one felt that he had anything to do with his son's drowning, not even the one person who suggested it in public.

He nodded. Then his wife tugged on his sleeve. She still didn't look at me. He glanced over at her and patted her hand before he turned back to me.

"We heard something about what was going on out by those tracks and want to know why you never said anything about it," he asked.

I have to admit that he caught me off-guard with that. "What did you hear?" I asked him.

He looked at his wife, then leaned in to me. He tried to make it a whisper, but his emotion wouldn't allow him.

"Wildness," he said.

I was pretty certain I knew where this was headed, but I had to be sure. "What kind of 'wildness' are we talking about here?"

He gave another glance to his wife who lowered her head. It was clear that neither one of them was comfortable talking about this.

"Do you want your wife to wait outside?" I asked him.

He turned to her, but she was shaking her head even before he did. He looked back at me, then leaned in again. This time he did manage to keep his voice low, although I am sure his wife could hear.

"You know what I'm talking about," he said. "Don't make me say the word."

"Sex?" I asked, letting him off the hook. His wife looked up briefly, then back down as soon as I made eye contact. Mr. Vogel made a face like he just drank some bad milk, but he nodded.

I let things settle a bit before I asked him what kind of sex. He looked frustrated.

"How the hell do I know what kind?" he said, no longer trying to keep his voice down.

"Well," I told him, "It might be important. Some kinds aren't illegal."

"Right out in the open?" he asked.

"If it's out in the open, it's probably against some law," I admitted. "Though we don't often run into that." He stared, waiting for me to go on. "When we do, it's usually kids," I explained. "Teenagers. In cars. You know. We don't punish them. Having us shine a flashlight on them is usually enough to give them a scare. It's not even worth writing them up."

"This wasn't kids," he said.

"Who was it then?" I asked.

"That's what I'd like to know," he said. "All I do know is they weren't kids. They were adults." He said "adults" as add-ults, making it seem even more damning.

"And where did you hear all this?" I asked him.

His wife looked up at that, first at him and then at me.

"Were you telling the truth when you said my boy wasn't molested or is that just another lie you told?" she asked.

Her husband gently laid a hand on hers and kept it there. He looked at me as if he was waiting for my answer as well.

"First of all, I never lied about anything," I told them. "The district attorney and I agreed not to let out all the information that we knew in an effort to make the perpetrator think he was in the clear. That's something that's often done in criminal investigations."

"Was he or not?" Mr. Vogel asked, a bit more forceful then.

"The doctor told us that there were no signs of molestation," I said. "None whatsoever."

"That don't mean he wasn't, does it?" she asked.

"I don't suppose it does one-hundred percent," I admitted. "But generally there would be signs. So I think it's safe to say that Mikey wasn't."

"It's not Mikey," she said angrily. "It's Michael. Says so right on his birth certificate."

I took a deep breath and apologized for the mistake. "I just assumed that's the name you preferred."

"Well, you shouldn't assume anything," she said.

I couldn't think of anything to say at that point so we sat there silent for a time.

"What about all that business out by the tracks?" Mr. Vogel asked finally.

"Well, I need to ask you again where you heard that," I said.

A look of concern passed between them. Then Mr. Vogel turned toward me as if he and his wife had discussed this very point and might not be of the same mind on it.

"What difference does it make?" he asked.

I felt enormous sympathy toward both of them, but I was tiring of all the cat and mouse and was hoping to bring the conversation to a speedy and peaceful end. "Obviously," I said, "some sources are more reliable than others. Especially on matters like this."

He stared at me for a bit before he spoke. "Cyrus Robbins," he said. "Cyrus told me."

I was taken aback, although I probably shouldn't have been.

"Is there a problem with that?" he asked, reading my expression.

"Cyrus Robbins is not someone who I would consider trustworthy on current events," I told him.

"Why the hell not?" Mr. Vogel wanted to know. Suddenly, the air was full of all sorts of unspoken things.

"I think you know," I told him.

Mrs. Vogel looked at me then. "You didn't look that shocked when my husband told you what he heard," she said. "That means you heard it, too, don't it?"

I was not expecting her to corner me like that. Fritz Seiver might be able to do that to me, but not Wanda Vogel. For the second time in a few days, I worried that I was slipping. I mulled over how much to reveal of what I had been told over the previous two days.

"I was informed of something similar by two boys after the meeting the other night," I admitted. "I'm thinking now that they probably got it from the same source as you did."

Mr. Vogel looked suspicious. "How do you know?" he asked.

"I don't," I said. "For all I know, they may have told him. More likely, though, it's just a rumor started by someone hoping to make themselves a part of the story."

"Just because they're kids don't mean it's not true," Mrs. Vogel said.

"I agree," I told them. "But I've already looked into what they told us and, frankly, their story doesn't hold up. Like I said, they may have made it up to feel important."

"So that's as far as you're going to take it?" he asked. "Again?" We both knew what he meant by that. I felt my face go red and I fought to maintain my composure. I turned to his wife.

"I'm sorry," I said to her. "I know how difficult this must be for you."

Mrs. Vogel stood abruptly then. "No you don't," she told me. "You have no idea."

Mr. Vogel gently ushered his wife toward the office door. He turned as he opened it and shook his head at me. Then they left.

HAGER

Obsession is not pretty. Nor is it easy to manage. The psychology course I took in college taught me as much, although neither the textbook nor the professor used the word "pretty". Nevertheless, I got the idea. I don't know about the rest of those who were out there those two nights, but I was most certainly "obsessed", and it wasn't easy to control. You would think that with danger lurking around every corner in the form of the sheriff and whoever told him about my being at that diner, it would make me more hesitant to resume those activities. In point of fact, the danger had just the opposite effect. Following the visit by Sheriff Miggs, I wanted even more to start up again, without regard to any possible consequences. Like I said, obsession is not pretty.

I felt the same way going up that dirt road leading to the tracks the night I ran into those boys. Before I saw them, I was having thoughts of what had transpired in that same place on an earlier occasion, in particular, the only one on which we were uninterrupted. I was even hoping that a few of the others might have wandered out there that night, looking for someone else to show up. That was ridiculous of course. John had already told me that he had warned everyone about staying away, and everyone was probably fearful enough of him to obey, although I would have no way of knowing that for certain.

In any event, that's what led me to take out the suitcase from under my bed that Friday night and lay out all the masks on the bedspread. I fantasized that we were all going to meet once again, and I went about looking them over as if to decide which one I would wear for the occasion. The ritual of preparing like it was really going to happen was enough to stoke my obsession. My fantasy was rudely interrupted when my doorbell rang for the second time in three days.

I knew immediately that it was trouble. As I said before, no one would have a reason to come to my door, especially after dinner. I hurried to shut the case and slid it back under the bed, taking time to make sure that no part of it was visible before I left the bedroom and went to the door.

Even as I opened it, I knew that Sheriff Miggs would be on the other side. It was almost a physical sensation, one that I cannot to this day explain. He was alone this time and wore a solemn expression instead of a smile. There wasn't even a hint of him being sorry to bother me, as had been the case the previous time.

"Mr. Hager," he said, "I'm afraid I'm going to need to ask you a few more questions."

My first thought was to close the door in his face and wait it out. I wasn't a lawyer certainly, but I seemed to recall that he would need a warrant to enter my home, unless I invited him in. I watched enough Perry Mason to know that. My second thought was to call an attorney. The problem was that I didn't know any. John certainly would, although I never gave a thought to calling him, for obvious reasons. In that two or three seconds after Miggs spoke, I decided to keep playing the role of the cooperative citizen, hoping it would continue to make me appear innocent.

"Certainly," I said. "Come in. I was just about to make some tea. Can I get you some?"

He didn't look like a tea drinker to me, but he surprised me and said yes. That forced me to take him into the kitchen once more and, in turn, allowed him to pass the doorway to my bedroom. He took a long look in there as we passed, but I was certain that he could not have seen the suitcase under the bed.

I went about filling the tea pot and getting out the tea bags and cups while we spoke.

"The last time I was here," he said, "you told me that you were alone at that diner on Sunday. Do you remember that?"

I turned from the stove and looked at him with what I hoped was surprise on my face. "I do," I admitted. "Why do you ask?" I was hoping he would take my casual tone to mean that my being alone that day was beyond question.

"Well," he said, "I went back and spoke to the employees who were at the diner that day."

"Oh?" I said, trying to sound as curious as a stranger who might be following this story from afar.

"Yes," he said. "They recall seeing you there as well."

I had to believe we both knew where this was going. The only difference was that I was trying to guess what he knew, while he was probably thinking he had already caught me in a lie and was only waiting for me to step into his trap.

So I did the only thing I thought could save me. I nodded like I was caught with my hand in the cookie jar and sat down across from him. I gave him as earnest a look as I could muster. "I'm afraid that I wasn't entirely truthful with you the other day," I confessed.

Though he tried not to look surprised, he failed. "So you admit that you weren't alone?"

I nodded once more.

"Who were you with then, Mr. Hager?" he asked. His voice had gotten softer, almost as if he was a friend trying to help me out of a difficult situation.

I suppose this would have been the point where I might have called the lawyer, but I didn't. As I said, I didn't know any and felt it would only make me look guiltier. I still believed I could talk my way out of it. After all, I had done so on other occasions. In other places and other times.

"I'd rather not say," I told him, hoping that his question was an indication that he still didn't know who I was with.

"Why is that?" he asked.

I looked down.

"Mr. Hager?" he asked.

"It's personal," I told him, looking up when I finally spoke.

He didn't react right away, but I could read his thoughts. "Was it someone that maybe you shouldn't have been with?" he asked, confirming my belief.

I waited a second or two before I nodded.

He took his time before he asked the next question. I could tell that he was quite careful in choosing his words. "I was told that you were with another man." He said it like he wanted to make sure that I knew what he was thinking.

I had done a little bit of acting in college. Nothing big, just a few plays, but enough to know that I had some innate skill in that area. I sighed and felt my eyes water.

"I'm not sure you know how difficult it is to live with a secret," I told him.

He stared at me as the color drained from his face. Clearly, he had found himself in a place he didn't want to be. Certainly not where he thought he'd wind up when he walked in the apartment. I had confessed, but not to what he had hoped.

"I'm not a married man," I explained. "I live a solitary lifestyle of my own choosing."

He nodded, obviously understanding my meaning.

"It's bad enough that you know now," I said, "but I would feel forever guilty if I had to give you the name of my companion that day. I feel that only he should ever reveal himself if he so chose."

I could tell that this was not what he had hoped to hear. I don't know whether that was because he never considered that a man like me might have a lifestyle other than his and that of most of the other men in our community. Or perhaps he just didn't think that way about me.

He sat there silent for what felt like an entire minute. "Under the circumstances," he said, finally, "I'm not sure if I can agree to that."

I paused to consider what I might say next. I knew what I wanted to say, but was concerned that it might start the whole affair unraveling. Again, I decided to take a chance.

"It's my understanding that I am not required by law to answer your questions." I tried to say it as non-threatening as I could. Nevertheless, he frowned.

"That's true, I suppose," he said. "But that only makes you appear that much more suspect, I have to tell you."

I nodded, but committed to not backing down. "I have already told you my reason," I said. "There's nothing more to it than that. It certainly doesn't have anything to do with whatever nonsense that boy said he heard."

He straightened up, suddenly looking interested. "How do you know it was a boy we talked to?" he asked

I was immediately angry at myself for having presumed that's who he meant and for having said so. Of course, having already committed myself, I felt I had no other choice but to continue with that presumption, which was at least rooted in truth. "After your last visit I thought back on that day and could only recall one other couple in the restaurant at the time. They were there with a boy. Their son, I assume. He was the only person I could recall coming close enough to hear anything we said. He threw their trash in a barrel near our table." It was all true, but I couldn't be entirely certain that it was the boy who he had been referring to on his previous visit.

He stared, most likely trying to decide what to say next or how much to give away. I waited patiently, hoping that I hadn't incriminated myself. "But you don't know what he told us he heard." It was a confirmation, but not a concession.

"No I don't," I said. And waited for him to try to trick me with another question. I had already spoken too fast and without thinking. I was determined not to make the same mistake again.

"I'm going to ask you another question then," he said. "It's entirely up to you whether you answer it or not, of course."

I didn't like the way he put that. For the first time, it felt like I was not in control and that he might have taken the upper hand. I nodded, although I certainly had no intention of answering at that time.

"Did you and your lunch companion at any time while you were at the diner ever have a conversation involving sex?"

I swear I felt the air rush out of the room. It was like someone opening the door during a thunderstorm. My heart raced and sweat formed at my temples. I was sure that I must have turned red. The whole time the sheriff stared at me, waiting to see if I would answer and, if I did, what I might say.

It was the tea kettle that saved me. Its shrieking startled the sheriff even more than me. I shot out of my chair and over to the stove where I turned off the gas quickly. The whistling faded and eventually silenced. I lifted the pot from the stove and turned back to Miggs.

"Do you still want that tea?" I asked.

"That's fine," he said, not really answering me.

I poured the steaming water into the two cups, then brought them to the table, setting his in front of him before I sat down. I took my time before answering. John and I never discussed sex where people were around. He wouldn't have stood for it. However, I was conflicted. The boy must have told him we did, for whatever reason. If I denied it, it might only make things worse. On the other hand, if I admitted it, what else might I be admitting to? In the end, I decided to answer in a manner consistent with my earlier response.

"I certainly am not going to go into detail about any of our private conversations except to say that we were and are always most discrete," I told him.

I couldn't read his expression or tell if he was angry for my drawing the line at that.

"Let me ask you this final question then," he said. "Did you and your companion at any time ever utter the word 'mask' that day?"

My acting ability was not required in response to that. I was stunned and am certain that it showed. Thinking back on it later, I decided that my expression was absolutely perfect for the moment. However, I wasn't thinking so at the time. I truly was stunned. I searched through my memory bank to try to recall whether John and I might have used the word "mask" that day. I couldn't imagine that we had, but at that moment I could be certain of nothing.

"I'm not sure I have ever uttered that word at any time other than Halloween," I told the sheriff. It was an obvious lie, but it sounded convincing even to me.

He nodded. "Alright then," he said. "If I should need to get any more information from you, I'll be back. You can decide then whether you want to answer those other questions. Of course, depending on what you decide, I may have to take some further action."

That statement was probably designed to scare me into talking more, but I didn't take the bait. After all, it was not something I didn't already know. He got up to leave then and, without thinking, I pointed out that he hadn't had his tea yet.

He smiled. I'm sure he couldn't help himself. I guess it broke the tension. He looked at the still-steaming cup for the first time.

"I never touch the stuff," he said, and with that he left.

SAM

Richie said he was hurt. That's how he put it. He was hurt. It was such a Richie thing to say. We were over at the baseball field during the day when no one was around. Keith had called me to tell me that Richie wanted to talk to us. Keith and I got there first. Richie showed up fifteen minutes later. I could tell he did it on purpose. I knew he must have heard about Keith and me going to the sheriff.

"You should have told me," he said to both of us.

"I didn't tell anyone," Keith told him.

"You told him," he said, and he pointed at me.

"That's only because he came to tell me he lied about his parents hearing that stuff out at the hobo camp," I said.

Richie looked at Keith. "You lied about that?"

Keith looked at me and it dawned on me that Richie still didn't know the whole story. He still thought Keith was telling the truth about his father.

"What the fuck is going on with you guys anyway?" he asked.

Keith looked at me. I nodded finally. So then he turned back to Richie and told him the whole story.

Richie asked a whole bunch of questions that we both answered. Nothing new. Not to me anyway, but it was all new to him. Of course, the big thing was that both Keith and I saw those people out at that camp. Separately. Except that I saw Mikey out there, too.

Richie thought about that for awhile.

"So they must have killed Mikey," he said.

"I guess," I said.

"Cool," he said.

"It's not cool, you idiot," I told him.

"No, I know," he said. "It's not cool that Mikey's dead. But it's cool that we know something the cops don't."

I hadn't really thought about it like that, but I guess it was.

"That's why we made up the story about those guys at the diner," Keith said. "The cop found his sneaker not too far from there, so we wanted them to make a connection and start looking around. We thought maybe a couple of those people might get nervous and start to snitch on each other."

"Without us having to say it was us who saw anything," I said.

Richie smiled. I asked him what he was smiling about.

"We know something else they don't," he said.

"What's that?" asked Keith.

"You weren't out there by yourselves," Richie said.

I don't know how or why, but I had forgotten about Kimberly in all this.

"She saw it, too," Richie said. "And she was out there twice."

I felt my stomach go tight. "Once," I said.

"What's that supposed to mean?" Richie asked.

I wasn't sure whether I should say anything, but I figured I had to. I had no choice. I had already told Keith. "She never showed up with me," I told him.

Richie started laughing like a baboon.

I tried to ignore him and said that when I heard the voices coming from the camp, I thought it must be her and maybe some of her friends, so I went down the path to see what was going on. "That's when I saw them," I said. "And Mikey."

He stopped laughing when I mentioned Mikey.

"Serves you right for not telling me," Richie said. Then he

turned to Keith. "She showed up for you though, right?"

Keith took a second before he nodded. "Except she wouldn't do anything," he said. "I wasted three freaking dollars on a pint of Seagram's I bought off of old Robin Hood."

Richie went off on another laughing fit. I didn't join in.

"So what now?" Keith asked. "What if the cops don't believe us? What if they don't go looking for those people?"

Richie got serious then. "That's OK," he said. "I got a better idea."

MIGGS

The report from the state crime lab about Mikey's sneaker came back Friday morning. It went to Fritz's office, not mine, which was why I was reading it while sitting across from Fritz in his house on Saturday afternoon. When I was done, I looked up at him.

"No paint?" I asked.

He looked confused.

I reminded him of what the boys had said about the people they claimed were out there.

"I thought you didn't believe them?" he asked me.

"I don't know," I said. "Maybe we shouldn't rule it out."

"What's changed?" he asked.

I told him about my meetings with Hager. In particular, the second one. He didn't react at all when I explained about Hager's proclivities. I hate when he does that because I never know what he's thinking.

"You think maybe he's lying?" he asked finally.

"I don't know if we can say that anyone's telling the truth at this point," I said.

"OK," he said, after thinking some more. "Suppose just for a moment that the Somerset kid did hear that. And there were actually people - adults - having sex out there at some point. How are we supposed to confirm that?"

I shrugged. I didn't have an answer for him.

"More than that," he said, "how are we supposed to prove that they had anything to do with the boy's death?"

"Seems like too much of a coincidence," I said. "If it's true that a group of people were out in that field doing what those boys said they were doing and Mikey was out there nearby and lost his shoe, then there has to be some connection."

"Maybe," he said. "Except he was alive that day at the pool and disappeared before it got dark, which is when they supposedly do their thing."

"His body was discovered after sunset," I pointed out.

He shook his head. "Just after. Hardly enough time for him to get out there, see something, get himself killed, and then brought back to the pool."

"Well then, maybe he saw them earlier," I said. "On another night."

"And that's when he lost his shoe?" Fritz asked. "Why would the other one be in the locker room the day he went missing?"

I had to admit that he had me there. "So you still think those boys made it up then?" I asked.

He shrugged. "All we know for sure is that he's dead. And somebody killed him. It's your investigation. If you want to pursue that angle, it's your call."

We sat and stared for awhile.

"Who would be the kind of person to paint their body and put on a mask and go out in the middle of nowhere and engage in sexual activity with a bunch of others just like them?" I asked.

"I don't know," he said. "I don't think we can go house to house and take a survey."

"No," I said. "But maybe someone who had done this type of thing before might have gotten caught. And maybe there's a record of it somewhere."

"The state?" he asked.

I nodded.

"Probably worth checking," he said.

I told him I would, although I was hesitant to give them an opportunity to take over the case. I got up to leave and was at the door when a thought came to me and I turned back around. He asked me what was wrong.

"When I left Hager's apartment yesterday, I had a weird feeling," I told him. "There was something in there that bugged me, but I just couldn't put my finger on it. It just came to me."

"What was it?" he asked.

"A smell," I said. "There was a peculiar smell."

HAGER

After the close call of the sheriff's second visit, I knew I had to do something about them. I thought about a safe deposit box, but dismissed it as too small for my needs. I believe they have some that are rather large, but not nearly big enough. I thought also that I might get rid of most of them and keep only a couple of my favorites, putting them somewhere safe for use at a later time. In the end, though, I decided it was too risky to hang on to any of them. I couldn't take the chance that the sheriff could get a search warrant and find even a single one of them. So I packed them all up in the suitcase and carried it out to my car at dawn on Saturday morning, before anyone was up, and I was on the road five minutes later. I didn't see a single soul and I don't think a single soul saw me.

They say there are more than a hundred lakes and ponds within fifty miles of our town. Many of them are popular for swimming and beach activities. People have built cottages around the more desirable ones to escape the summer heat, but most are inaccessible by road. You have to park near the state highway and walk a path to get to them, in some instances, hiking two miles or more to do so. Some are closer to the road, but are so small and shallow that no one has bothered to build a road leading to them, let alone a house.

I had stumbled across Kitchiwa Lake purely by accident. I was looking at property when I first moved to the area and thought that a house outside of town, near the water, might be nice. I liked the idea of the solitude. Not having neighbors to worry about. However, I was told how difficult it might be to drive to and from town at times in the winter, and I didn't much like the idea of being trapped in my house for days at a time, solitude or not.

Anyway, when the broker was showing me around that day, we passed a sign that looked old and weathered. It simply said "lake". I asked about it and the broker told me about Kitchiwa Lake. It was about a mile from the nearest road, but at one time was worth the hike, she said. There were no houses or roads and the water was the clearest around. She said that when she was in high school it was a popular spot for kids to go to watch the "submarine races". When I told her that I didn't know what she meant, she blushed and told me that it was where the teenage couples went to "make out". She said it wasn't so popular any longer. I asked why, and she said that something had blocked the stream that fed the lake and it had caused the water to get murky. While before you could see a penny on the bottom twenty feet down, now you couldn't see your hand in front of your face. In addition to making out, apparently those kids liked to swim there as well.

When I thought about what to do with those masks, Kitchiwa came to mind. I rejected it at first, thinking that the drive and the transporting of the suitcase would be too risky. Of course, simply burning them would have been my first choice, except that I had nowhere to do so. There was a barrel in the backyard of my building that my landlord used to burn trash and leaves, but I would have had to ask him first. Plus, I would be visible to at least three other houses, not to mention him. Someone would see what I was doing, and not letting anyone see them was the whole point. So when I crossed that off the list, along with every other possibility that came to mind, Kitchiwa seemed like the best choice. It helped my decision that it was drizzly and unusually cool for a Saturday in August, my feeling being that no one would likely be going up to that lake, even had the water been pristine.

After parking a short distance from the highway, I hiked the one mile path through the woods, lugging the suitcase, until I came to a clearing at the edge of the lake. I could immediately see why that broker and her high school friends would have liked it. It was private and beautiful, even on a dreary day, save for the water, which was quite turgid, as she had described. It had turned into a swamp, really. And that presented me with a problem. I couldn't exactly wade out into the water to check the depth. When I stepped close to the water line, my shoes sank into the muck almost up to my ankles. So I backed away and found a good sized branch and tried to lean out and gauge how deep it was. The problem became apparent right away. At least near the water's edge, it was no more than six inches from the surface to the muck below. That wasn't even enough to cover the depth of the suitcase, unless you could push it down into the mud, which I wouldn't be able to do without getting myself stuck.

I searched for a way around the lake, perhaps to a point where the water might be deeper, but I would have had to walk through swamp in either direction in order to do that and I was afraid I might end up in mud up to my hips if I tried.

So then I held out the suitcase at arm's length to evaluate its heft and get a fair estimate of how far I might be able to throw it. The problem with that was that I would only have one chance, and if I miscalculated, the suitcase might still be visible and I'd have to wade out into the mud to retrieve it, again possibly getting stuck in the process. For that reason, I decided I better practice first. I twisted my body as far to the right as I could, with the suitcase extended out behind me, and my feet planted firmly to the ground. I then spun forward quickly, while still holding onto the handle, hoping to get a feel for how far I might be able to heave it.

However, before I even got halfway around, both of the clasps gave way under the weight of the masks, and they flew out in an arc along the shore. Fortunately, they landed in the grass, not the water, and I was able to gather them up and put them back in the suitcase, cursing as I did. I then attempted to secure the clasps as best I could, but they were either cheaply made or defective, and when I tried again, I ended up with the same result. So I gathered them up once more and made a fateful decision.

Unlike at my apartment building, I was out there all alone, a mile from the nearest road. I reasoned that I could make a small fire and burn the entire batch and then kick the remnants into the water and cover them with dirt or mud. With any luck, the rain would get heavier and wash away whatever remained of them.

I don't smoke, but I always carry matches since so many other people do. I find it helps me to make an acquaintance if I am able to offer someone a light. So I gathered some small branches, along with some dried grass I managed to find and got a fire started rather quickly. When the flames were going nicely, I took the masks one at a time and fed them into the fire. It took some time to feed each one into the flames and watch it until it burned beyond recognition.

It was unpleasant work, especially since the rain had picked up, and I soon resented the fact that John had assigned me the task of keeping them. Prior to that, I only had the one that he had given me to wear when he decided to allow me to join with the others. He must have collected the rest from them. The night after the boy was discovered in the pool, he came to my house with a bag full of them and instructed me to hold onto them until he came to get them at some unspecified point in the future. Naturally, I protested, but he said we had bigger things to worry about and that he would be taking them back eventually. He said they would be safer at my house than his, since I would be the person they would least likely look at, should anything happen. I asked him why he felt that way, and he said that I was relatively new and unknown in town. In retrospect, he obviously thought just the opposite, and I regret that I hadn't seen that sooner.

When I asked where they all came from, he told me that he had obtained them from various places over the years. Different countries he had visited. He said that whenever a new person was asked to join our group, he gave them one to wear. I didn't study them enough to determine what they were made of. However, I found them all to be fascinating and, well, provocative, causing me to reflect fondly on the one and only time we had taken part in what we had set out to do. I only mention this because, whatever they were made of, they soon caused the fire to emit a dark, swirling smoke. The rain may have had something to do with it as well, and the smoke kept building and rising, as I added one after another to the hissing fire.

Finally, anxious as I was to escape to the warmth and safety of my car, I grabbed the last few and threw them in, hoping to get on my way before anyone noticed the smoke. I considered putting the suitcase on top of them, but I suspected that burning it might cause an even larger plume of smoke and I had no idea how long it might take to incinerate. So once the last few were pretty well consumed, I closed the suitcase and took it with me. After all, it had cost me quite a bit of money and I figured I could use it again, so long as I had no reason to throw it any great distance.

Going back down the hill, I watched intently for anyone coming up the trail. Fortunately, I made it down without seeing anyone. However, I was not so lucky at the bottom. When I got to the car, I turned back and looked up to see if the smoke was still visible and could easily see it swirling. I quickly threw the suitcase in the trunk and made my way around to the driver's side door just as a car come around the wide bend in the road less than a quarter mile away.

When I saw the red lights atop the distinctive black and white sedan, I knew it was trouble.

SAM

School was starting in two weeks. Not mine, theirs. When it did, Keith and Richie would have plenty of chances to see Kimberly Miggs and talk to her, but I'd already be down at that new school which was starting a few days sooner. So that's why Richie said we couldn't wait and that he was going to call her.

I was against the idea. So was Keith, but only at first. He was embarrassed, since she never talked to him again after that night they were together. She even ignored him at the pool the day Mikey went missing. Of course, I had my own reasons for not wanting to see her.

"Why would she ever agree to meet you?" I asked Richie. "She obviously doesn't want to talk about it."

"Don't you worry," he said. "She'll come."

Richie had been the first to tell us about Kimberly and how she'd let you feel her up if you gave her some booze. He claimed he did it that spring. Keith and I didn't believe him at first. He's always making stuff up like that. But the Monday after he said it happened, she said hi to him in the hallway at school and she never even looked at him before that. Plus, he gave us all sorts of details, like where he bought the rum and where they did it (under the bandstand). He even took us up to Vorelyn Park to see the empty bottle and the grass all walked over. It seemed like some pretty good evidence, but with Richie you never know for sure.

"She won't ever go back out to that camp," Keith told Richie.

"Even if she's in love with you, which we all know she's not."

"Who said anything about going out there," Richie said. "I'll tell her to meet me in town somewhere. We just need to get her alone. It doesn't matter where."

"And then what?" I asked.

"Then we get her to tell her father what she saw," he said.

"I already told you she won't do that," Keith said.

"That's what she told you," Richie said. "I'll be the one asking now."

Typical Richie. Thinking he could get anybody to do anything he wanted. I still didn't think it made any sense, but I suppose it made as much sense as anything else. So that was our plan.

The first one anyway. It turned out that when Richie called her, she told him that her father wasn't letting her go out unless she was with a bunch of her girlfriends because of what happened to Mikey. She said she couldn't go out with just him.

"Bullshit," Keith said.

"What?" Richie said. "You don't believe her?"

"No," he said. "I don't believe you."

"What other reason would there be, smartass?" Richie asked him.

"Maybe your thingie's too small," Keith said.

"Who cares?" I said. "Can't we just drop this whole Kimberly Miggs thing now?"

I thought Keith would back me up, but he sided with Richie again and said we should try to get her to meet us some other way. I think maybe he was hoping that since she didn't like Richie anymore, she might like him again.

We went back and forth on a bunch of different plans. One of them was to have one of us follow her out of her house one morning and use walkie-talkies to tell the other two where she was headed. Then we could head her off and wait for her. Richie loved that idea. He said it was like The Man From U.N.C.L.E. or 007. But then I pointed out that she'd probably be with a bunch of her friends anyway and besides, we'd stand out like sore thumbs if we were walking around town holding walkie-talkies to our ears. "The idea is to avoid the cops," I told him.

Keith got mad, seeing as it was his idea, but he finally admitted that it wouldn't work. Richie then said he wished she had a boyfriend, someone we knew, so that we could get him to help. That's when Keith came up with the idea to use Tom Nevins, the lifeguard at the pool who every girl over the age of seven had a crush on.

"Why would he ever help us?" I asked.

"Because we'll pay him," Keith said.

"With what?" Richie said. "None of us have any money."

"No," Keith said. "But I've got something better."

"Like what?" Richie asked.

"Leftovers," he said.

MIGGS

After my meeting with Fritz, I decided I better go out to the place they call the old hobo camp and take a look around myself. I wasn't ready to admit that I believed the Somerset boy's story, but I couldn't dismiss it either. If I was being completely honest with myself, I probably should've gone out there sooner. Instead, I had sent Brisby out the day after the boys first came to see me. He said there wasn't any sign of a recent fire or anything else unusual out there, which was about what I expected, but I still thought I should go see for myself. After all, I was the one who convinced Fritz to let me handle the investigation.

On that Tuesday morning, I drove out of town and pulled the car onto the dirt tractor road that Larry Gehring uses to get to his fields, and then I parked as close to the tracks as I could get. Fortunately, Larry wasn't plowing and I didn't have to explain what I was doing there. I could have gone in behind the houses down on West Main and gotten there quicker, but in broad daylight someone probably would have seen me, and the Vogels were among the people who lived down there and I sure as hell didn't want them to find out that I had been seen walking back there and have to explain why. Not after what they told me a few nights before.

There's a third way to get the camp, from north of town, through a patch of woods and fields, but I would have been pretty far out of my jurisdiction had I chosen to go that route. So I walked down the tracks, the same as Vic did the night he found the boy's shoe. There's a strip of crushed stone on each side of the steel rails that makes walking easier, but it also makes it so that leaving any kind of track would be pretty much impossible. If someone had been out there, it would be awfully difficult to tell from that route. Eventually, I came to the spot where you catch the path to the old camp area through an opening in the woods.

It was actually a pretty clever place to set up a camp. Unless the train stopped right there, a bull guard would have to walk in some distance from the east or west to find it. For the tramps, that wasn't much of a hardship. The remoteness kept them safe from discovery and arrest, along with giving them a secure place to rest. There's also water from a nearby spring, so it was easy to see why they chose it.

I had only been to see it one other time. Like most people in the area who had ever gone out there, I went for historical purposes. The camp had been used pretty regularly by tramps and hobos from the time of the Depression until just before World War II. Everyone knew about it and the whole idea of riding the rails sounded pretty exciting to a kid. Of course, parents warned their children to stay away from the camp, but not because they were afraid that they would run into any tramps and hobos. They were long gone by then. They did it mostly to keep them from getting hit by a train. My friends and I went out there when we were around fourteen and, like most any kid that age, we never told our parents. All I could remember of it was a big empty space and a large circle of rocks where the tramps used to build their fires. Not much else. Of course, we were there in the daytime.

Not long after we had gone out there, someone told us that teenagers would go there at night to make out, without fear of getting caught. It provided them the same kind of privacy as the hobos who used it before them. Plus, as I said, you could walk there from the western end of town. This was before kids had the same access to cars as they do today. I do remember seeing a mattress out there that earlier time, so maybe there was something to that.

I made no such discovery on this latest visit out there. No mattresses or any other indication that people used the grounds for sexual reasons. However, the large circle of rocks was still there, or something like it anyway, and there were some scraps of burnt wood in the circle, but that was about it. Nothing that looked like a bonfire. Besides, there had been several thunderstorms since Mikey was found dead, as there often are in August, so any possible evidence of a fire, if there ever was one, would have been long gone.

I walked the entire perimeter of the area and looked for anything that seemed out of the ordinary, but found nothing. I suspected that my first instinct was right and that the two boys had made up their story and nothing funny had ever taken place out there.

However, I had to admit that if there had been people out there doing what the boys said they were doing, they probably would have been able to do so without anyone discovering them. And that kept me from dismissing the notion entirely.

HAGER

I'm a pitiable fool when it comes to tradition. It's one of the things I've enjoyed most about living in this town. There's the flooding of the high school football field every winter to form a large lighted skating rink that just about everyone in town uses, adults and children alike. Then there's the all-day cartoon marathon at the movie theater on the day after Thanksgiving, free for all the kids. That's followed two weeks later by the Christmas parade, featuring an authentic-looking Santa and a team of real reindeer. Best of all, though, are the summer band concerts, which are truly delightful and attended by people of all ages and from all walks of life. They alternate from week to week at the two main parks that sit on the eastern and western ends of town and, like most of those other traditions, they provide a sense of community that I've come to embrace in the short time I've lived here.

People take different approaches when it comes to how they choose to enjoy the concerts. Some bring blankets and folding chairs and make a picnic out of it. Others park their cars along one of the four streets that surround each of the parks and they sit inside with the windows open to take in the brassy sound, mostly marches by John Philip Sousa, along with other patriotic fare. The town council allows vendors to set up booths to sell snow cones and cotton candy, while many kids make popcorn at home and put it into small brown paper bags and carry them around on homemade cardboard trays, selling the bags for twenty-five cents apiece.

I always buy from the same boy, who is quite generous with the butter, so much so that just the sight of it staining the bag is enough to get my appetite going.

I don't have a favorite spot, unlike almost everyone else who goes, staking their claim on the grounds or on one of the benches. I never drive there. I wouldn't want to sit alone in my car. Instead, I walk from home to whichever of the two parks is hosting the concert, and I make a continuous circuit around the perimeter the entire time, savoring the music and watching the fireflies flicker in near rhythm to the songs. The concerts usually last for the better part of two hours, and one time I counted making twenty one full laps before it ended. Together with the walk from home and back, it is the most exercise that I get during the week. I also like that it allows me to feel a part of the community, even if that's mostly an illusion on my part. Oh, I often see people from church or work, and I always stop to say hello, but mostly I keep to myself while still sharing in the atmosphere.

That particular Wednesday night was the next to the last concert of the summer, and there was already the specter of autumn in the air. The school year was about to begin and another summer was about to end. I always find that to be a sad time. It was even more so that night considering the circumstances. I am certainly not unaware of the contradiction that I present. After all, I had recently engaged in behavior far outside the norm, albeit with much regret, so much so that I actually considered making a full confession that night as I walked around the park.

That may come as somewhat of a surprise. You have probably surmised by now that I am a bit of a survivor, but I do have a conscience, and walking around that park brought me face to face with scores of children and an even larger number of adults, almost all parents or grandparents. I could only imagine the sorrow they would feel had it been their child in that pool that night. Most were probably harboring some anxiety that whoever did it might strike again, and with that in mind were probably watching their children more closely than they might have just a month before. I imagined the relief it would bring them to be able to let go of that fear and return to the peace and security they must have felt back then. However, that was as far as I would allow my imagination to take me. I tried to envision my life afterward were I to confess to my part in all of this. I would no doubt be sent to prison for a long time, perhaps for life, and I knew that I could not survive incarceration. Not again, not after what happened on a regular basis the first time.

In the end I concluded that it was a price I simply could not pay, and so I dismissed any of those thoughts as I walked around the park enjoying the final strains of the lively music, hoping against hope that fate once again would allow me to survive.

SAM

It turned out Tom Nevins wanted five bucks to go along with the whiskey that Keith didn't use up on Kimberly. It was a pretty expensive deal, but we went along with it because it was the only way he'd agree to do it without us having to tell him why we wanted him to get Kimberly up to Vorelyn Park on Saturday night. Vorelyn Park isn't one of the parks where they have the band concerts. It sits way up above town and is used more for cookouts and family reunions and stuff like that. There aren't any lights to speak of, so we knew there wouldn't be anyone there on a Saturday night.

We met Tom to arrange it all at the band concert on that Wednesday three nights before. College kids like Tom don't go to the band concerts. They're too cool for that. We wanted to feel the same way, but we knew we were still young enough not to be made fun of for being there. Besides, we didn't have a car like him or anywhere else to go.

Tom couldn't wait to get out of there once we made the deal. He said he had somewhere he needed to be, but I think he probably just didn't want to be seen with us. I understood that. If I was in college, I wouldn't want to be seen hanging around with a bunch of twelve-year-old kids, especially at a band concert. Once he drove off, that left us having to go find something else to do.

When I was younger I used to sell popcorn at the concerts. It was a pretty good way to make some extra money for baseball cards and ice cream. Last year I decided it didn't seem so cool to be seen carrying a tray of popcorn around the park anymore. No one ever made fun of me. I just noticed one night that everyone else selling popcorn was younger than me. The older guys were all trying to talk to girls instead. I wasn't interested in girls then. All I cared about was baseball and goofing around with Keith and Richie. Somewhere during seventh grade, I started looking at girls more. They were still stupid, but I found myself noticing how they smelled and what kind of clothes they wore. A few times I caught myself wanting to reach out and touch their hair. I never did, though.

By the end of seventh grade, Richie already claimed he went all the way with someone. He wouldn't tell us who it was, which is why Keith and I didn't believe him. Richie can't keep his mouth shut. He brags about everything. You'd think he'd brag about that, but for some reason he wouldn't tell us who. I asked him once if it was Kimberly and he said no. I started to ask him about someone else and he said to forget it, he wasn't going to play that game.

I only mention it because we were looking at a bunch of girls by the bandstand that night and Sylvia Vogel was one of them. She saw us looking and kept right on staring at us. Me mostly. Richie saw her and said we should go over and say something to her. Maybe tell her we were sorry about her brother. I told him I thought that was a real bad idea.

I thought he might ask me why, but he just shrugged and didn't bring it up again.

MIGGS

I was home alone on Friday night, one week after my second meeting with Yancey Hager, when Irwin, the detective from the state who Brisby knew, called and asked if he could come by to talk. My wife was out with one of her girlfriends. She told me what they had planned, but frankly I didn't pay much attention. She took my youngest daughter with her, and my younger son went camping out of town with one of his friends and his family. I was keeping a pretty tight rein on the kids then, given the circumstances. Even Kimberly. That night she said she wanted to go over to a friend's house to watch TV. My wife agreed to drop her off there, so I didn't put up a fuss about it. Like I said, she had always been the most reliable of the four kids, and I always felt that until she proved otherwise, she deserved my trust.

I offered to meet Irwin down at the station, but he said there was no reason to make me to go in to work. "It could even wait till Monday," he said. "But my wife is off to see her mother, and I don't have anything else to do so I thought maybe you'd want to see what I came up with."

He was right. I did. I was getting a little antsy since we had no leads, other than a guy in a diner who was with another guy who he probably shouldn't have been with. Fritz assured me that wasn't enough to get a search warrant. In fact, he was pretty well convinced that it had no connection to the case whatsoever. I wasn't quite so convinced, but without Fritz's approval and a subpoena that only he could apply for, I couldn't really do much about it.

Irwin was younger than I thought he'd be. Younger than me by several years. Truth be told, that made me a little jealous and uncomfortable. I didn't want to give him the upper hand. After all, he was coming to see me, but I couldn't very easily ignore that he had the better job, at least in the eyes of most people.

He brought a folder with him and got right down to business. The folder contained some carbon copies of state police reports on known child molesters. He took me through each one and told me what happened and where the perpetrators were now. Except for two, they were all either in prison or dead. One of them was in Florida out on parole. Irwin said he called the police down in Daytona Beach, and they checked on the man and confirmed that he was in the state at the time the Vogel boy was killed. Irwin said he had hoped that wasn't the case since the man had ties to the area (a sister two towns over), but he said there was not much doubt that he wasn't the one we were looking for.

The only other known offender was missing. No one had heard from him in some time, and his probation period had ended and he had essentially vanished since then.

I asked if he had any connection to the area.

"Not really," he said. "He was known to have been in the state a number of years ago. He was picked up for indecent exposure in a state park. Did a short stint in county downstate, but that's about as close as it gets."

I asked if he thought he might be the guy.

"Could be," he said. "That's why I brought it over."

He gave me the carbon copy of the report. I looked at it briefly, then back at him.

"Have you got a mug shot?" I asked.

"We did," he said. "Looks like it got misplaced, though. We're looking for it now. When we find it, I'll send it along."

I told him I'd appreciate that. I thought then about telling him what those boys had told us, but stopped myself. I guess I was afraid to look like a fool on some sort of wild goose chase. So instead I just asked if he had heard anything down at his office about any kind of activity out by the old hobo camp.

He look at me curiously. "What kind of activity?" he wanted to know.

"Nothing specific really," I said. "Just anything out of the ordinary."

"Does this have to do with that shoe your man found?" he asked.

I told him it did and he nodded.

"Can't say that I have," he said. "But I'll ask around."

Once again, I told him I appreciated the cooperation and we shook hands before he left. To my surprise, he never said a word about taking over the investigation, which I took to mean that he approved of how I was handling the job.

HAGER

I never asked John where he came from. I only knew that he wasn't born around here. Like me, he grew up somewhere else. We once had a conversation about my past and my prior "activities", but when it came time for him to reciprocate, he refused. I was about to ask some more questions when he said we should change the subject. He thought that it was too dangerous to know too much about each other. From that moment on, I became frightened of him.

I suppose I should have been afraid from the very beginning. The first time we met should have put me on alert. I have lived here for more than eighteen months and, until this past spring, I had never seen John around. Then one day I was out in the woods on the north side of town, wearing my binoculars and looking for an oriole that I suspected might be nesting nearby. This was a solitary activity for me. I don't know other bird watchers nor do I really want to. I prefer the solitude. For me it is not a contest, nor am I looking to share my exploits and accomplishments with some amateur ornithologist over a glass of sherry. I simply look for a rare member of the species and record the time and place that I spot him or her in one of the many journals I keep. It is purely for my own amusement. I prefer it that way.

Therefore, I was rather surprised that afternoon when someone behind me asked what I was doing out there. I turned and that was the first time I ever laid eyes on John. He was not wearing bi-

135

noculars, nor did he appear to be dressed for a hike. He was wearing the same clothes he would probably wear to shop for groceries downtown. He also did not look like a bird watcher, if there is such a look. He was simply standing there. I was so startled that I did not respond at first. To be truthful, it was rather unnerving, the way he was looking at me. It was as if he knew everything about me just from that one look. I know that sounds strange, but it is simply the truth.

"See anything interesting?" he asked, when I did not speak.

"I'm looking for an oriole," I said, finally. "A female."

"No luck?" he asked.

"No," I said. "I think I may have the wrong place."

"Maybe you should look for something else then," he said. Something about that comment made me shiver. He wasn't talking about a bird. Of that I had no doubt.

"Maybe," I said, part of me hoping he would just go away and leave me alone. Then again, another part of me was hoping he wouldn't.

"I'm afraid I couldn't be of any help to you," he said, as if sensing my caution. "At least not if that's what you're looking for."

It went on like that for a minute or so before we agreed to walk back to the cars together. His was parked right next to mine. We sat in his sedan for a brief time, talking about me and my hobby and how beautiful those woods were when autumn came around. Then he suggested we might go to his house. I suppose he must have been able to read me and my predilection. Or perhaps he did that with anyone he suspected of having the same "penchant" as him.

In any event, we did go back to his house, which turned out to be in Oliander, explaining why I had never run into him in town. Even though I accompanied him back there, I don't want to suggest that anything of a physical nature happened. It didn't. I probably would have gone along had he suggested it, but that didn't come until later. Instead, he showed me the books he kept locked up in his basement, the ones he had procured in his travels abroad, and I knew instantly that his tastes ran along more exotic and dangerous lines. Soon the conversation shifted to religion, though not one I was familiar with. Certainly not the one I practiced in town. Before I left that night, I had acknowledged that what he had shown me would be of interest to me and that I could be trusted to keep our discussion a secret.

"That's good," he said. "I think you might enjoy getting together with some people I know."

Perhaps if I never saw him again, none of this would have ever happened and I wouldn't have had to worry about the situation I found myself in. However, the excitement I felt upon meeting John and viewing those books was simply too much to resist. I went along willingly when he contacted me later with his suggestion to join the "group", and I thoroughly enjoyed the one successful "gathering" we had, so much so that I looked forward to many more, although none ever did take place because of the boy. Still, I must acknowledge that there was a different path I might have chosen had I been stronger.

I thought of all this as I was burning the suitcase in the metal drum that my landlord used to burn leaves every fall. After being questioned about it by that state police officer that day out at Kitchiwa, I felt that I had no choice but to dispose of it, without regard to who might see me. Although the encounter with the officer ultimately proved to be innocent, and I was able to leave without raising any suspicion, I felt that I had been given a warning, one that I must heed.

It was late Saturday afternoon and, fortunately, no one was around. I had asked my landlord earlier in the day if I could use the drum and he said yes, after making me tell him a lie about spilling something that smelled strongly inside of the suitcase. That was why I needed to burn it, I told him. He nodded, apparently accepting my explanation. Thankfully, he didn't stay to watch me. Nevertheless, I did pour some acetone inside before I brought it down, just in case I needed a smell to back up my lie. Ironically, the chemical only made it burn faster.

Flames burning in a near empty barrel make a considerable noise, which I suppose is why I didn't hear John approach. Just like that day in the woods when we first met, he asked me what I was doing. This time, I knew precisely who it was, and I hesitated before turning to him. He could clearly see the suitcase, or what was left of it, so I told him the same story I told my landlord, adding that it was beginning to cause my whole apartment to take on the aroma.

He smiled. The same lie that satisfied my landlord only seemed to amuse him. "What did you say you spilled?" he asked.

"Acetone," I told him once more.

"What on earth would you be doing with acetone?" he wanted to know. "And why would it be anywhere near that suitcase?"

Of course, I hadn't thought about any of that. Why would I? My landlord was neither as curious nor suspicious as John. Even if he had asked the same question, whatever fabrication I made up probably would have satisfied him.

"I was cleaning the paint off of something," I told him. "I used the suitcase as a stand while I sat on the edge of the bathtub." I thought that was a pretty clever lie, especially coming right off the cuff the way it had. Obviously, John did not find it so clever.

"What kind of paint?" he asked. His voice was calm, but threatening just the same, the way I would imagine a lawyer's might be when questioning a defendant whose guilt was all but certain.

I simply lost patience with him then. Perhaps I no longer cared what happened to me. Suddenly, I was tired. Tired of my entire life and everything about it. I certainly was tired of feeling like I was under John's thumb. "None of your business," I told him, more firmly than I had ever spoken to him before.

He smiled once more. "Would it have been something like this?" he asked.

That's when he held up a small can of red paint that I had used to paint my face on two separate occasions and which I had stored in the back of my landlord's garage. I had meant to dispose of it at the same time as the masks, but in my haste to get rid of them I had completely forgotten about it. He must have retrieved it before letting me know he was there. That he knew it was in there was even more troubling.

"Why don't we go for a little ride," he said. "We can talk about all this in private."

I briefly thought of running or shouting. I guess it might have brought my landlord out. Perhaps a few of the neighbors as well, if any were home. But to what end? I really didn't care anymore. I was prepared to accept whatever fate had offered.

"Let me get my windbreaker first," I said, pointing to where it was hanging on a hook in the back entranceway. He nodded.

So I went inside and retrieved it and then we walked together to the car and went for that ride.

SAM

Tom Nevins sent word through his sister that he wanted to talk to Kimberly. Sure enough, she called him back the same night. He told her to meet him out at Vorelyn Park at eight o'clock on Saturday night. He promised to bring some booze. He told her that he had his eyes on her for a long time and was just waiting for the right time to ask her out.

We met Tom in town at about seven thirty. There was an argument over whether we should give him the money before we found out if she'd actually show up. Richie said we should hold back on the booze at least, but we finally gave in when Tom said he'd drive us up there so we wouldn't have to walk. Besides, he said he was a "hundred percent sure" she'd show and that if she didn't for some reason, we could meet up with him the next day and he'd give us all the money and booze back. I found out later that he left to go to college the next morning, but it didn't matter because Kimberly did show up, just like he said. I guess if you're a cool guy like him, you have a pretty good idea about whether some girl is going to do what you tell her to do.

Kimberly didn't get a ride from anybody. She just walked into the park all by herself, bold as anything. We watched her walk right up the road to the pavilion, just like Tom told her to. We talked before about how we should meet her when she got there. We didn't want to all come out at the same time and scare her to death. Since Keith was the tallest and would look the closest to Tom in the dark, we decided to have him come out of the woods first. Richie and I would come out after, once she figured out who it was.

So that's what we did. Keith waited about two minutes after she got there and then walked out of the woods, straight toward her. She watched him the whole way without saying a word until he was standing right in front of her. She didn't even bat an eye when she saw who it was, which surprised me. Richie and I came out then, just like we planned. When she saw us, she just shook her head.

"You must really think I'm stupid," she said. Then she pointed at Richie. "First he calls me up out of the blue. Then some college boy who every girl in town wants to go out with asks me to meet him up here. Christ, did you really think I'd fall for that?"

"You're here, aren't you?" Richie said.

"I am," she said. "And I know why." She looked at Keith, then back at Richie. She ignored me.

We all looked at each other then. She was right. There was no point in denying it. We all knew what we were doing there. Then she said that we weren't going to say anything about this to anybody else, including her father, and that we all better agree on that or she would just leave. It seemed to me that telling her father was the whole point, but I guess we felt that we had no choice so we said OK. I guess Kimberly didn't think that was good enough because she said we had to swear first. So we all just put our hands together and swore and that was it.

"One other thing," she said. "No one is ever going to touch me again. Ever. Understood?"

I was going to remind her that Keith and I never touched her in the first place, but it didn't seem like a good thing to bring up at that point.

"So what now?" Richie asked. "If you aren't going to tell your father, what's to talk about?"

She told him to shut up and follow her. So that's what we did.

Good thing there weren't any clouds. If it weren't for the moon being out, I don't know how we would have found our way through the woods above the park. Like I said before, Vorelyn Park is up on a hill overlooking town. Down the hill there's just one road leading into the upper part of town. On either side of the park are just woods that go on forever, east and west. North of the park is more woods for about a mile till you get to the county road leading to Herford. The trees are pretty thick in that part and nobody goes there much because there's nothing to see, unless you're looking for diamonds, and nobody does that after they're ten years old. If you are going to go in there, the best way is from the upper end of the park. That was the way Kimberly took us.

"What the hell are we doing?" Richie asked, after we were walking for awhile.

Kimberly kept walking and didn't say anything. Richie stopped.

"Where are you taking us?" he asked.

She stopped this time and turned around. "Just shut up and follow me," she said.

Keith and I looked at each other and smiled. I could tell Richie hated her saying that in front of us, but he did shut up. We started up again and kept on walking until we came to a clearing, some sort of open space in the middle of the woods where the trees didn't grow. The moon was bright enough to let us to see what she brought us there for.

Right in front of us was a big hole. Not a natural hole or a pot hole like you see sometimes in the rocky areas outside of town. This was a hole that somebody dug in the dirt. Deep. Probably over our heads. Maybe shoulder high if a grownup stood in it. It was kind of rectangular and there was a huge pile of dirt next to it. We all walked around it and looked at it for a few minutes.

"What is it?" Keith asked.

"What do you think it is?" Kimberly said.

"A hole?" he said.

She gave him a look.

"How'd you know it was here?" Richie asked.

"Larry Trupa," she said.

"Larry Trupa?" Keith said. "He's eight years old. Are you saying he did this?"

"Of course not," she said.

"How did he know it was here then?"Richie asked.

"He told his sister he saw it when he was up here looking for diamonds with a couple of his friends," she said. "She told me."

"Does anybody else know?" Keith asked her.

She just shrugged.

Finally, I asked the question everybody was probably thinking. "You think it has something to do with Mikey?"

"What do you think?" she asked.

I was about to tell her when I heard leaves crunching, coming from the woods in the other direction from where we came in. I thought at first it might just be a raccoon or something, but then we all heard the voices and froze.

MIGGS

Fritz stopped by my house that Saturday night. It was quite odd for him to do so. In fact, I can't recall if he had ever even been to my house before that. He was with his wife and he said they were on their way out to their usual Saturday night dinner at the Rotary Club. He told me he needed to talk to me for a few minutes to fill me in on something. He was going to have his wife wait in the car, but I insisted that he bring her in, and she went into the kitchen with my wife to have coffee while Fritz and I sat down on the porch.

When we were settled in our chairs, Fritz told me that he had received a call from someone he knew with the state police to ask about the investigation. It seemed that they were getting antsy and were asking about when he might want them to take over. I told him that Irwin was just at my house the night before, sharing some information with me and he hadn't said anything about any of that.

"That's how they do it," he told me. "They pretend to be helping and the next thing you know they're in my office telling me why the locals aren't equipped to handle a thing like this."

That was disappointing to hear, especially since I thought Irwin was being straight with me. But what Fritz said made sense, and I didn't want to give it up.

"So then maybe we should try for a warrant now," I told him.

"An arrest warrant?" he asked.

"Search," I said. "For that Hager fellow."

He was quiet for a second. I thought he might be thinking it over.

"Funny you should say that," he said.

"Why's that?"

"The guy I was talking to over there asked me if we were looking at anybody for the crime. I told him we didn't really have anybody we thought was a serious suspect. But then I did mention Hager."

I sat up at the mention of his name. "And?" I asked.

"Well," he said. "He told me to wait and then he went and got one of his guys, a trooper. It seems this guy was out on route seven in his cruiser last week when he spotted what looked like a fire up by Kitchiwa Lake."

"A fire?" I asked, not sure what this had to do with anything.

"Yeah," he said. "So he told me he drove on down to check it out and spotted a man next to a car in the parking area."

"Hager?" I asked.

"One and the same," Fritz said. "He asked to see his driver's license and wrote down the name. The statie said he was carrying a suitcase when he spotted him."

"A suitcase?" I repeated.

"That's right," he said. "Odd no?"

"Very," I said. "What was in it?"

"That's the thing," he told me. "He said he and Hager went back and forth for a bit. He said it sounded like Hager knew his criminal procedure, but he finally relented and opened it up for him."

"And?" I asked.

"Empty," he said. "Not a thing in there."

I took a moment to think about that. "So he let him go?"

"Yeah," he said. "But not before after asking him if, by any chance, he had started a fire up at the lake."

"What did he say?"

"Hager said he was never up there."

I nodded, suddenly seeing where this was going. "So what's he doing out there with an empty suitcase?"

"Exactly. He told the statie he was just taking it out of the back seat and putting it in the trunk. Said it was sliding around in the back and driving him crazy, so he pulled off the road to take care of it."

"The statie didn't believe him, right?"

"That's the thing," he told me. "He said he was sure Hager was coming out of the woods when he first saw him.."

"Meaning he might have tried to dump something out there?"

"It's a long shot, but yeah."

"So did he find anything?" I asked.

"He didn't look," Fritz told me. "He said he got a call to respond to an accident. He said it was raining pretty good by then so he wasn't worried about the fire spreading."

"And he had no reason to think there might be anything criminal going on since he didn't know anything about Hager," I said.

"Correct," Fritz said. "Not until I mentioned him to my friend."

"Do you think that's enough to get us a warrant?" I asked.

He shook his head. "Not unless we find something up there."

"You're saying I should check it out," I said.

"Probably a good idea," he said.

I thanked him for his advice, as usual, and he told me not to worry about it and to get in touch with him if I found anything of interest.

Not five minutes after he left, the phone rang again. I figured it was probably just Vic calling me about some drunk somewhere, but it was the fire chief. He told me that he had gotten a call from Jim Abernathy who owns the apartment building where the Hager fellow rents his apartment. He called to say that Hager had been acting suspicious lately. Lots of coming and going at all hours.

Immediately, I thought of what Hager had told me the last time I had been to his apartment. It made sense that his landlord would find this suspicious.

I asked the chief why Abernathy would call him instead of me. "I'm getting there," he said. "Tonight Hager asked Abernathy if he could burn something in the barrel Abernathy uses to burn leaves and trash."

I took a second before I spoke. Two fires in one week. That was sure as hell suspicious. "Was it a suitcase?" I asked.

"How the hell did you know that?" the chief wanted to know.

"Never mind," I said. "So what happened?"

"Abernathy told him it was OK, but he said he didn't believe Hager when he told him why he wanted to burn it. Something about spilling something on it. So Abernathy kept checking out the window to see what he might be up to."

"And?"

"And about ten minutes later some guy came to see Hager while he was out there burning the thing," the chief said.

"Any idea who?"

"Couldn't see his face too well," said the chief. "He said they left not five minutes after the guy got there. Left the suitcase burning right there in the barrel."

"Is it still there?" I asked.

"It is," he said. "That's why he called me. Then he asked me to call you."

"You been out there yet?" I asked.

"Not yet," he said. "But I just sent a guy out to put out the fire."

I told him to meet me there and that I was on my way.

HAGER

I didn't kill the boy. I wish to make that clear, if I haven't already. I would never hurt a child. I understood everyone's concern when he suddenly appeared out at the abandoned camp that night, and I certainly understood everyone's desire to keep our secret, but I would never take the life of a child in order to do that.

I did kill John. I wish to make that equally clear, and I did so for two reasons. First, I was certain that he was going to kill me. I am not ignorant. I knew early on that he might someday want to cause me harm. However, in the end, he underestimated me, as he always had.

The second reason is that I believe he most certainly killed the boy. I don't know that he drowned the child himself. He may not have. John liked to use other people to do his dirty work. I was proof of that. However, even if he had someone else do it, he was just as guilty in my mind. So I did it for the boy and his family, as much as for me.

I was remarkably calm as we drove away from my house that night. As I said, I had no doubt about what he had in mind for me. I don't think he cared that I knew his intention either. He was quiet as we drove, confident I'm sure that he was in control. Confident also that I was incapable of doing anything about it.

When we were outside of town, I asked him what was bothering him. After all, he said we should go for a ride to "talk about it", whatever "it" meant. He didn't answer right away. When he finally did, he said that I was becoming too unreliable. Too many meetings with the police. "I'll remind you that you were the one who said putting the boy in that pool would end all our problems," he said.

I reminded him that if we had simply buried the boy, as he had proposed, then it would have become a missing persons case, one involving a child, and that would stir up even more interest and controversy. There would be searches and manhunts. It would make local news. Maybe even national. It would take weeks to die down. True, I hadn't thought about the chlorine in the water and admitted as much, but it was still a mystery to them or we'd be in jail already. He didn't respond.

We were on a deserted stretch of highway when he slowed the car and pulled off the main road onto a dirt road leading into the woods. I didn't recognize the area. He pulled in far enough so that we wouldn't be visible from a car passing on the highway in either direction. Although I had a pretty good idea of what was in store for me, I asked him what we were doing out there.

He said he had something to show me. He got out and turned on a flashlight, aiming it toward the woods, but not before checking the highway in both directions to make sure no cars were coming.

"This thing you're going to show me," I said. "What does it have to do with my being unreliable?"

"You'll see," he said. Then he turned toward the woods as if he expected me to simply follow him.

"No," I said. "I don't think so."

With that he turned around and smiled. Then he took his hand out of his pocket to reveal a pistol. It was small enough to hide like that. However, I was sure it was big enough to accomplish what he had in mind. I looked at it, then him.

"Is that really necessary?" I asked.

"I'm afraid it is," he said.

He smiled when he said it, then gestured for me to walk into the woods in front of him.

SAM

It was only a few seconds after we heard the voices that we saw the flashlight. About a minute after that, two guys walked into the open area where we had just been standing near the hole. Kimberly and I were hiding behind a large rock then. Keith and Richie were both behind a tree. We didn't have time to run once we saw the flashlight. They would have heard us if we did. They probably would have seen us too, if they shined the light in that direction.

I didn't recognize the bigger one, but I knew the other one right away. It was Mr. Hager, the guy who got up at the town hall meeting that night. The guy who's on my paper route. The guy Keith told the cops had said that stuff about having sex at the old hobo camp, except that he didn't really say it.

Mr. Hager was in front of the other guy, the bigger one, who was holding a gun to his back. I had never seen a gun before, other than in the movies. It was a pistol, not a rifle. My father didn't like guns or hunting and would never let me have one of my own. I looked over at Keith and Richie, but they were both staring at the two guys. I wanted to get out of there, but we were trapped. Kimberly had a hold of my arm and was digging her fingers into my skin. I had to pry them off. When she realized what she was doing, she pulled her hands away quick and didn't look at me.

When the two guys got in front of the hole, they stopped. Then Mr. Hager turned to the other guy and said, "Looks like you planned this."

"I don't like to take chances," the other guy said. Judging from his looks, I believed him. Like I said, he was bigger than Mr. Hager and looked a lot stronger. He had a crew cut, not longer hair like a lot old older guys are starting to wear, and that made him look even scarier.

Then Mr. Hager did something that surprised me and everybody else, I guess. Especially the big guy behind him. He fainted. Or at least that's what it looked like. His legs gave way and he sort of fell right toward the bigger guy. I guess that's why he didn't shoot him. It was probably just instinct that he tried to catch him. He put his left hand, the one without the gun, under Mr. Hager's right arm. He still had the gun in his right hand, so that's probably why he didn't try to grab Mr. Hager's other arm. That was a mistake, because Mr. Hager swung that hand around real fast and hit the bigger guy in the neck. When he pulled his hand away, I could see the knife sticking out.

It all happened fast. Mr. Hager must have been carrying it in his pocket the whole time. He must have been left-handed, too. Or else he was just lucky to be carrying it in that pocket, but I don't think it was luck. I think Mr. Hager was just smarter than the other guy. He not only brought a knife with him without getting caught, but he also got out of the way as he stabbed him. That was a good thing because the big guy fired the gun then, only he was too close and he didn't get it around fast enough to hit anything. It looked like he wanted to shoot again, but Mr. Hager kept moving away until he was behind him. Then, before the big guy could get all the way around to aim at him, Mr. Hager shoved him to the ground. He landed face first and it must have pushed the knife in a little more because he groaned real loud.

Mr. Hager just stood there for a minute or so, staring down at the big guy who was still moaning on the ground. The knife was still in his neck and he rolled over the other way. Then he reached up with his left hand, the one without the gun, and pulled it out.

But he seemed real weak then and just let it drop out of his hand. When he did, Mr. Hager reached down and took the gun from his other hand. He didn't even put up a fight. He just let him do it. You could tell then he was dying.

Mr. Hager put the gun in his jacket pocket and looked all around. He even looked in the direction of where we were. For a second, I was afraid he might be able to see us, but the flashlight was laying on the ground near the big guy, shining off in a different direction from where we were. Mr. Hager finally picked it up and put it in a spot so that it shone on the hole.

Mr. Hager then put his hand in the bigger guy's jacket and took out what looked like car keys. I could see the big guy's head move, like he was trying to look at Mr. Hager, but he was bleeding pretty good then, so he couldn't do much about it. He was still alive, though. You could see that. Mr. Hager then picked him up by the heels and dragged him over to the edge of the hole. But then he stopped and stared down into the hole. I think he was trying to figure out whether to put him in there. That's how it looked to me anyway. Finally, he let his feet drop and started walking back the way they came. We waited until he was gone for what seemed like a long enough time, then we all looked at each other.

"Holy shit," Richie said.

Keith was already out walking toward the guy. When he got a few feet away, he stopped and looked down at him.

"What're you doing?" I asked. "Get away from there."

He didn't answer, so I went over next to him to see what was up. Richie and Kimberly were right behind me. The four of us just stood there looking at the guy who looked like he stopped breathing. I thought he must have finally died, but then he opened his eyes and took a big breath all of a sudden and we all jumped back. He looked up and you could tell he must have been trying to figure out who we were and what we were doing there. He looked at each one of us, but stopped when he got to Keith.

Keith didn't say anything. He just kept staring at the guy.

"Why's he looking at you?" I asked him.

"That's him," he said. "That's the other guy."

"What guy?" Richie asked. But I knew right away what he meant.

"From the Custard Cup," Keith said. "That's him."

I was about to say we should get out of there when Richie pointed at the flashlight that was coming toward us again from in the woods.

MIGGS

When I got to Hager's place, the fire chief was standing there with Dick Nevins who's been on the fire department for about as long as I've been a cop. They were next to the barrel which was still smoking. On the driveway sat what was left of the suitcase. It was mostly just the handle and the top part of the frame. It looked like they put a hose to it after they took it out. The rest of it was gone, probably still smoking in the bottom of the barrel.

I shook hands with each of them before I took a look in the barrel.

"What do you make of it?" I asked them.

Nevins looked to the chief, who said, "Not much. Except for the smell."

"Yeah," I said, noticing it for the first time. It reminded me of the smell I encountered at Hager's house that day. "What do you think that is?" I asked.

"Don't know for sure," the fire chief said. "Hager told Abernathy he spilled some acetone on it."

"Acetone?" I asked. "What the hell is that?"

"It's a solvent," the chief said.

"What the hell would he use that for?" I asked, looking first at the chief, then Nevins.

Before either one could answer, Abernathy came out of the house. He must have been watching from inside and saw me arrive.

After we shook hands, I asked him to tell me again about Hager. Why he was so concerned about him. He basically told me the same thing the fire chief said over the phone.

"Anything else?" I asked. "Besides the visitor and the late hours?"

He shook his head. "Not that I can think of," he said.

I nodded and turned back to the fire chief and Nevins.

"You just about done here?" I asked. They exchanged a look, then the chief said that they were, if that was OK with me.

"Alright then," I said. "I'll take it from here. Thanks."

"You want us to take that?" the fire chief asked, pointing at what was left of the suitcase.

I shook my head. "I'll send somebody from the station to get it," I told him.

He nodded. "Tell 'em to watch out," Nevins said. "It's still hot."

I told him I would, then Abernathy and I watched them leave. When they were gone, I turned back to Abernathy.

"I'm going to ask you some questions now," I said, "but I have to have your word that you won't talk about any of this with anyone. And I mean anyone. Especially not with Hager. This is an ongoing investigation. It's deadly serious."

He looked a little frightened, but said he understood. "Does this have to do with that boy?" he asked.

"Never mind what it has to do with," I said, "If I hear you talked with anyone about this, even another cop, I'm going to be awfully angry with you. Anything you might say, even if you think it's not important, could interfere with our investigation and that might add up to obstruction of justice in my eyes and you don't want any part of me if that happens."

He looked even more frightened then, but he nodded. "I won't say nothing," he said.

I didn't know Abernathy particularly well, so I wasn't sure if he

156

could be trusted, but I had no choice but to rely on my threat, so I went ahead and asked him if he had ever seen Hager with the guy who came there that night.

"Nope," he said.

"So you don't know the guy?" I asked.

He shook his head.

It was about what I expected. I asked him to give me a physical description, which he did. It wasn't nearly enough to identify the guy, but it was enough to compare to what someone else might say. Someone like the Somerset kid, who I intended to talk to once I got through with Abernathy.

"I think he might not be from around here," Abernathy added then. That got my attention.

"Why do you say that?" I asked. "Did he say something?"

He shrugged. "Don't know exactly," he said. "A feeling I guess. The way he acts and all."

"Like Hager?" I asked.

He laughed. I think he knew what I meant. "No," he said. "Just the opposite. More John Wayne than Wayne Newton."

I tried not to laugh, but really it wasn't funny. I thought long and hard about what I was about to ask next, but I could see no other way except to just ask it. So that's what I did.

"You ever see Hager wearing a mask or carrying one or having one in his apartment?"

Abernathy looked at me like I was nuts. Then he shook his head. "He has a thing for red paint, though," he said.

"Who?" I asked. "Hager?"

"Yeah," he said. "I seen the tin in the garage and knew it wasn't mine. So I knocked on his door to ask him whether he was painting his apartment without my permission."

"What did he say?"

"Said he wasn't painting anything. Said it was for a hobby. Though I ain't ever seen any paintings. Must be he stores 'em somewhere else or he's got 'em hidden up there somewhere."

"You wouldn't happen to know where that paint is now, would you?" I asked.

He nodded. "Just saw it in there this morning," he said. Then he pointed at the garage.

I asked him if I had his permission to go into the garage and see if it was still there. He told me I did. So I went in and looked around for a few minutes before I came back out and asked him to show me where it was.

He followed me back in and went right over to a spot near the back where there were a few other cans of paint. He stopped short. Then he started looking around, moving cans and other things as he did. He seemed put out. Finally, he gave up and turned back to me.

"It was right here this morning," he told me. "I swear."

I believed him, which only made the whole thing more troubling.

HAGER

It was considerably more of a challenge to dispose of a grown man than an eight-year-old boy. Especially a man who was over six feet tall and probably weighed two hundred pounds. It was a good thing I didn't put him in that hole before I went back to the car or I don't know how I would have gotten him out.

When I first heard the whispering after coming back from the car, I was frightened but also certain that it couldn't be the police. They couldn't have learned what happened and gotten there that fast. Then I thought that perhaps John had arranged for others to be there in case he needed assistance. However, as I stood there waiting to be confronted, I realized that whoever it was must have chosen to run away, since no one came forward and there were no more sounds. That was quickly confirmed when I walked to the area where I first heard them, but I saw no sign of anyone.

After that, I knew I had no choice but to take John with me. If whoever was out there had seen what happened, as I assumed they had, they would surely call the police and I couldn't afford to have them find the body there. Not just any body, but the body of a man I had been seen with just two weeks before in a very public place and who, even more recently, I was questioned about by the sheriff.

I had gone back to the car in the first place to look for a shovel. I knew John would have to have one if he was intending to bury me in that hole. Sure enough, I found it in the trunk. My original plan was to bury him in the same hole where he had obviously hoped to put me. That seemed both fitting and convenient, but once I realized that someone had been out there, I knew I couldn't do that. I thought briefly about filling the hole so that if the police did come back, there would be no hole anywhere to be seen and they might begin to doubt the story of whoever had been out there. But in the end I decided that it was too great a risk to spend the time that it would take to accomplish. There was a lot of blood on the ground near the hole that they would easily spot if I just left it, so I covered that with some dirt before I left. In total, between dragging John back to the car, getting him in the trunk, and cleaning up the scene, I was out there no longer than half an hour after whoever was out there had left. The entire time I was certain that I would hear sirens coming for me. Why it didn't happen that way, I don't know. I suppose I was simply fortunate once more. I don't mean to suggest that God was on my side or anything. I know better than that.

You may wonder why I didn't simply run away, leaving the body there. I surely considered it. Flight is a normal response, as I learned in that college psychology course. Nevertheless, I forced myself to remain calm and tried to think of the best plan for survival. I reasoned that if I left John there and ran off, there were at least three people who could connect me to him. That boy and his parents saw us together at that diner and had already spoken to the sheriff about us. The workers at the diner would probably confirm that as well, and if whoever was out there moments before had seen what happened, they would be able to identify me. So I concluded that my only chance of avoiding all that was to do what I did.

However, that left me with an even bigger problem. As I said, I somehow managed to get him back to the car and into the trunk, but that was just the beginning for me. By the time I had done so, I was covered in dirt and blood. I knew I couldn't very well drive through town like that and risk being seen, which left me with the dilemma of where to leave the car and the body.

Naturally, hiding both of them somewhere far outside of town seemed like my best option. However, if I abandoned the car, I would be faced with walking all the way back into town in those dirty clothes. I briefly considered simply driving the car back to town and leaving it there somewhere with his body in the trunk. I rejected that idea, though, as I knew I would be faced with the same dilemma of having been seen with John prior to that night, regardless of where the body was found. After all, dead was dead.

Once again, I managed to calm myself and think it through until I came up with what seemed like an acceptable solution. It was the only one that made any sense, really. I simply determined that I should separate the two problems and handle each one on its own. The first thing I needed to do was to get the body as far away from me as I could, preferably to a place where, unlike the boy, he wouldn't be discovered. Not right away, anyway.

I mentioned before that there are approximately fifty lakes in our region. My initial thought was to weigh him down and drop him into one of them. I suppose the connection to the boy made that a natural choice. However, I knew I couldn't very well risk taking him to Kitchiwa, where I had already been spotted by a state police officer. Plus, I'd never get him a mile up that path all by myself. All the other lakes I knew of seemed to present the same challenge of getting the body from the car to the water, so I dismissed that notion right away.

My next thought was a rather gruesome one, I admit. Most people don't know that pigs will eat human flesh. In fact, they'll devour it quite readily, leaving next to nothing behind. Such efficiency was certainly appealing to me. However, trying to sneak onto the property of a farmer and taking the chance of being caught dumping a dead man into a pig pen was far too great a risk. It was soon after rejecting that idea that I came up with the most fitting of all.

I mentioned before how John and I had met. Me bird watching, him hunting, in a manner of speaking. What I failed to mention was that the spot where our paths first crossed was atop a very steep hill, both high enough and rocky enough to satisfy my needs. John obviously had a deep puncture wound in his neck from where I had put the knife. If he were eventually found, that would be a clear indication of his cause of death. Therefore, I needed to not only dispose of the body, but to do so in a manner that might throw off the investigators for awhile, should he ever be found.

That's why I drove out to where we met earlier that spring. Like then, it was isolated, as you might expect after midnight. Once there, I took John out of the trunk and laid his body on a blanket he kept in there, and I used it to help pull him up to a place on that hill overlooking the bubbling creek some fifty feet below. Before rolling him over the edge, I broke off a stick I found nearby, leaving one part with a somewhat sharp end. I then examined the knife wound in his neck. I determined that the stick would provide a nice explanation for how he died, so I placed the tip of the stick in the center of the wound and pushed it in with considerable force.

The groan caught me completely by surprise, and I found him staring back at me, not quite dead. Fortunately, he couldn't speak. Not that he didn't try. He made some sounds that were quite disturbing, so I rather quickly pulled him over to the edge and unfurled the blanket so that he tumbled neatly over. It was pretty dark so I wasn't able to determine if he fell all the way down to the water, but I had to hope so.

Of course, if he didn't, there was nothing I could do about it anyway. So I left.

SAM

We took off running and didn't stop until we were about a block from town hall. Richie was in front and stopped first. He bent over with his hands on his knees, breathing hard. Keith came up next, then Kimberly and then me. We were all trying to catch our breath and coughing and no one said a word for what seemed like forever. Then we all stood up and looked at each other.

"Where's your father?" Keith asked Kimberly.

"What do you mean?" she asked.

"We got to go see him," he said. "There's no choice. We have to tell him what we saw."

She shook her head and backed up. "No way," she said. "I told you. I'm not telling him anything."

"We just saw a guy kill somebody!" Keith told her.

"You promised you wouldn't tell!" she said. "You swore!"

"That was before!" he said.

"Forget it!" she said.

"Alright then," Keith said, "we'll just go ourselves."

"Don't you dare!" she told him.

"How're you going to stop us?" he asked.

She put on the scariest look I have ever seen on a girl. "If you say anything, I'll tell him that your father was one of those people I saw out there that night."

I don't know about the rest of them, but I was wondering if she really meant it or was just making a threat. Keith looked furious. His face got all red and I was afraid he might go after her. "That's a lie!" he said to her. "My old man wasn't there!"

Keith looked at me then. "Tell her!" he said. "You didn't see my father there!"

"I couldn't tell who any of them were," I said.

Keith turned back to Kimberly. "See? You can't prove nothing."

"I don't have to," she said. "I'm his daughter." She was right. The sheriff would definitely believe her over any of us.

She didn't wait for him to argue with her. She just turned around and took off running.

"So what do we do now?" I asked.

Keith shook his head. I wasn't quite sure what that meant, so I turned to Richie. He hadn't said a word the whole time, which wasn't like him at all. "Let me think about this for a second," he said.

I watched Kimberly turn the corner at the end of the block and head up the street that would take her to her house.

"She's right," Richie said then. "I mean, why say anything to the cops? The big guy was the one with the gun. And he was taking the other guy into the woods where there was a hole already dug."

"What's that supposed to mean?" I asked.

"It means he was probably going to kill the other guy and bury him in it," he said.

"That was Mr. Hager," I said.

"You know him?" Richie asked, looking surprised.

"Yeah," I said. "He's on my paper route."

"You never told me that," he said.

"I don't tell you a lot of things," I said.

He made a face at me. "Well, if you know him so well, why would anyone want to kill him?" he asked.

"I have no idea," I said. "But it sure looked like self-defense to me."

"I don't care who's right or wrong," Keith said. "We have to tell them what we saw. Let them figure it out."

"I thought you said he's the same guy you told the sheriff was in that diner," Richie said.

"Yeah, so?" Keith said.

"So even if we tell the sheriff everything we just saw, he's still going to think he's tied up in this thing because of what you said you heard at the diner," Richie said. "Unless you want to admit that you lied about all that"

Keith looked at me. I could tell he hadn't thought of that. Neither did I.

"Are you going to tell the sheriff you lied?" Richie asked.

"That's obstruction of justice," I told Keith, remembering what my father and Mr. Pickens were talking about that night. "You could end up in juvie."

We all looked at one another. It was a mess, no doubt.

Richie shook his head. "Kimberly's right. I'm sure as hell not going to the cops. And neither is she, so it would just have to be you two. Again."

I looked at Keith and he frowned. Then he shook his head. And so we decided we better keep our mouths shut and pretend like nothing ever happened.

MIGGS

After I left Abernathy's, I went right over to see Nathan Somerset to ask his son to give me a description of the man he saw with Hager that day at the diner. I had asked him before if he knew the man, and he said he didn't. I hadn't bothered to ask for a description. I didn't think it was important then. I was hoping now it might match what Abernathy said and that I might get some idea of who he was and how he might fit into this whole thing.

Unfortunately, when I got there, Nathan said his boy had gone out with his friends. One of them was the Fisher kid who came with him to the town hall that night. The other was the Hamilton kid. Richard was his name. The poor kid was destined for trouble, and I was afraid that I was at least partially responsible for that. It was his older brother who Cyrus Robbins had run down that night I let him go. Richard was only five at the time, so all his suffering came after. His father was a drunk, just like Robbins. Only worse. Not a year has gone by when he hasn't been involved in some sort of bloody fight outside a bar. Never bad enough to lock him up for more than a night or two, but enough to make most folks afraid of him and to keep my men on alert. To my way of thinking, his kid has almost no chance of turning out OK. Again, I take my share of the blame on that.

I asked Nathan Somerset if he and his wife could provide me with any more information about the man with Hager, but they stuck to their story that they only saw him from the back and didn't really pay any attention. I didn't have any reason to doubt them.

"Do you think this person might have something to do with the Vogel boy's death?" the wife asked as I was leaving.

I should have seen that one coming and was mad at myself for not being more careful. I told her we were just checking out every lead and being cautious not to let anything get by us.

"On a Saturday night?" Somerset asked.

I stared at him and he clammed up pretty fast. I then asked them to give me a call on Monday so we could arrange a time for me to talk to their son. They didn't seem too happy about that, but Somerset was just scared enough of me to give me his assurance that they would.

I left there and was on my way home when I saw my daughter Kimberly walking up the hill from downtown, heading toward our house. I never asked her how she was planning on getting home from her friend's house that night, and I felt guilty seeing her walking by herself in the dark, even if she was only two blocks from Main Street and the town hall. In any event, I figured I better give her a ride, so I pulled up alongside and beeped the horn. She about jumped out of her skin and backed away a few steps before she realized it was me. I pulled the car over and put it in park.

"Sorry," I said. "I didn't mean to scare you."

Something about her didn't look right. I couldn't put my finger on it, but something was clearly wrong. She tried to smile, but I could see that she was still spooked.

"You didn't scare me," she said. "I was just surprised. That's all."

I nodded, even though it was obviously not true. I suppose she has lied to me a hundred times over the years. The usual kind of lies that kids tell. Nothing of any real consequence. This seemed different, though. She stood there on the sidewalk almost like she was afraid to get in the car with me.

"Don't you want a ride?" I asked. "You're going home, right?"

She nodded, but didn't move. I was starting to get concerned at that point. "Is there something wrong, honey?" I asked.

She shook her head and walked over and opened the door on the other side. I thought maybe I might be reading too much into it, but I didn't say anything, and she got in. I started the car and drove off heading for home. She kept her head turned away from me the whole time.

"You sure there's nothing you want to tell me?" I asked her. I tried to keep my tone from sounding like I was interrogating her. I get accused of that by my wife sometimes and I've become more sensitive about it.

She shook her head again.

"Hey," I said. "Look at me, will you?"

She did, but turned back again real quick. I could see immediately that she had been crying. I pulled the car over again, still two blocks from home.

"OK," I said. "Tell me what's going on."

"Nothing," she said, still avoiding my stare.

My daughter and I have always had a pretty nice relationship. I love her and I believe she loves me. Even more important, I think she respects me, but that doesn't mean we've had a lot of heart to heart talks. Our conversations have always been on a surface level and, more often than not, of a joking nature. It's where I'm most comfortable, and I've always thought that if she had anything serious to talk about, it would be a conversation she would have with her mother. In most cases, I'd rather not know what they talked about, so long as her safety wasn't involved. I suppose that was why I found it so difficult to think of what to say next.

"Does this have something to do with that Nevins boy?" I asked her.

She turned and looked at me then, her mouth open in surprise. "No," she said. "Why?" She sounded pretty defensive which told me I might have found the source of her tears.

"Your mother told me you spoke to him the other night," I said. "He didn't ask you out, did he?"

She didn't answer right away. "Sort of," she said, finally.

"Sort of?" I repeated. "Either he did or he didn't."

She just shrugged.

"That's not where you were tonight, was it?" I asked, sounding more like a sheriff than a father. I immediately regretted it.

"No," she said, sounding surprised. "He wasn't really serious anyway."

I nodded, assuming that I had learned enough to know what was going on with her. So I put the car in gear again and headed toward the house. "Good," I told her. "He's too old for you anyway."

She didn't say anything.

"You just have to be careful," I told her. "Boys can be cruel. Especially boys like him who think they're better than everyone. It's their problem, not yours. They eventually grow out of it. Most of them anyway."

I was feeling pretty good about how I handled it, but then we got to the house and parked and were getting out of the car when she asked me something that told me I had missed the whole point and had no idea of what was going on inside her head.

"Do some people deserve to die?" she wanted to know.

"Why on earth would you ask that?" I asked her. "You don't want to kill Tom, do you?" I was joking, but she didn't laugh.

"No," she said. "I don't even care about him. I'm talking about Mikey Vogel."

I definitely didn't see that one coming. "You think Mikey deserved to die?" I asked.

"Of course not," she said, in that same annoyed teenage girl voice I had become accustomed to. "I mean the person who killed him."

I had to give that one some thought. I supposed she was talking about the death penalty, and I wanted to make sure I gave her what I hoped was the right answer.

"Maybe," I told her. "But I don't get to decide that. That's up to a judge and a jury. After a fair trial. We do have the death penalty in this state. If we catch the guy who did it and manage to prove that in court, there's a good chance he'll be executed."

"Shouldn't God be the only one who decides that?" she asked.

Once again, she caught me off-guard. "Maybe," I told her. "Maybe in some way he does. Maybe he looks down and helps those people on that jury when they're having trouble deciding whether they should convict that person."

The mention of God was a bit of a sore point for me. After the incident with Cyrus Robbins and the Hamilton boy, I stopped going to church. I had always thought I was a good man and most always did the right thing and I couldn't imagine why God, if he existed, would allow me to make a mistake that cost a boy's life. My wife and I had argued about it for a time, my abandoning religion. She thought I was setting a bad example for the kids, and Kimberly's question that night made me wonder if she had been right.

"What if God decides there doesn't need to be a trial?" Kimberly asked me then. "He can do that can't he?"

"He's God," I said. "I imagine he can do about anything he wants." To me, that was no idle statement and probably sounded more harsh than I had intended.

She stared at me for a bit before answering. "Then maybe he'll take care of it for you," she said. "Maybe he already has. Maybe you'll never find the person who did it."

I was going to tell her that I preferred that he at least let me have a hand in it, but she didn't wait for me to answer. She just went up to her room, which was probably a good thing, since I wasn't sure that I had earned any right to that.

HAGER

I checked the trunk for blood before I left the car in the parking lot behind the school. When I put John in there, I spread out the blanket underneath so that any blood that dripped out of his wound would go on the blanket. It wasn't much. Most of it had come out next to the hole back in the woods, and that was now covered with dirt. Still, I wanted to be careful, so I folded up the blanket after I used it to roll him down that cliff and threw it out along the highway some five miles or so out of town, hoping that anyone who found it or the body wouldn't be able to make any connection between the two. I did the same with the knife a mile or two beyond that.

I also wiped down the car for fingerprints before I left it, and I disposed of the keys down the sewer where I prayed no one would ever find them. The only other thing I had to worry about was my clothes, so I turned my windbreaker inside out before I got out of the car and brushed off my pants as much as I could. They were still rather dirty, but I assumed that if I was seen by anyone, it would be unlikely that they would notice dirt stains on my pants in the dark. If they did, I could always say I fell down on the way home. I would act drunk and that would probably end any curiosity. As it turned out, I made it home without seeing another soul.

You're probably wondering why I chose to leave the car at the school. This is where I thought I was being rather clever. There's one high school, two junior highs and three elementary schools in our town. I left the car in the parking lot behind one of the elementary schools. Based on the newspaper reports, I knew it to be the one attended by the boy. It was my thinking that the car would eventually be discovered there, and they would be able to trace the license plate back to John. If they didn't find his body right away, he would be thought to be missing or to have run away. That would certainly look suspicious, his car having been left at the same school attended by the dead boy. The police would have no choice but to link the two, making him the prime suspect in the boy's death. He would at least have to be someone to consider. If they did eventually find his body, they might easily conclude that he intentionally threw himself off that hilltop and died because of the neck wound caused by a tree branch. Either way, he would be the preliminary focus of the investigation, and they would probably come to the conclusion eventually that he was the one responsible for the boy's death. Even better, since he was also dead, there would be no one to dispute it.

All in all, I was quite pleased with myself when I arrived home that night. I had taken a potentially dangerous situation and turned it around so that the focus of the investigation might point away from me. Of course, once John was determined to be missing or was found dead, Miggs would probably learn that John was the person I was seen with at the diner that day. However, I could then feel free to identify John as my companion without fear of denial or retribution and that would be the extent of it. I could say I had no idea of any involvement John might have had with the boy, and Miggs would have nothing to contradict that. Or so I hoped.

The only wild card was whether I was seen earlier that night by whoever was out there in the woods, but that was a problem for me regardless of where I parked the car or where I left John's body. I was just going to have to trust that I hadn't been seen or, perhaps, that they wouldn't be able to identify me in the dark.

The first thing I did when I got home was take a long hot bath to wash off all the dirt and grime. Then I washed the clothes I was wearing. I had to do it in the bathtub since I shared a laundry in the basement with my landlord and the other tenants and I didn't want to risk having one of them find me washing clothes before sunrise on a Sunday morning. When I was done, I wrung my clothes out into the tub. Then I hung them on the shower rod to dry the rest of the way. I had just gotten into bed and was about to drift off to sleep when I heard a soft rapping on my door.

I don't know if it was confidence that my plan would work or if I just didn't care anymore, but I did not even get out of bed. I simply lay there and listened as it continued for another twenty seconds or so, then stopped. Whoever it was had obviously gone away. After all, it was nearly six o'clock on a Sunday morning. No one could be expected to answer the door at such a time, especially if they weren't expecting someone. If anyone asked later why I didn't answer, I could say that I had been asleep and didn't hear it. If it was the sheriff, he would need a warrant to enter without my permission. Since he didn't do so, I could safely assume it was either not him or, if it was, that he didn't have the necessary warrant. In any event, I was asleep within a few minutes, and I slept soundly until early the next afternoon.

SAM

My parents were pretty mad at me for coming home after curfew Saturday night. They wouldn't let me leave the house the next day except for church. It was just as well. I wasn't in any hurry to see Richie and Keith again. I didn't want to even think about what we saw. It was too much. I had never seen a dead person before. I guess, technically, I still hadn't. Like I said before, the big guy was still alive the last time we saw him near that hole.

Richie and I talked till almost midnight after Keith left us that night. I told him that if they ever caught Mr. Hager, we would be the only people in the world who could prove he killed the guy in self-defense. I told him he didn't have to say anything, but I couldn't just ignore it and let him go to jail.

"Why not?" Richie said. "You don't really know the guy or what was going on. You should just stay out of it."

It was a good point. I didn't really know him. Collecting for the paper every week didn't mean we were friends or anything. Still, he was always friendly when I came by. One time, when it was snowing like mad outside and I got soaked, he invited me in and made me hot chocolate while I dried off. We talked about movies and TV shows we liked, and the Beatles even. To tell you the truth, I kind of felt sorry for him, being a bachelor and not having a family. He seemed kind of lonely. I suppose that doesn't mean he's a nice guy, but I kind of liked him for some reason.

I didn't say any of that to Richie. I just told him I wouldn't do anything unless Mr. Hager got arrested. Then I might have to make a decision. Richie said it didn't matter what I did, he wasn't ever going to talk to the cops. He said if he did, his father would beat him to within an inch of his life. I knew what Richie's father was like and it was true. He would.

With nothing else to do, I spent most of the day thinking about what we saw the night before and trying to decide if it had something to do with Mikey. It sure looked like it to me. I mean, an eight-year-old gets himself killed and then a couple of weeks later, a guy stabs somebody who looks like he was planning to kill him out in the middle of the woods. Like I said before, murder never happens in our town. The last one was a guy who killed another mechanic at the gas station where they worked when he found out the man was fooling around with his wife. That was no great mystery. Everybody knew who did it and why. The guy didn't even try to get away. He just stayed right in the garage while one of the other mechanics called Kimberly's father who came and arrested him. I heard he confessed to the whole thing right there.

I was up in my bedroom trying to figure out what I'd tell Kimberly's father, if it ever came to that, when the phone rang downstairs. A few seconds later, my mother came up and said it was for me.

"It's Sylvia Vogel," she whispered. "The Vogel boy's sister."

I thought she was being a little dramatic. I knew who Sylvia was. Still, I got sort of nervous when she said her name.

I had to go downstairs to pick up the phone. A couple of my friends have an extension upstairs in their house, but we only have one phone and ours is right in the middle of the den. My mother went into the kitchen, but our house is so small I knew she'd try to hear everything I said, so I closed the kitchen door for the second time in as many weeks.

I said hello and Sylvia told me it was her. I don't know if she thought my mother wouldn't tell me, but if she did, that was pretty dumb. She was the most famous kid in town at the moment.

"What's going on?" I asked her.

"Do you think we could meet somewhere?" she asked.

"What for?"

"Because we need to talk," she said.

"What if I don't want to?" I said. I have to admit, I was a little annoyed to be talking with her at all.

"Well, I do," she said. "It's important."

"Why can't you just tell me now?" I asked her.

"Are you trying to make this harder?" she asked back.

I wondered what that was supposed to mean. It seemed like a weird thing for her to say. "I'll be over at the football field in an hour," she said. "Near the stairs to the pool. But I won't wait all day." Then she hung up.

I looked at the phone for a few seconds then hung it up. My mother came back into the den right then, so I knew she was listening or trying to anyway.

"That was fast," she said.

"I guess," I said.

"So what did she want?" she asked.

"She just wanted to wish me luck at that new school," I lied.

I could practically see the air go out of her. I could tell she was hoping for something juicier. "Didn't you tell her you're not leaving until Friday?" she asked.

"She knows," I said. "All my friends do."

She looked at me kind of suspicious then. "I didn't know you two were friends," she said.

"Sort of," I told her.

"And she called just to tell you that?" she asked.

"I guess," I said.

She probably knew I was lying, but she didn't say anything. If she did, she'd have to admit that she was trying to eavesdrop and I knew she would never do that. She just wiped her hands on her apron and went back into the kitchen.

I was getting pretty used to lying to my parents at that point. It was getting to be so easy that I wondered if I would ever be able to tell them the truth again.

MIGGS

I thought that what transpired the night before was important enough for me to stop by church, not for any religious reason, but because I knew that's where I'd find Fritz.

I waited for him outside, and he agreed to go have coffee with me after I told him that I might have uncovered some new evidence. We were at a booth in the back, far enough away from everyone so that they couldn't hear what we were talking about when I told him about Hager burning the suitcase and the missing paint in Abernathy's garage.

"Paint?" he asked. I could tell he wasn't getting why I thought it was important.

"Yeah," I said. "I was hoping to send it down to the state lab. See if it was the kind people might use on their skin."

He looked like he was deep in thought. "Then again," he said, "it might just be the kind people use on their walls."

That was about what I expected him to say. "I asked Abernathy to look around for some acetone, too," I told him. "I knew you probably wouldn't be able to get a warrant to look for that."

"Acetone?" Fritz asked.

"Yeah," I said. "It's what people use to take off makeup. Or paint. I looked it up." Then I explained the excuse Hager gave Abernathy for burning the suitcase.

"I'm more curious about that," he said.

"You mean why he'd be burning it?" I asked.

"Yeah," he said. "I doubt he was telling the truth about that acetone business. He was obviously trying to hide something. People don't go and burn their suitcases in their backyards because of a bad smell. They just throw it out or take it to the dump."

"That's what I was thinking," I told him. "So what about that? With the paint, would it be enough to get an arrest warrant?"

"Not nearly," he said.

"What if Abernathy finds the acetone?" I asked him. "Will that do it?"

He shook his head. "We won't be able to use it," he said. "No warrant."

"But we wouldn't be doing the search," I said. "Abernathy would."

"By asking him to look for it, you've made him an agent of the police," he said. "If he finds anything, we can't use it."

I had heard about the agent theory one time down at the capital. It never even occurred to me when I asked Abernathy.

"So then we wouldn't be able to use the paint, either?" I asked.

"Probably not," he said. "It's gone now anyway. The chain of custody is broken. His lawyer could say we don't know if it's Hager's and he'd be right."

"What if we find his fingerprints on the can? I asked.

"Maybe," he said. "It all depends."

I nodded, though I wasn't entirely clear on where we stood at all.

"Don't worry," he said. "If he finds the acetone, it'll just confirm what we already suspect. I can have Abernathy testify about both in a grand jury. We just need something bigger to get an arrest."

"So we're back where we started," I said. "The longer this goes on, you know, the harder it's going to be to catch this guy."

He shrugged. He knew I was right. "Tell me what you have again," he said.

I told him again about the smell I observed in Hager's apartment. The Somerset kid's story about the diner. The state cop seeing Hager with the suitcase at the parking area by Kitchiwa. Then the whole business about Hager burning the suitcase and the missing paint.

Fritz rubbed his chin for awhile. "It certainly does look like all those things might be connected," he said.

"That's what I've been saying," I told him.

"Except the best it shows is that maybe there were people out in that field engaging in some hijinks and that he might have been one of them," he said. "But it doesn't mean he killed Mikey Vogel."

"You're forgetting the sneaker," I reminded him.

He nodded. "Yes," he said. "There's that. Except it doesn't tie in to Hager other than that it was found out near the place where the hijinks may have taken place, and Hager's connection to the hijinks is tenuous at best. It's all very intriguing, but definitely not enough to get a conviction. Hell, not even enough to get an indictment."

"What about a search warrant then?"

He just shook his head. "Even if I thought I could get it, I'm not going to ask for one."

I stared at him, hardly able to believe he could say that. It must have shown.

"If he burned that suitcase, he must be thinking that he's being watched and has to get rid of any evidence," he said. "What do you think the odds are that he'd have anything incriminating left in his apartment?"

It was a good point, but it didn't make me feel any better. I wanted to do something. Anything. He must have been able to read my mind.

"If we get a warrant we'd just be tipping him off," he said. "Better we let him think he's in the clear. Maybe he'll screw up and incriminate himself some other way. I'd rather take him by surprise."

I wanted to disagree, but couldn't. It was essentially the same rationale we gave for not disclosing the water in the boy's lungs and it was just as sound.

"I take it you didn't find anything up at that lake," he said.

My heart sunk. I hadn't gone up there yet, and I had to admit as much to him. True, I had only found out the day before, but that was no excuse. I should have gone before coming to see him. He looked at me and I know what he was thinking: here we go again. Fortunately, he didn't give me a hard time, like he could have. When the thing happened with Cyrus Robbins and the Hamilton boy, Fritz was one of the few people in town to support me. Being backed by the DA was probably the only thing that allowed me to keep my job and get re-elected. Still, I was asking him to back me over the state police in conducting this investigation, so I was putting him in a bad spot by not covering every angle as soon as I could. I should never have put him that position again.

He must have read the guilt in my expression. "It's Sunday," he said. "It can wait a day. Head up there first thing tomorrow morning. And do it yourself. It's probably a good idea to keep this as quiet as possible."

I said sure, then we left. On the way back to the station, I considered taking a trip out there right then, but I knew my wife would be disappointed if I made her cancel the cookout she had planned that afternoon. I figured morning would come soon enough.

HAGER

It was the first Sunday all summer that I had missed church. I know it must sound rather incongruous, the idea of me and religion, but I am quite spiritual in my own way and enjoy being part of the congregation. I especially like being in the choir, and I think they have appreciated my presence, too. I have a strong voice and carry the tenors, truth be told, and was truly sorry to be letting them down, but I was in no shape emotionally or psychologically to interact with anyone that morning. My thoughts were too consumed by what had happened the previous night.

I was tempted to drive out to the hilltop where I had been the night before, just to be certain that I had done a thorough job of it. However, I knew the risk was too great. I also considered going back out to that place in the woods where John brought me, to see if there was any sign of anyone having gone out there after I left. For the same reason, I dismissed it. Instead, knowing that it would be lightly attended, I took in a movie, a late afternoon matinee.

It was called The Naked Prey and it was about a group of men on safari in Africa who come upon a tribe of savages. The rich man who sponsored the safari refuses to give a gift to the tribal chief and this is taken as an insult, angering both the chief and the tribe. After that, all except one of the men in the safari are killed in rather gruesome fashion. The chief then decides to give the lone remaining man a fighting chance to survive by releasing him, only to be hunted down by a handful of the tribesmen.

Although the film was obviously set in a different time and place, I found the parallel to my situation rather unsettling. Like me, the hero was an outsider who knew the customs of the tribe and could even speak their language, even though he was not a member. Also like me, this man had done nothing to cause the trouble with the tribe. He just happened to have associated with the wrong people. In fact, in the film, the main character had urged the safari sponsor to give the chief the gift, just like I had wanted John to let the boy go and do nothing about the fact that he had seen us. Just like me, the hero of the film was made to pay for someone else's transgression.

Naturally, I felt quite an affinity for the hero as he raced to save his life. I was rather shaken when the movie finally ended, even though the man did indeed survive. They didn't show what he did once he was safely back inside the fort, surrounded by British soldiers. Presumably, he lived a long and happy life. As for me, I went right home and finished what was left of the bottle of Irish whiskey that my employer had given me at Christmas.

I suppose I should have felt comforted, since John was no longer around to threaten me, but I realized that I had overlooked something about our relationship and our "activity" and it was haunting me. I knew who John was and he knew me. After all, he had recruited me to take part in our activity. I was told that he had recruited all the others, as well. However, he told me that he had rules when it came to what we were doing and rule number one was that none of us could know who the others were. Only he would know everyone's identity. He was very strict about that.

He said that when he recruited each person, they were told the same thing. They would only know his name and no one else's. He would be their only contact. He would tell them when and where we were going to meet. He even arranged how we would get to that place by the railroad tracks and where we would park our cars. Most importantly, we were all told that under no circumstances could there be any words exchanged during our time together. That way no one would be able to recognize a voice and identify someone. For the same reason, we had to arrive wearing a mask and make sure it was securely attached and never came off at any time. No unique or otherwise identifiable clothing was to be worn. Likewise, no jewelry of any kind was allowed. We were to apply paint to our bodies before we came out for the ritual, so that when we undressed, there were no identifying marks. We were to put on the masks before we left our cars.

Based on how we conducted ourselves out there, I would say everyone did as he said. If they were like me, they did so out of fear. John made it clear to me that anyone who disobeyed would suffer. I had no doubt that would be the case, and I for one wasn't willing to test him. Besides, in an odd sort of way, the anonymity made it all the more alluring.

He explained to me that he insisted on all that strict secrecy in case someone ever got cold feet and decided to tell what we were up to. That way they would only be able to name him, and he assured me that he was willing to stand alone for our benefit. As a price for that, he warned that if anyone disobeyed the rules, they would also have to answer to him. I think most people would have assumed that to mean that he would do something terrible to them. I know that's how I interpreted it.

I have to admit that the paint and the masks did make identification difficult. Nevertheless, I have spent time in church or at the grocery store looking at various people, trying to imagine them without their clothes on and their skin painted a variety of colors. I've had my suspicions about who some of the other participants might have been but, all in all, John's plan was quite successful. I would never be able to say with any certainty who anyone of them were. It would be pure speculation. Certainly, it would never hold up in a court of law, which was his point I suppose.

Nevertheless, I felt a nagging fear that Sunday when I returned home from the movies. What if he had lied to me? What if he did tell someone else? What if there were others he trusted, in the event that something like this happened? Would they know about me? Had I put myself in danger by killing John, the only one of them who I thought posed a threat to me? That he might have lied was hardly far-fetched. After all, according to him, the whole reason for meeting in such a remote location, masked and adorned, was that we were taking part in a religious ritual, one that the more conservative members of the community might find offensive. A form of pagan worship, he called it. However, it was quite clear to me that the only reason we were all there was carnal. There was nothing religious about it. In truth, it was all a big lie.

As I've said before, I did not kill the boy. I wasn't there when the decision was made to kill him, nor was I present when the boy was actually killed. I was only involved because John had called me that day to dispose of the body. Naturally, I was not happy to have been summoned and would have turned him down had he not made it clear that my refusing to do so would lead to serious "consequences". He didn't elaborate. He didn't have to. I knew what he was capable of.

John made all the arrangements so that the task could be accomplished without detection, which it was. I didn't ask what he did and he didn't offer any information. I only followed his orders. Oddly, I felt little guilt in doing so. After all, the boy was already dead and not by my hand. I would have felt far worse if had he been buried out in an abandoned field as John had originally suggested. The thought of that poor boy resting in some pit, covered in dirt in the dead of winter made my skin crawl, even more so because his family might never know what had happened to him. I felt it would be far easier on the boy's family to know that their son had drowned (which apparently he did) and that he had done so at the pool (which he did not). They would at least have an explanation of how he died, along with the comfort, cold as it might be, of being able to bury him in a marked grave where they could pay their respects.

Ironically, in the end, my effort to ease their pain ended up putting me in greater jeopardy than if I had gone along with John's idea. If it were ever to come out that I had placed the boy in that pool, I had no doubt that any jury would find me guilty of his murder, regardless of what I might say about the events that took place prior, especially since I would be unable to identify anyone else who had been out in that field that night. It would sound like some wild story, a desperate attempt to avoid responsibility. I might even sound insane. And I would be all alone. Just like the hero of that movie.

SAM

I killed Mikey Vogel. I may as well say it because it's true. I don't mean that I drowned him or put him in that pool, but I may as well have. See, it turns out that I was the reason he was out at that camp that night and I was the reason he saw what he saw. Which means I was the reason somebody came and found him the next day and killed him so he wouldn't say anything about it. It's weird how you can kill somebody and not even realize it, but that's what happened. Until I met Sylvia out at the football field that Sunday, I had no idea. But it turns out it's true. I killed Mikey Vogel.

Sylvia was waiting for me right where she said she would. I had to run all the way over there because I was afraid that if I took my bike, my mother or father would see that it was gone and know that I snuck out.

It was actually pretty easy to do. I told my mother I was going to take a nap and to wake me up for dinner. Then I went up to my room and shut the door and climbed out the window onto the porch roof. From there, I hopped down to the side yard and took off. My father was watching the Yankee game in the den on the other side of the house. My mother was busy in the kitchen in the back. I figured once Sylvia was done telling me whatever she wanted to tell me, I could climb back up on the roof and into my window before dinner was ready.

Sylvia was sitting on the bottom bench of the stands waiting for me when I got there.

"I was afraid you weren't going to come," she said when I sat down.

"You should talk," I told her.

"I know," she said. "I'm sorry."

Sometimes you can think things are true just because they're the worst thing you can think. I guess that's why I didn't call Sylvia the day Mikey died.

"So what happened?" I asked her. "Did you chicken out?"

She looked confused. "Didn't Mikey tell you?" she asked.

"Tell me what?" I said.

"My mother had another one of her fits right before I was supposed to leave," she said. "My father made me stay with her until she fell asleep. I knew it would be awhile and that I wouldn't be able to meet you, so I sent Mikey out there to tell you. You mean you didn't see him?"

"You sent Mikey out there?" I said. I was pretty confused then.

"So then you did see him?" she asked me.

"I couldn't figure out why he was there and you weren't," I said, not really answering her question.

"He didn't tell you?" she asked again.

"Didn't he tell you?" I asked back.

"Tell me what?" she wanted to know.

"Mikey didn't say anything when he got home that night?" I asked her.

She shook her head. "I was still with my mother and couldn't talk to him," she told me. "He went straight up to bed. I was going to ask him in the morning what you said, but he went out before I got up. Then you wouldn't look at me at the pool that day, so I figured you were mad at me."

"I was," I said. "I thought you stood me up."

"I knew you might think that," she said. "That's why I wanted to talk to Mikey. I wanted to ask him what you said when he saw you. That's why I asked the pool lady to help me find him."

That's when I first realized that Sylvia didn't know anything about what happened. What I saw. What those people were doing out there and why Mikey got killed.

See, I was never going to meet Kimberly Miggs out there that night. I only told Keith and Richie that because I was too ashamed to tell them who I was really going to see. The girl they made fun of all the time. The girl whose mother sometimes had fits in public places like church or work. The girl they thought was too plain and too poor to be seen with. Definitely too poor to make out with.

I guess they never noticed that I didn't say things about her when they did. That I always hung around in the background when they said stuff to her. She noticed. She came up to me one time when they weren't around to ask me why. So I told her. I liked her. She asked me why I palled around with them, and I just said it was because they were my friends. They might be stupid, but they were still my friends. She said she understood and that she liked me too.

That's why I asked her to meet me somewhere where we could be alone. Away from school. Away from those guys. We arranged it the day before. I told my parents I was going to sleep over at Richie's. They'd never call his house to check. I brought my sleeping bag. Sylvia was going to bring soda and food. We were going to stay out there all night. Just the two of us. Except I didn't find out until that day at the football field that she couldn't go because of her mother and that she sent Mikey out to tell me. He was just doing a favor for his big sister and he died because of it. What a stupid thing to die for.

"So Mikey never told you about what happened that night?" I asked her one more time.

"No," she said, suddenly looking scared. "Why? What happened?"

So I told her.

MIGGS

As Fritz requested, I didn't tell anyone what I was going to do that Monday morning, not Brisby, not Vic, not even my wife. I didn't want to explain why I was going out to that lake or that it might have something to do with Hager. I was still sorting out my thoughts on it, but I definitely didn't want anyone thinking of Hager as a suspect and risk having them make a mistake and alert him. Sure, Abernathy knew something, but I had to have faith that my threat would keep him quiet. For awhile, at least. The Somersets also had to have some idea, based on what Elsie Somerset said to me, but I had to hope that they kept their mouths shut, too.

I stopped by the station early to get some bags to store any evidence I might find. Not that I was optimistic about that. I was just concerned about doing my job right. Luckily, I managed to miss everyone except Vic who had pulled the overnight shift. He barely looked up when I came in, and he paid no attention when I went into the equipment room to get the paper bags we use to store evidence. On my way back out, I told him I'd be gone for the morning and to tell everyone that if they needed me they could reach me on the squawk box. He just said "OK" and didn't ask any questions.

I had just thrown the empty bags into the trunk when Brisby pulled into the lot in back of the station. I waved and got into the car before he could park and get out of his. I was already backing out when he got out, and he gave me an odd look. I just waved again and counted on Vic to tell him what I told him to tell everybody minutes before. I didn't like keeping my own men in the dark, but like I said, I didn't want to mention my renewed focus on Hager

When I got out to the lake, I backed my car into the dirt road turnoff and parked it as far back as I could. I didn't want anyone to see it there, not even the state police, who I knew patrolled the area.

I briefly checked the area around the turnoff to see if maybe Hager might have dropped something there, but I didn't see anything. I didn't get down on my knees, but I searched pretty good. I didn't really expect to find anything. It hardly seemed likely that Hager would have dumped whatever was in that suitcase anywhere near where he parked. When I was done looking around, I grabbed the bags I brought with me and started up the mile-long path to the lake.

My wife and I used to go to Kitchiwa back when it was known for its clean water. Of course, swimming was secondary to what we were actually there for. Oh, we did swim on occasion, but only after we did what young couples often do when looking for a place to go and be alone. In that way, it felt odd to be walking the same path for the reason I was there that day.

It took me about a half an hour to get to the end of the path and up to the lake itself. It was a splendid sunny morning and the lake looked rather beautiful, even though the water was no longer fit for swimming. I stopped to take it all in and couldn't help but let my eyes go to where my wife and I used to spread out our blanket and make out for hours. Sometimes other couples would be there at the same time as us. It would always be awkward at first, everyone barely out of sight of one another. But then, we'd all realize that we were there for the same thing, and we'd try to find a little privacy and get down to business. Odd how we did that without ever talking about it. Odder still that we never really spied on the others and, to the best of my knowledge, they didn't spy on us. Sex is a private affair. To most people anyway.

Of course, it was deserted up there that morning. It didn't look like anyone had been there in years. I wasn't there long, though, when I smelled something familiar. It didn't even take me a second to recall where I detected that smell before. I followed the scent away from the path a bit and soon spotted what looked like an old campfire, right on the edge of the water. It was somewhat circular in shape and appeared fresh.

The thing is, with a campfire, there are usually some rocks around the edges to contain the fire. Even a cub scout knows to do that. Also, the ground around it would show signs of people sitting or standing. Other than in one spot, there were no indications of that, and there were no rocks whatsoever, just what appeared to be the remnants of a fire. Of course, Fritz had told me that it was a fire that had caused the statie to swing by Kitchiwa when he encountered Hager out there. Still, I was surprised when I actually came across its remains more than a week later.

I found a stick nearby and poked around the ashes. Right away I could tell that they weren't from wood. Not entirely anyway. First of all, there was that smell. It wasn't the usual odor you get from pine or oak, which is all that's around that lake. It was more foreign than that. Using the stick, I moved things around and saw that there were still clumps of whatever had been burned there. One by one, I picked out the larger pieces and put them in one of the paper bags. I certainly hoped that whatever I was gathering would turn out to be evidence. The trouble was, I wasn't sure that anyone, even the state police crime lab, would be able to tell what it was before it was burned or what it might be evidence of.

When I picked out everything that I thought might have any possible evidentiary value, I took a walk along the shoreline to see if there might be anything else that I might be able to connect with Hager.

That's when I spotted it.

At first, it looked like just a clump of dirt. It was nestled in some tall weeds, as if it had been dropped into the spot and left behind unnoticed. I'm still not sure what caused me to look closer, but when I did, it soon became apparent what it was.

It wasn't like the kind kids wear on Halloween. Those are plastic and shiny and usually have a rubber band around the back to hold them on. This one was carved out of some sort of wood that was not native to our region. It was also quite primitive looking. There was a sort of skull piece on top that allowed it to be held in place by the shape of the wearer's head. There was also a string that must have been used to tie it around the back to make it fit even more securely. Though mostly made out of wood, there was some sort of hair or fur, along with some kind of paint around the holes for the eyes and mouth. When I held it out in front of me, I couldn't help but think of the National Geographic magazines I read down at the barber shop.

Of course, I knew right away what this meant. Finding it so close to the fire, along with the remnants of what had been burned, I had no doubt that someone, a jury hopefully, would conclude the same as me: Hager had been up there trying to dispose of a number of masks, the significance of which was obvious.

I have no idea how the brain works. I think we all believe that it's our conscious mind that gives us our ideas or dredges up certain memories. I don't know why I still cling to that notion when so many times in my experience those things have occurred to me out of the blue, from somewhere deep in the brain, without any connection to what I may have been thinking or doing just prior. That's how it was that day and in that moment. Out of nowhere, a random thought came to me: it was the Fisher boy who had told us where the Somerset boy had heard the story about the camp activities, not the Somerset boy himself. I had asked the Somerset boy other questions that he answered by himself, but when I asked him that one, he paused. Then the Fisher boy "reminded" him of where he heard it. Why would he have to do that? On reflection, it made no sense. Hager all but admitted to me that he and his companion had talked about sex at the diner. So I simply assumed the boys used that as the basis for making up what they said they heard. Which meant that the Somerset boy wouldn't need to be prompted when I asked where he had heard it.

That got me thinking that while they were most certainly lying, they just might be doing so for a different reason.

HAGER

When I woke up Monday morning, I had the strongest urge to pack a bag, get in my car and drive away as far as I could, to Canada or Mexico maybe. Somewhere that would make it difficult, if not impossible, for them to find me. I would dye my hair and get eyeglasses. Had I listened to my instincts that day, none of what took place later would have come to pass. Now it's true that other things may have happened, things I could not have predicted nor controlled. I might have gotten caught despite a change of name and appearance. I might have gotten into a car accident on the way to wherever I had decided to go. I might have even gotten struck by lightning. If God were truly a punishing sort, that's what would have happened. If I were God, it's what I would have done to me, only I would have done so at the beginning of the summer, not the end. Of course, how God chooses to work remains a mystery, which is probably why things turned out the way they did.

As you can probably tell, I didn't leave. I stayed and resolved to act as if nothing had happened. As if I had never put that boy in the pool, nor killed John that night in the woods. Still, I had a sense of foreboding from that moment on. Sleep was no longer peaceful. Waking hours were even worse. I felt as though any moment might bring the sheriff to my door with a set of handcuffs and an arrest warrant.

When I left for work that morning I felt only slightly better than when I went to sleep. As I came down the stairs, my landlord opened his door before my foot hit the last step. Perhaps I was becoming paranoid, but it appeared to me that he had been waiting there for me. Avoiding him seemed to be impossible, so I just said good morning. He didn't reply. He simply stared at me as I walked by. I got to the front door and was going to let it go, but decided to turn around to see if my instincts were correct.

His reaction was quite odd. He took a step back into his own apartment and began to close the door, almost as if he were afraid of me. Now I must confess, that has never happened to me before. Not just with him. With anyone. As a child, I was always the one who was picked on, never the one picking. Try as I might, I couldn't summon the name of a single person who was ever afraid of me. Child or adult. Ever.

"Did you want to ask me something?" I asked Mr. Abernathy, still standing in the doorway, clutching the door.

He seemed to gather himself before he answered. "No," he said. "Why would you say that?"

"You were staring," I told him. "It looked like you had something on your mind."

He shook his head. Quite deliberately, I might add. "I was just leaving for work myself," he said. His tone was neither friendly nor apologetic. He didn't make a move out of his apartment.

"You didn't say anything when I said 'good morning'," I pointed out.

He looked flustered at that. "Oh," he said. "I'm sorry. Good morning."

I nodded once more and turned back toward the front door.

"How long do you plan to stay here?" he asked, before I could exit.

I turned backed once again. "What do you mean?" I asked.

"How long do you plan to stay in the apartment?" he wanted to know. His inquiry sounded anything but friendly.

I have rented the four-room flat from Mr. Abernathy for the

entire time I have lived in this town. I found it listed in the paper not long after the broker showed me the houses out near Kitchiwa, and I agreed to rent it within five minutes of viewing it. I didn't have a lease. Neither of us wanted one. My tenancy is what they call month-to-month. That might sound, well, temporary, but it simply felt right. I have always paid my rent on time, and Mr. Abernathy has always left me alone. The one time I had a problem with a leaky faucet, he fixed it right away. I thought the arrangement was working out for both of us. Until that morning.

"I thought you didn't have anything to ask me?" I said.

He seemed taken aback by my question. "I didn't," he said, rather defensively. "But now that I ran into you, I thought this might be a good time to ask you."

"Why do you want to know?" I asked him back.

He took a second before he spoke. I took that to mean he was thinking of what to say. "I have a cousin who may be moving to town and I told him I'd try to give him an apartment here," he said. It did not sound the least bit convincing.

"Have you asked any of the other tenants?" I asked him.

Again, he took some time before he answered. "No," he said. "They all have leases."

I nodded. "As you know," I said, "you could give me notice and I'd have to move out after a month. That's what we agreed to when I moved in. Are you giving me notice now?"

He seemed to think that one over. Then he shook his head. "I just wanted to get an idea, in case you were thinking of leaving. That's all."

I wanted to say that he must have been reading my mind, but of course I didn't. The coincidence was unsettling, though. "I don't have any plans to leave anytime soon," I said. "So does that mean I can stay? I rather like it here."

He pursed his lips like he was disappointed by something I said. "Of course," he told me. "I was just asking. Forget I said anything."

I nodded and turned to the door once again. Then turned back.

"When is your cousin coming?" I asked, intending to press him further. But he had already gone back into his apartment and closed the door.

SAM

I didn't go over to the field to play ball with Keith and Richie on Monday, and I didn't answer the phone when it rang at nine. I suppose it could have been someone else, but that's when they always called, so I was sure it was them. I didn't call them either. I didn't want to tell them about Sylvia and I didn't want to lie anymore either. Before I left Sylvia on Sunday, I got her to agree not to say anything to anyone. We agreed that we would meet again on Tuesday to figure out what to do next with what we knew.

I would have met with her on Monday, but she said she had to go shopping with her mother for the day, so I was stuck by myself. It helped that my father wanted me to clean the garage. That was part of my punishment for coming in so late Saturday night. At least it gave me something to do. I don't think they believed my excuse for missing curfew, but there wasn't any way for them to prove I was lying. I just told them we were goofing around at Richie's house and lost rack of time. It's always a good idea to blame Richie in those situations. Because of what happened to his brother, they feel sorry for him, but they don't exactly like him either. They've never actually come out and said it. They would never do that, but they wouldn't have minded very much if I made some new friends. It was kind of like letting my hair grow longer. They hoped it was just a stage, but they weren't going to tell me to get a wiffle either. Anyway, I pretty much straightened out the whole garage by lunch time, so I went inside to get cleaned up and eat something.

About an hour later, I came back out on the porch, just as the sheriff pulled up in front of our house in his big black and white car. I almost went right back into the house, but he already saw me and I knew it wouldn't look too good if I did.

He got out of the car and came around to the front of our house. He stopped for a second to look around, then he walked up to the porch.

"Sam, right?" he said.

I nodded, but didn't say anything.

"Is your mother or father home?" he asked.

I told him that my father was at work and my mother was out shopping. It was true. She went to Herford to get me a suitcase to take to school. She tried to get me to come with her to pick it out, but I told her she could pick it out herself. I know she was only trying to be nice about the whole school business, but I didn't care. I didn't even want to think about it, even though I was leaving in just four days. Of course, I didn't tell the sheriff any of that. I just said she went shopping.

"Do you know how long she's going to be gone?" he asked me.

I shook my head. Like before, I didn't say any more, thinking about what Mr. Pickens, the lawyer, had told me that night he was at our house.

The sheriff looked around again, this time at the houses on either side of us and the ones across the street. It was almost like he was afraid of being seen with me.

Then he walked up and sat on the top stair with his back against the railing. He wasn't exactly facing me, but he could still see me pretty good.

"If you don't mind," he said. "I'll just wait here for her to come home then."

I said OK, even though I minded a lot, and then I sat down in the rocker in front of the living room window. We both sat there like that without saying a word to each other for what seemed like forever. I was starting to think I should have gone with my mother and that it probably served me right to be sitting there with the sheriff after all the lying I'd been doing. Finally, I couldn't help myself and asked him if my mother and father had done something wrong.

"No," he said. "I'm here to talk to you, actually."

"You can't talk to me without my parents, though, right?" I asked.

"That's right," he said.

I probably could have gotten up and gone into the house then. I probably should have. It would have been the smart thing to do. I don't think he could have come in without me letting him. There would have been nothing he could do except wait for my mother to come home. In the meantime, I could have gone out the back door while he was waiting, and then he would have had to come back. By then, my father would have had that lawyer back there, so he wouldn't be able to ask me anything that Mr. Pickens didn't want me to answer. For some reason though, I stayed right where I was.

"Have you talked to Kimberly lately?" I asked after awhile.

I guess he wasn't expecting that because he gave me sort of a weird look. "She's my daughter," he said. "Of course I've talked to her."

I nodded, but he kept looking at me. "Why would you ask me that?" he wanted to know.

I shrugged. It seemed pretty obvious to me. I mean, he said he was there to talk to me, so I figured she must have told him about Saturday night. I wanted to be ready just in case.

"Any more news on Mikey?" I asked him.

"Look," he said. "I can't really talk to you without your parents here, so if you keep asking me questions, then I'm liable to start asking you questions, and I can't do that. Not without one of your parents here."

"OK," I said. I was about to say I was going to go inside to wait, when the radio in his car started talking. It was loud enough to hear, but not loud enough so that I could make out what the person on the other end was saying.

The sheriff looked annoyed and got up and walked over and opened the driver's side door. Instead of getting in, he just reached in and grabbed the microphone part you talk into. It's attached by a cord, like a telephone. He must have pushed a button on it because I could only hear his side of the conversation then.

He listened for a bit. "Can't it wait?" he asked the person on the other end.

He listened some more, then he looked over at me and made a face. "Alright, I'll be right over," he said.

He put the microphone thing back inside the car and walked back up to the porch and told me he had to go.

I asked him what I should tell my mother and father when they came home. He said not to worry about it and that he'd call them when he had a chance. Then he looked at me for what seemed like another really long time.

"Should I be talking to Kimberly about something?" he asked me.

I just shrugged. He stared at me some more, then got back in the car and drove away.

MIGGS

I was disappointed that I couldn't talk to the Fisher boy or his parents when I got back from the lake Monday afternoon. It was just the boy at home and, for legal reasons, I couldn't ask him anything without his mother or father there. I have to admit that he turned the tables on me when he asked about my daughter and whether I had talked to her. He didn't say about what, but it left me feeling uneasy, especially after her behavior on Saturday night. I was mighty tempted to go ahead and ask him all the questions I had anyway, since I felt like he was holding back on something, but then I got the call about the car they found over at the elementary school.

When the call first came, I thought it was just a routine thing, an abandoned car from somebody who had too much to drink and left it there and hadn't gotten around to picking up yet. When I look back on it now, I believe that was the beginning of the whole affair unraveling.

I still had the mask in the car with me when I pulled into Gary Wheaton's garage down on Elm Street. I hadn't wanted to bring it to the station and log it in, so I threw my hat over it on the seat so no one would see it. I didn't want to have to answer to anyone why I had the thing in the car with me or where it had come from. It's a small town. Something like that would get around, especially if those boys had talked to anyone else about what they claimed they heard. I made sure no part of it was visible, and then I got out and walked over to Vic and Brisby who were both standing next to a 1965 green Buick four door. It looked recently waxed, except for some mud splatters on the side panels, and appeared to be well-maintained. It was also vaguely familiar to me, though I couldn't place it at the time. You live in a town this size, you get to know what everyone drives, so it was odd that it felt familiar, yet I didn't know the owner.

"What's so important about this that I had to come right over?" I asked Vic. He was the one who called. I didn't know that Brisby would be there, but his presence told me that something important had to be going on.

"We got a call this afternoon," Vic said. "The principal over at St. Joe's Elementary says this car is parked there. Never seen it before. Doesn't belong to anyone who works at the school. One of the neighbors tells him it was there all day Sunday too. Hasn't moved. He tells me he hates people parking anywhere in their lot and asks me what he can do about it. So I tell him to leave a note telling the owner to call us when he picks it up. I figure it's only a matter of time before the guy comes to get it and I'll just warn him not to do it again. But the principal says he doesn't want it there. Says what if he doesn't show?"

"Maybe it wouldn't start," I said. "Maybe whoever left it just hasn't gotten around to getting it jumped. Maybe they were going to do it after work today."

"Yeah," he said. "That's sort what I was thinking, too."

"And?"

He shrugged. "I figure I make the principal happy," he said. "I call Gary. Tell him to tow it down here. Give him a little business. He's always helping us out, you know."

I stared at him, waiting for him to go on. He got the message and continued.

"Anyway, the car's locked, so Gary uses his bar to open her up so he can put it in neutral to tow it. He looks in the glove compartment for the registration, so he can call the guy to come down and get it and pay him what he owes him."

"Which he obviously hasn't," I pointed out.

Vic looked at Brisby who just shrugged, like Vic was doing fine and should continue.

I looked back at Vic to see what the problem was.

"Yeah," Vic said. "See the thing is, the guy who's car it is never showed up for work today. And no one's heard a word from him for at least two days."

I looked back and forth between the two of them. Clearly, there was something else they weren't telling me.

"So what's the big mystery?" I asked him. "Who is he?"

Vic looked to Brisby. He was definitely handing it over to him at that point.

"Johnny Irwin," Brisby said.

I took a second for me to process that. "The guy from the state police?" I asked. "Your friend?"

Brisby nodded.

I got a sick feeling in the pit of my stomach then. "Well did anybody go over to his house?" I asked. "Maybe he had a heart attack or fell down or something."

"The company commander sent a guy over around noon," Brisby said. "Nobody there. Mail and newspaper haven't been picked up. He was supposed to play golf with one of the other detectives yesterday and didn't show. He was on the schedule to be at work at seven this morning. No call either time. He's gone. Just disappeared. No one knows where."

Something about what he was telling me didn't add up. "Well what about his wife?" I asked. "What's she have to say?"

"He's not married, chief," Brisby said.

I turned to look at him. I must have had a hell of an expression on my face because I scared him, I think. I asked him what the hell he was talking about.

"He's divorced, Daryl" he said. "He lives alone."

"You're wrong," I said. "He just came to my house last week to give me some files they had on child molesters. I offered to come out there but he said something about being alone that night because his wife went to see her mother." I made sure to emphasize the word "wife".

Brisby looked as surprised as I must have. I asked him what was wrong.

"Nothing," he said. "Just that I knew he was divorced. Five years. I can't imagine why he'd tell you that."

"Are you sure?" I asked him.

"Positive," he said. "You can check with his commander, but I know what the answer's going to be."

We all stood there looking at the car, like it might provide us with a clue.

"What do you want us to do?" Vic asked.

I stared at the two of them for what seemed like a whole minute. "What're the state police doing?" I asked him. "It's their guy."

"They said they're looking for him," Vic said. "You know, the usual stuff."

I took a deep breath and tried to assess the situation, which was getting crazier by the day. "Well," I said, "they're probably going to want the car. Tell Gary to hand it over to them if they come. We'll cover the tow if we have to."

"Right," Vic said. "Oh yeah, there's one more thing."

I was almost afraid to ask, but of course I did.

Vic hurried back to the workbench in the garage and returned with a small silver can. He held it out to me, but I knew what it was before he could tell me.

"We found this on the floor of the back seat," he said. "Probably doesn't mean anything, but I thought you might want to see it."

I took the can, which had a single red drip mark running down the side.

"Looks like blood," he said. "But it's just paint. Odd place to keep a can of paint, though, don't you think? "

I took a few seconds to look around. They were both staring at me, waiting for me to answer I guess.

"I don't know what the hell to think anymore," I told them.

HAGER

I couldn't help myself. I had to drive by the school on my way home from work. I slowed as I passed the driveway leading to the parking lot and that's when I saw that John's car was no longer there.

Part of me was happy that they had found it. That might mean my plan was on the way to working. However, the sight of the empty spot where I had parked it left me feeling more than a little uneasy. I even had the silly thought that John had somehow survived and climbed back up that hill and retrieved the car himself. Of course, I knew that couldn't have happened. The only logical explanation was that someone had called in to say it was there and the police were notified. That would also mean that they had probably learned that John was missing.

When I got to the apartment, I once again went over all the scenarios that could link me with him. Of course, the biggest was that I was seen with him in that diner a couple of weeks before. The employees might recall that. The same was true for the family that was there, the one with the boy who told the sheriff that he heard me talking about sex. However, in the end, the authorities only knew that John was missing. They didn't know he was dead, and they didn't know the part I had played in that. I felt that if they came to see me because of the diner, I could admit to having lunch with him and then say that I hadn't seen him since then. That would just be further confirmation that he was missing. Of course, if whoever was out at the clearing on Saturday night had seen us and could identify me, none of that would matter.

After waiting an hour for my nerves to settle, I decided to go down to the market to shop for groceries. I don't necessarily believe in fate. An all-powerful God, yes. Fate, I'm not so sure about. However, something had to have been at work that day. I was pushing my cart down the frozen food section when I heard a commotion in the next aisle. A girl's voice was telling someone it was going to be alright. That was accompanied by the sound of banging or thrashing. Whatever it was immediately drew the attention of the other shoppers who all seemed to hurry toward that aisle. Like them, my curiosity got the best of me, so I steered my cart around the end of the row so that I could see what was going on.

There were quite a few folks gathered in the middle of the aisle, all looking down at something or someone. I assumed it to be the girl whose voice I heard, who was continuing to assure someone that it was going to be alright. I left my cart where it was and moved closer to get a better look at what was happening and, perhaps, to see if I could help.

I managed to get near enough to peek over the shoulder of a woman who was in the choir with me. She didn't see me at first. She was looking at what I soon came to see.

A middle-aged woman was spread out on the floor, and she appeared to be in the midst of a seizure of some sort. Next to her was the girl. She was holding the woman's head in her lap and it appeared that she had placed a flat stick of some sort in the woman's mouth. It looked like one of those tongue depressors that doctors use when looking at your throat. I assume it was there to prevent the woman from biting her tongue. I had read something about that in Reader's Digest not even a month before. The girl was continuing to soothe the woman, and she called her "mom" several times. Only after the woman's body had stilled and the seizure passed did the girl turn around and look at all of us gathered there to watch.

In that moment, I could see the resemblance. I had seen the father at the town hall and observed no trace of the boy in him at all. That was because the boy looked just like his sister who, in turn, looked just like her mother. I remember the boy's face quite well. It remains etched in my mind, although it was pale and lifeless when I last saw it.

The girl looked sheepish as she realized the commotion her mother's condition had caused. She started to say she was sorry, but the woman in front of me put her arm around the girl and told her not to worry a bit, that everyone understood. Someone else asked if there was anything they could do. The girl just shook her head. By that time, the mother appeared to regain her faculties, and several of the bystanders came to her aid while others began to disperse and return to their shopping carts. Although I wanted to do the same thing, I was rooted in place watching the poor girl who was now helping her mother to her feet.

"Let's go, Mom," the girl said, gently turning her mother back in the direction they were heading. Her mother seemed to comply and put her hands on the shopping cart for support. The girl used one hand to guide her mother and the other to help push the cart ahead. As she did, she turned back to me and the few others still standing there.

"Sorry," the girl said, offering a much sadder smile than any girl her age had reason to. Then she turned and followed her mother to the end of the aisle where they turned toward the checkout.

Looking back on it, I believe she was the most composed and mature child I have ever seen. In my estimation, she deserved all of the joy that life could bring, and none of the heartbreak that I had a hand in providing.

The woman from the choir turned to me then and just shook

her head. You could read in her eyes all that was going through her mind and probably the minds of everyone else in the store that day. She then walked back to her cart and continued with her shopping, never saying a word to me. I suppose she felt that there was nothing to say. I suppose she was right.

Of all the things that happened in this affair, that incident may have been the saddest of all to me.

SAM

Sylvia didn't blame me for Mikey being dead, but that's only because she blamed herself. No matter how hard I tried to talk her out of it, she wouldn't listen. She told me if she hadn't said she'd meet me out there that night, Mikey would still be alive. I told her that whoever killed Mikey was the one who should feel bad, not us. If they weren't out there doing what they were doing, none of this would have ever happened. I suppose that was really true, but I was having trouble believing it myself.

This was Tuesday when I met her at the football field near the pool, like we planned. She told me she cried the whole night after we talked on Sunday, and she looked like she was going to start again right then. It was the first day of practice for the high school football team and they were using the football field. I told her we should go somewhere else because they were all looking at us. It was Sylvia who said we should go up to the pool.

Normally, the pool would have been packed on a Tuesday, a week before school started, but it was empty and locked up, just like every day since they closed it down at the town meeting. The lady who runs it wasn't even there. We walked all the way around the back and didn't say a word as we did. Sylvia stared at the pool the whole time. I couldn't help thinking that it was the last place anybody saw Mikey alive. Maybe that's why she wanted to go there. Maybe she wanted to see it for herself one more time. Maybe she hoped it was all a dream and Mikey would still be there. You think crazy things when stuff like that happens. I know.

When we came around to the front again, I said that maybe we should go up into the woods above the pool. We'd be alone up there and the football players wouldn't be able to see us. I saw that some of them were still watching us when we walked up the stairs, and I didn't like it. Sylvia said OK and so we hiked up the path into the part where kids usually go to make out.

I don't know if Sylvia was thinking about that when I asked her to go up there. I know I wasn't. It didn't even occur to me until we sat down. As soon as I did, I was going to tell her that maybe it was a bad idea to be there. That's when she grabbed my hand and asked me if I would kiss her.

I had never kissed a girl before. I thought about it a lot. Keith and Richie talked about it all the time. How you were supposed to do it and what it felt like and what girls liked, but I wasn't sure about what to do exactly. Sylvia probably could tell because she kind of showed me. I don't know how long we kissed for. I sort of lost track of time. I don't think it was that long. When we stopped, she just looked at me and asked if I wanted to do it again. So we did. Then she asked me if I wanted to do more than that.

Before all the stuff with Mikey, I would have jumped at the chance. I mean, guys my age are always talking about how they're going to do things with girls and can't wait, but this was different. It was like we were in our own world, and not just because of the kissing or where we were. I think it was because we were the only ones who knew the whole story about Mikey and we were the ones who caused everything to happen the way it did. I guess that's also what made it feel so wrong to me, and I told her so. She surprised me though, and said she was happy I said that. She said she felt the same way and only asked because she was afraid I might not like her anymore if she didn't let me. I told her I liked her just fine. Even better actually.

"Does that mean you won't forget about me when you go off

to that new school?" she asked.

I told her that I'd never forget her no matter what happened or where I went.

She smiled and kissed me again. Then she said she had one more thing to ask me.

MIGGS

Fritz had already heard about Irwin when I got to his office at around six that night.

"Well?" I asked. "What do you think?"

He asked what I meant by that.

"The Vogel boy," I said. "Do you think it could have any connection?"

He gave me an odd look. "Why would it?" he asked back.

"Seems awful coincidental, doesn't it?" I asked, growing frustrated by his making me spell it out.

He rubbed his chin and sat back. "I honestly hadn't thought of that," he said. I stared. Waiting. "Are you saying you think he might have killed the boy?" he asked. "A state cop?"

"No," I said. "But doesn't it seem like they have to be connected somehow?"

"You seem to be getting way ahead of yourself here Daryl," he said.

"Well, what else could it be?" I asked.

"Hell, it could be anything," he said. "Maybe he got fed up with his life and took off. Ran away to Las Vegas. Or Mexico. God knows where. That's not against the law, you know."

I didn't like that last remark, but I swallowed it. "You really think this has nothing to do with that boy?" I asked.

"Tell me why you think it might," he said.

Again, I was getting annoyed at the way he was reacting. It was more like something I would expect from a defense lawyer. "For starters," I said. "We're getting closer to a suspect."

"Are we?" he asked.

I pulled out the mask I found out at Kitchiwa and showed it to him. Then I told him about my trip up there. I also showed him the bag of burnt things I plucked from the ashes.

"Well now," he said. "That is something."

Then I told him my thinking about the Fisher boy prompting the other boy about where they heard the story and how that might mean that there was more to their lie than we had originally thought. Fritz considered that for a bit. Then he nodded. "Yes," he said. "Now that you mention it, I do recall that. I should have picked up on it then."

I was happy to hear him admit that he had slipped up as well, especially since the mask was a reminder that I should have gone up to that lake sooner.

"Still," he said, "none of that means Irwin was involved. The state police haven't taken over the investigation. And unless you told him about all those other things, he wouldn't have any way of knowing about them."

That part was true. I hadn't told Irwin anything about Hager or the mask or the two boys. "So what do you think it means then?" I asked him. "Him being gone?"

"Like I said, he could be shacked up with some chippie in Atlantic City."

"That's another thing," I said. Then I told him about Irwin lying about his wife the night he came to see me.

That seemed to strike a chord with him. He asked me to go over my conversation with Irwin again.

"Maybe you're right," he said, when I was done. "Maybe he is involved somehow. But I just can't see a state cop killing a child, can you?"

I shook my head, again wondering why he was going down

that path. "No, but I could see someone killing him. Someone who did kill the kid."

"For what reason?" he asked.

"I don't know," I said, honestly. "Maybe he learned something on his own."

"And didn't say anything?" he asked. "To you or me?"

I just shrugged. "What about Hager?" I asked, picking up the mask. "He has to be involved somehow, don't you think?"

"Are you suggesting he might have something to do with this Irwin business?" he asked.

I thought about that a bit before shaking my head. "I can't see how, no," I said. "But we can't ignore the masks. And what those boys told us. There has to be some connection to the Vogel boy."

Fritz seemed to ponder that for a moment. "We can't even prove the mask belonged to him," he said. "Circumstances would seem to indicate that it does, but not enough to arrest him."

I think he could read the disappointment on my face. He gave me a look then.

"I can understand why you would want to do that, Daryl," he said. "But nothing we do now is going to bring that boy back to life. We certainly don't want to make another mistake."

In twenty one years, I have never said a cross word to Fritz. I certainly have never wanted to throw a punch his way. However, in that moment I wanted to do both, and not because he was wrong to say what he did. He was right and I knew it. And I hated that it was so.

HAGER

The waiting had become unbearable. There was nothing in the newspaper about John's disappearance. Not even a mention of the car, and it wasn't as if I could ask around. I wanted desperately for them to make the connection and turn the focus of the investigation onto him, but I couldn't force them to. I couldn't even suggest it.

I was beginning to think that it would be better if they did find his body. That way they'd know he was dead and not just out of town somewhere. The longer they went without finding him, the more they might conclude that he simply ran away. That might still make him a suspect, but it wouldn't close the case. Not without some other evidence which I couldn't very well provide. Certainly not without implicating myself. I thought that if they did find his body, they might be more likely to think he had to have had something to do with the boy's death. If my theory held up about them concluding that he had committed suicide, they would have to draw a connection. Of course, there would then be the link back to me, which I most certainly did not want. Even though I was unaware of any evidence that might connect me to John and the boy, I couldn't be certain that it didn't exist in John's house or elsewhere. So, as hard as it was for me to do so, I had to remain silent and stay patient. An unsolved case was better for me than one that pointed in my direction.

With all this going through my mind, it was becoming increasingly difficult for me to go about my normal routine. That's why I told my boss that morning that I wanted to take a few days off before Labor Day. I asked for Thursday and Friday off, so that with the holiday on Monday I could have a full five days to get away. Ordinarily, you have to give four weeks notice if you intend to take vacation, but I was well-liked at work and never missed a day for illness. Plus, it was the end of the summer and a slow time. He told me to enjoy myself and to maybe give him a little more notice next time. If he only knew.

Because of what had happened in my past and my never-ending struggle with temptation, I had made some arrangements in the event that I ever needed to disappear. With the help of an "associate" of mine down south, I had acquired a driver's license in a different name in Georgia. Different from the one I was already using, which had so far served me well. I also opened a bank account in three separate states and had put enough money in each to help me start over somewhere, if I ever needed to. Still, I knew that if I disappeared, there would be no doubt that I would be a prime target of the investigation into the boy's murder. They might even put me on a most wanted list. I would need to do more than have a phony drivers license and some spending money to avoid capture then. So I wasn't quite ready to run at that point, but I was thinking about it.

I opted instead to rent a cabin at one of the lakes north of town. I had done so the year before, and when I called the owner to inquire about renting the same one again, I was fortunate to find that it was available for all five days. It had been my intention to bring some books and some sun tan lotion and try to relax somehow. I figured that I would be away and alone, but close enough to keep track of what was going on. I'd be able to buy the local paper up there and would even bring along a radio to listen to. I planned on leaving word with my landlord where I was going, just in case the sheriff came looking for me, so that it wouldn't look like I was running away. Of course, if I heard that they found John's body, I would do just that. And pray that they'd never find me.

SAM

Sylvia asked me to meet her at the band concert on Wednesday night. It was the last one of the summer. They have fireworks at the end and everybody in town goes. Kids like it because school starts the week after and they can stay up until at least ten o'clock which is when the fireworks usually end. It's the last big thing before summer's over. Of course, that wasn't why Sylvia and I were going there. Anyway, that's what I was thinking about when I came home that afternoon after playing baseball with Keith and Richie. I almost walked right by my mother who was sitting by herself on the couch in the living room.

No one uses that room or sits on that couch, except on Christmas morning or maybe when we have company. We're always in the den, watching TV, or in the kitchen eating. My mother doesn't even like us to be in the living room. I asked her what she was doing in there and she looked at me for a second or two and then told me to come in and sit down. Something definitely seemed weird, but I did what she said and sat on the other end of the couch.

"Do you have anything you want to tell me?" she asked.

I had forgotten all about the sheriff stopping by on Monday. I figured he must have called her and she wanted to know why he wanted to talk to me again. I asked her if that's what she was talking about.

"He was here again?" she asked, looking surprised. That's

when I knew I might be in some trouble. I just nodded.

"What did he want?" she asked.

I told her the truth, which was I didn't know. I told her what he said about not being able to talk to me without her or my father being there. Then him getting a call on his walkie-talkie in the car and having to leave.

She seemed satisfied with that. "Well, we'll talk about that later," she said. "I wanted to ask you about this."

She reached under the pillow next to her then and pulled out a book. Not just any old book. It was the one I took from the library after Mikey died. The one I hid in my room, though not as good as I thought. She laid it on the couch next to her so I could see it.

"What's this?" she asked.

I wanted to try to sound like it was no big deal. I was still thinking maybe I could talk my way out whatever trouble I might be in. "It's just something I got out of the library," I told her.

"Why would you take a book like this out of the library?" she asked. She didn't sound that mad. More like she was curious. I was hoping she wasn't so curious that she looked inside it, especially at the part in the middle with the pictures.

"It was for school," I told her. "A project I had to do."

"In the summer?" she asked.

"Last spring," I lied.

"Are you telling me the school had you write a report about this kind of stuff? In the sixth grade?"

"No," I said. "Not really. Different religions. Stuff like that."

She looked like she was thinking about that. "So then why did you have it hidden under a bunch of clothes in the back of your closet?" she asked.

I just shrugged. I couldn't think of an excuse off the top of my head. I kind of figured she would press me on that, but she didn't. I thought that was weird. Instead, she just nodded.

"Well, this belongs to the library," she said. "You need to

bring it back. If you took it out in the spring there's probably a late fee on it. A big one. And you're going to pay for it."

For a second there, I thought maybe the worst had passed and that I was going to be alright. I was wrong.

"Let's see how bad it's going to be," she said then. I wanted to stop her and tell her I would take care of it, but before I could, she opened it to the back where they stamp the due date. She looked at the little piece of paper there, then back at me.

"This hasn't been checked out in ten years," she said. It was kind of funny. She didn't act surprised at all. I realized then that she probably already looked back there before I even came home. So I didn't say anything. I figured anything I said then would only make things worse, and they were already pretty bad.

"So do you want to tell me why you would take this from the library and not check it out?" she asked.

She stared at me for what seemed like forever. I wanted to tell her, but I just couldn't. So sure enough, she opened it up to the page with the drawing of the naked people in masks dancing around a fire. She turned it around so I could see it. Not that I needed to.

"This has to do with what you and Keith told the sheriff, doesn't it?" she said. I remember thinking then that Mr. Pickens could probably take a lesson or two from her. She asked me all those questions already knowing what my answers were going to be and she had me trapped pretty good. I figured there was nothing else I could say at that point, so I just nodded.

"So the sheriff was right then?" she asked. "You and Keith did make all that up? About hearing that man in the diner talk about this?"

"Yeah," I said. I mean, technically that was true. We did make that part up.

"And this is where you got the idea from," she said. "That business about those people out by the tracks. You saw it in some book."

I thought about lying again. I mean, it would have been the easiest thing to do. But I guess I was tired of the whole thing at that point. So instead, I just shook my head.

She looked confused. "What's that supposed to mean?" she asked. "You're saying you didn't get it from this?"

I shook my head again and she looked even more confused. "Where did you get it from then?" she asked.

Like I said, I was tired of lying. I just wanted it to be all over and for everything to go back to the way it was before. For Mikey to be alive again. For Sylvia to be happy. For me to be going to the same school as all my friends. Even though I knew that none of those things could ever happen.

"I saw it with my own two eyes," I told her.

MIGGS

I had just arrived back at the station from a meeting over at the county seat on Wednesday when Vic came in to tell me that the state police had called. They found Irwin.

I guess Fritz had an influence on me, because I expected Vic to tell me that Irwin was shacked up somewhere with a busty blonde barmaid. Although I shouldn't have been, I was taken by surprise when he told me that someone had found his body in the stream up near Six Mile Point that morning. Apparently, the fellow who found him goes out there to trap beavers and woodchucks. It's his favorite spot and when he went to check his traps that morning, he saw Irwin laying face down in the water.

The detective I spoke with when I called the state police barracks told me it looked like Irwin had fallen down a steep embankment and had died as a result. He said they weren't ready to rule it an accident yet, since there were some things about it that didn't add up.

I asked what those might be. He hemmed and hawed and told me that the investigation was ongoing and that it wouldn't be advisable to share with me what they knew at that time. Under normal circumstances, that kind of brush-off wouldn't bother me. I'd be pissed, but I'd just tell him I understood, and then I'd wait until I got to see Fritz and he'd tell me whatever it was that they refused to share. Not this time though. I was fed up with the state police at that point.

I reminded the guy on the other end that we had a murder investigation going on ourselves and that Irwin just happened to have been providing assistance in that. I reminded him also that it was a young boy who had died and that I had a town full of people who wanted answers. I told him that two suspicious deaths in such a short period of time in our part of the state was unheard of, at least in my twenty-one years on the force. I then suggested that any detective worth his salt would naturally wonder if the two might be related and that one investigator refusing to share with another was the exact opposite of what they preach to us every summer down at the state capital when we all meet to discuss proper police procedure and get drunk for three nights. I suggested that perhaps I might find more cooperation down at the state police headquarters in Albany and said goodbye.

Of course, I didn't hang up. I held the phone to my ear just long enough to hear him ask me to hold on. I took a second or two before I spoke and asked if he had said something. He sighed. Then he told me what they had discovered.

Irwin was dressed casually. Not for work. His body was free of wounds except for his neck where there was part of a stick or small branch protruding from it. A preliminary examination by the coroner revealed that his carotid artery had been severed. The thing was, it didn't appear to him that the stick had done it. It was in his neck alright, but not in the artery. It didn't reach that far, and it had a blunt end, not a sharp one. He said the doctor told them he was going to have to do a full autopsy before he could conclude anything, but that's the way it looked to him.

"What about the fall?" I asked. "Could that have done it?"

"Like I said," he told me. "The coroner doesn't think so. Plus there's the other thing."

"What other thing?" I asked.

"You guys found his car in town, right?"

I told him that was right.

"Well," he said. "It didn't drive there by itself."

I felt stupid for not having thought of it earlier. "There was no car out there?" I asked.

"Nope," he said.

"Nothing to indicate how he might have gotten there?"

"I suppose he could have walked," he said. "But it would have been a hell of a hike and for what reason?"

I let all that sink in for a bit. "So you guys are thinking maybe he was killed someplace else and dumped in the stream?" I asked finally.

"That's one theory right now," he said.

"And whoever left his car at the school is probably the person who killed him," I said. Not a question. I knew it had to be true.

"I'd say that's a pretty safe bet," he said.

"I probably already know the answer to this one," I said, "but do you have any leads?"

"No," he told me. "What about you? Any ideas?"

I had plenty, none of which I was ready to share with him or anyone else for that matter. I told him that I'd let him know as soon as I had something and then I hung up.

HAGER

I had just finished packing and was getting ready to leave for the final band concert of the summer when there was a knock on my door. It must have been around seven thirty or quarter to eight.

I had grown rather wary of that sound. I couldn't think of anyone who would be coming to see me at that time of night. No one I wanted to see anyway. When I opened the door, a rather large man was standing there. I didn't recognize him at first, but he smiled as if we were old friends. Then it dawned on me why I didn't know him right away. He wasn't wearing his uniform. He was the other police officer who came with Miggs to see me that first time. Brisby was his name, as I recalled.

"Can I come in?" he asked.

I guess it was instinct, or maybe I had simply honed my senses over the years to detect predatory behavior. Whatever the reason, I found myself holding the door with one hand and putting my foot behind it to keep him from pushing his way in if he tried.

"What do you want?" I asked him.

He looked down at my foot blocking the door. Then he looked back up at me and smiled. It sent a small current up my spine.

"Are you afraid of me for some reason?" he asked.

"Are you here to arrest me?"

He laughed, although there was no mirth in it. "No," he said. "I just think we should talk for a minute."

"About what?" I asked.

"About your friend," he said. "The one whose car we found behind the school. You see, he was my friend too."

My blood went cold at the mention of John. Immediately, I wondered how he could know about him. A swirl of thoughts went through my head, none of them pleasant.

"I really think you ought to let me in," he said. "You're going to want to hear what I have to say."

I thought about my options in that moment. There weren't many. I could have closed the door on him, but then what? Call the police? No matter what I did, I wouldn't be able to escape. Not really. Not anymore.

So I did the only thing that I thought made any sense. I let him in.

SAM

My mother didn't wait for me to explain or ask me anything else. She just told me to go up to my room, and she went straight to the phone and called my father. She almost never calls him at work, so he must have known it was serious. I didn't hear what she told him, but it must have been enough because he came right home. I never saw him so mad in my whole life, not even when I got paint on the new Bonneville the day after he brought it home from the dealer.

"Before you say anything," he told me, "you need to know that if I find out later that you lied to me or left anything out, you'll get the belt. I know I should try to be understanding, and I'm going to do my best. But this is serious business. That boy is dead and his family is suffering and the cops still don't know who did it. This is no time for games. Somebody else could die because you decided to keep some sort of secret."

"That's why I did it," I said.

"What's that supposed to mean?" he asked. If anything, he was even madder.

"I did it so somebody else wouldn't die," I said.

I guess he wasn't expecting that. "What the hell are you talking about?" he asked.

I didn't say anything, mostly because I wasn't sure how much I wanted to tell him. I thought maybe it might be better to just take my punishment and not say anything at all.

He frowned. "What did I just tell you?" he asked. "You need to tell me everything and you need to tell me now."

I looked down at the floor. That only made him madder.

"I'm going to give you one more chance," he said. "If you don't say anything, I'm calling the sheriff myself."

I didn't want him to do that and so I decided I might as well just come out with it. "Me," I said. "I was afraid that whoever killed Mikey might come get me next."

"Why on earth would they do that?" he asked.

"Because I saw the people who killed Mikey," I told him.

Just like with my mother that afternoon, it got real quiet then. He just stared at me with this weird look on his face. "You know who killed Mikey?" he asked.

I shook my head. "Not exactly," I told him. "It's kind of hard to explain."

"Well, you better start trying," he said.

So I told him. Everything. Well, almost. When I was done, he looked sort of stunned and asked me why I didn't tell him about any of it before.

I didn't say anything. He just kept staring at me. I could tell he was starting to get pissed off again. "Why Sam?" he asked again. "Why didn't you tell me?"

I still wouldn't answer, and so he grabbed me and shook me and yelled at me to tell him why.

"Because you don't give a shit about me!" I yelled back. "All you care about is that stupid school and those stupid tests! You don't care about how I feel or what I think! Why would I ever tell you a thing!?"

Thinking back, I didn't even know that was the real reason I kept it from him. I just knew it was true once I said it. I didn't want him trying to protect me. Because that's what fathers do. And I didn't want him to be my father anymore. I guess I must have told him that, too.

I figured he was going to go get the belt then and give me the beating of my life, but he didn't. He didn't even move. At first I wasn't even sure what was going on, but then he made a weird sound and I saw the tears and I could tell he was crying.

I can't really explain why, but it almost made me puke.

MIGGS

I had stayed at the office late that night, thinking about everything that had happened in the previous few days, trying to make sense of it all. Irwin was dead and it looked like murder and that came just a few weeks after what happened to the Vogel boy. The two had to be connected, just like I told Fritz. At the same time, I agreed with Fritz that it seemed illogical that Irwin could have been involved in the boy's death. I had always thought of myself as a pretty good judge of people. It's part of my job. Maybe the biggest part, and one I take very seriously. Maybe Irwin was investigating the Vogel case on his own and had gotten too close to the killer, just like I told Fritz before they found his body. But something about that theory bothered me. Irwin had lied to me. He said he was married when he wasn't. Why would he do that?

To try and satisfy my curiosity, I called the state police and ended up speaking with a different detective than the one who gave me all that trouble earlier. This guy was a bit more pleasant. I asked him if they had talked to Irwin's ex-wife yet. He told me that they put in a courtesy call to her that afternoon.

"How did she take it?" I asked.

"They've been divorced for awhile," he said. "She didn't seem that broken up."

"What did she say?"

He wanted to know why I wanted to know. I told him the story of Irwin coming to see me and telling me about his wife off visiting her mother. Which obviously wasn't true.

There was silence on the other end for a time.

"What's wrong?" I asked. "Did she say something?"

He sort of laughed. "Yeah," he said. "When I told her he was dead, she said 'it figures'. Like she was almost expecting it. I took it to mean him dying in the line of duty."

"You think it might mean something else?" I asked.

"I don't know," he said. "Do you?"

I asked if he'd mind if I talked to her. He said he couldn't see any reason why not. He went to find her number and gave it to me when he got back on. He told me to let him know if I learned anything new. I told him I would and thanked him. Then I tried the number.

It took about ten rings before she finally answered. When she did, her voice sounded funny, even though I had obviously never spoken with her. I told her who I was and why I was calling. I lied a bit and said that I was a friend of Irwin's and was working on an investigation with him before he died. She didn't say anything.

"You told the state police that you weren't surprised he was dead when you heard about it," I told her, rephrasing what the state cop had actually said. "Would you mind telling me why that is?"

She was silent for time. Then she admitted that she had been expecting a call like this for a long time. I asked her why that was.

"Because when you stick your nose in other people's marriages it's only a matter of time before you piss someone off," she said. "Pardon my French." I realized then that she was drunk. That's why her voice sounded the way it did.

"And how did he do that?" I asked. "Stick his nose in other people's marriages?"

"How do you think?" she asked back.

I thought about it for a few seconds before I answered. I wanted to be careful, even though they were divorced. "Are you saying he may have slept with someone else's wife?"

She let out a laugh. A bitter one. "If only that's all it was. A woman can live with that."

"What do mean?"

"What do you think I mean?" she asked me back.

"I'm trying to be respectful here," I told her. "But I think it would be better if you just told me what you meant by that. It might be important."

"All I'm saying is he probably got what he had coming to him," she told me. "And he sure as heck isn't standing at the pearly gates right now, if you know what I mean."

I started to ask her if she could be more specific, but she said she was all through talking and hung up. I was still staring at the phone when Vic stuck his head in my doorway. I asked him what was up.

He told me that he had just picked up Cyrus Robbins down on Main Street. He said he was drunker than usual and had passed out right on the sidewalk in front of Newberry's. My experience with Robbins has always been that he could drink more than most men are capable of and still manage to walk the streets all night. In fact, that was his routine. He must have been pretty drunk for Vic to have hauled him in.

I told Vic to stick him down in one of the holding cells till morning. He said he already did, but that there was something else. I got an uneasy feeling then, as if the ground under me had suddenly shifted. I asked Vic what was up and he said Robbins was asking to speak with me.

As I've said before, Robbins has had no use for me since the accident. Other than in a courtroom, we haven't spoken to each other for seven years.

"What the hell does he want?" I asked him.

"He won't say," he told me. "He just said he'll only speak to you."

Figuring I better just take my medicine, I told Vic to man the phones and I started down to the basement to hear what Robbins might have to say to me after all that time.

HAGER

I asked Brisby if John was dead. I think I was just trying to throw him off with the question. Then again, I suppose I hadn't completely rid myself of the irrational fear that John had somehow survived and was coming to seek revenge, so I can't say for sure why I said it.

He smiled once more. It was neither pleasant nor reassuring. "You know the answer to that better than anyone, don't you think?" he said.

I told him I didn't know what he was talking about.

He shrugged. "Have it your way," he said. Then his eyes went to the packed bag sitting just outside my bedroom. Since I burned my only suitcase, I had to use an old army duffle that I have owned for years. "Looks like I got here just in time," he said.

"What is that supposed to mean?" I asked him.

"It looks like someone is hoping to get away," he said.

"I'm going up to the lake for a few days of relaxation, if you must know," I told him. "It's nothing more than that."

He nodded. "Well," he said, "I'm afraid you might have to put that off for awhile."

I thought that was quite an odd thing for him to say. "Unless you have some official police business here, I'm going to have to ask you to leave," I told him, feeling a lot less confident than I sounded.

"Oh, I am going to leave," he said. "But you're coming with

me."

"So I am under arrest," I said.

"No," he said. "Not just yet."

"Then where are you taking me?"

"Down to the station," he said. "The sheriff wants to ask you some more questions."

There was something about him and his appearance at my door that didn't feel right. Maybe it was him being out of uniform. Maybe it was the fact that he came alone. "No," I said, rather defiantly. "I'm not answering any more questions. And if you insist on it, then I am going to call a lawyer."

He seemed to ignore what I had just said. Instead, he walked over and unzipped the duffel bag and opened it. He looked through it briefly, then let it stay open there on the floor.

"You can call your lawyer from the station," he said. "First you need to unpack and put all that stuff away."

I froze in place. Why on earth would he want me to unpack? What difference did that make?

He must have sensed my confusion because he then pulled out a handful of my clothes from the duffel and brought them into the bedroom and tossed them on the bed. "Let's go," he said. "Put it all away. Now."

"You aren't really going to bring me down to the station are you?" I asked.

He smiled that smile again. "Well, look who got smart all of a sudden," he said.

SAM

After my father left my room, I went out into the hall, near the top of the stairs, where I could hear him and my mother talking down in the kitchen. He was filling her in on what I told him. He skipped over the part where I said I hated him. I understood why he wouldn't want to tell her that. Maybe he was going to say something later. Maybe not.

When he was done, he said he was going over to the sheriff's house to tell him what I told him. He said I was a witness to a murder and that they needed to know that, as soon as possible. My mother didn't say anything at first. Then she said that maybe he should talk to the lawyer again before saying anything to the police. She said I might get in trouble for not telling the sheriff everything in the first place. I thought my father might argue with her, but he didn't even put up a fight. He just said she was right.

The next thing I knew, I was in the car with him and on the way to see Mr. Pickens. We met him at his office. I call it that, but it's basically just a room in the front of his house, separated from the rest of the place by a sliding wooden door. He met us out on his porch and brought us inside. I never even got a look at the rest of the house or saw his wife, if she was even there.

My father had me repeat to Mr. Pickens everything I told him an hour earlier, except for the personal stuff. I knew the lawyer had to be mad at me for not telling him the truth before, but he didn't say anything. Maybe it happens to lawyers all the time. The only thing he wanted to know was why I thought Kimberly didn't want to say anything to her father. I told him that I thought she wouldn't want her father to know what she was going to do out at that hobo camp.

"You mean with your friend?" he asked. "The Somerset boy?"

I nodded. Mr. Pickens then asked my father if it was alright if he spoke to me alone. My father didn't look too happy about it, but he said OK and went back out to the porch.

Mr. Pickens asked if there was anything else I wanted to tell him that I didn't tell my father. I thought about that for a bit before I answered. Then I told him that I didn't think Mr. Hager had done anything wrong. I told him that the other guy seemed like the bad guy to me. I said I didn't know why, but that was what I thought and that I hoped Mr. Hager wouldn't get in trouble for what he did. I never said that to my father. I just told him what happened. I didn't think I needed to tell him what I thought about it. He wouldn't care what I thought anyway.

"Do you know who that other man was?" the lawyer asked me.

I shook my head. Then I told him I was sorry I didn't tell him about all that other stuff before, but that I was too scared. He sort of smiled and told me it was a lot for someone my age to have to handle. Then he went outside and called my father back in.

My father asked Mr. Pickens what we should do and whether we should go down to the station to see the sheriff. Mr. Pickens then said something that I never knew. He said the law can't make you report a crime or punish you for not saying anything when you see something like we did that night with Mr. Hager. He said the reason was the same as why I didn't say anything in the first place - the law can't make a person put themselves in danger. He said the story that Keith and I made up about the guy at the Custard Cup was actually pretty clever. Just like we figured, it got them to look into the case and made it so nobody thought me and Keith saw anything. He looked at me then and told me I was a very smart young man. Those were his exact words.

I could tell that my father didn't know whether to be proud or mad. He asked him about me not telling the truth when the sheriff was at our house that night and wanted to know if I could get into trouble for that.

Mr. Pickens thought about that for a long time. Then he said it seemed to him like my answers that night were pretty truthful. I didn't really know what Keith heard that day. I wasn't there. Then again, I knew that Keith never heard anything to begin with, so the sheriff could say I lied. "No doubt that interfered with the investigation," Mr. Pickens said. "Normally that's obstruction of justice."

I could tell my father didn't like the sound of that. Neither did I. My father asked him if he thought they would charge me now.

Mr. Pickens said he didn't believe so. "The only reason Sam lied was because he was afraid he might get himself killed."

My father asked him if he could promise him that.

Mr. Pickens got a real serious look on his face and shook his head. So my father asked him again what we should do.

Mr. Pickens told him he wanted to sleep on it. He said he'd call my father first thing in the morning and tell him what he thought we should do. He walked us out to the porch and told us to go home and get a good night's sleep and not worry about it. He said he didn't think it would be a big deal to wait until morning and that it wasn't like anything was going to happen that night.

Boy was he ever wrong.

MIGGS

Robbins was sitting up, staring at a cup of coffee when I walked into the holding cell area. He looked up and immediately set the coffee aside. I didn't open the cell door or go inside. I just took a seat in the folding chair we keep there for visitors.

"Coffee's cold," he said, in a bitter sounding voice.

"Is that all you've got to say to me after seven years?" I asked him.

He stared at me for an uncomfortably long time. I couldn't say for sure that it was hate behind those eyes, but I knew it wasn't far from it. If he'd been as drunk as Vic described, he seemed to have sobered up considerably. Don't get me wrong. I could still smell the alcohol and see the redness in his eyes. He just seemed more in control than I expected.

"If you're planning on using this as a chance to tear into me for ruining your life, you're wasting your time," I told him. "We've been through all that." I started to get up.

"I was just making a comment about the coffee," he said.

I sat back down. "Look," I told him. "I have things to do, so if you have something to tell me, you best get on with it."

He made a sour face and then asked me if I could protect him if he told me something important.

I had no idea what he meant by that, but I figured I may as well go along with whatever game he was playing so I could get the hell out of there and back to the Irwin thing. "I can protect you as long as you're in here," I told him. "If you walk out and go wandering off to some bar and pass out in the street, there's not much I can do for you."

He nodded, as if that was the answer he expected. "In that case, I think I'll just stay in here until this all blows over," he said.

"Until what blows over?" I asked him, losing patience.

He rubbed his beard and stared. "You know what I'm talking about," he said.

In all honesty, I didn't. "Why don't you just tell me why you wanted to see me?" I told him.

He looked around and then leaned in to whisper, even though there was no one else even on the same floor as us. "I know something about that car that was parked behind the school the other night," he said.

That certainly got my attention. I inched the chair closer and asked him to tell me what the hell he was talking about.

He smiled then, like he was enjoying the fact that he was in possession of some information that I obviously wanted. He took his time before he spoke. I expected another wisecrack, but instead he went on to relate the story of seeing someone drive Irwin's car up the driveway of the school and around to the parking lot in the back. He said he was sleeping under a bush next to the garage at the house next door. It's one of his favorite spots, he said. There's an overhang to the roof and it keeps him dry in case it rains while he's passed out. The sound of the car pulling into the driveway woke him up, he said. He described it all in great detail.

I asked him if he knew the person who dropped the car off.

He nodded, but didn't answer. I told him I'd do my best to protect him, but I needed him to tell me what he knew and to tell me right then.

He gave me a half-smile. "That Hager fellow," he said. "The queer one."

I know I should have been surprised, but given all that had

happened in the previous three weeks I wasn't. I still had my doubts about Hager being capable of murder, but if Robbins was telling me the truth, that meant that Hager was obviously caught up in the whole business somehow. I asked Robbins if he was sure about that.

He told me he had no doubt. No doubt about the car. No doubt about Hager. He was also sure that no one else was in the car except for Hager. I asked him how he could be so certain, considering his condition.

If he was offended by the question, he didn't show it. He said there was a streetlight right there and he clearly saw Hager get out of the car alone and walk away from it after he parked it. He said that after Hager was gone, he went up to the car and looked inside. He said it was locked and all he saw was a small can in the back, on the floor. I didn't have to ask him more about that. I knew then he was telling the truth.

Robbins must have known how important his story was because he just stared at me with a smug expression on his face. I sat back thinking about all those times I used to watch him stare at me with undisguised contempt during the trial. I certainly never expected him to be of any use to me, certainly not in a murder investigation. Of course, he wasn't going to make the most reliable witness, given who and what he was, but that didn't make what he was saying any less valuable.

I asked him if there was anything else I should know. He said yeah, that he also saw Hager throw something down into the sewer as he walked away. He didn't see what it was, but from the sound of it, he thought it might have been the car keys. "I didn't think much of it until I heard you found that cop dead," he said. "It was his car, wasn't it?"

I was stunned, to say the least, since none of that information about Irwin or his car was ever made public. I asked him how he could possibly know about all that.

He grinned and said he knew all kinds of things about this town, things that even I might not know.

I ignored the obvious insult and asked him why he was telling me this. Why he was being so helpful to me.

He just shrugged and didn't bother to answer. We both just sat there for another minute or so. I didn't know what else to say, so I got up and told him he could stay in the holding cell for as long as he wanted and that he'd be safe there. I told him we'd even send out for breakfast for him in the morning. Anything he wanted.

"Pancakes and sausage?" he asked.

I told him he would have them when he woke up.

"Just don't have that deputy bring it," he said.

"Which one?" I asked, although I was pretty sure I knew the answer.

"That Brisby," he said.

"What's wrong with Brisby?" I asked him.

"Just don't have him bring it," he said. "I rather starve to death than see him."

As is probably the case with most law enforcement outfits, I've gotten complaints about every one of the men in my department over the years. No more for Brisby than anyone else. Still, his fear of Brisby was troubling to me. I have to admit that I had seen Brisby take advantage of his badge on more than one occasion. Nothing big enough to make me take any disciplinary action, but troubling nonetheless. I wouldn't go so far as to call him a bully, but that wouldn't be far off either. I also suspected that there might be more people in town who might've had complaints about Brisby but never said anything out of that same fear. It certainly wasn't hard for me to imagine Brisby making life hard for someone like Robbins.

I told him that I would have Vic bring him his breakfast, and he seemed satisfied with that and lay back on the cot.

I took that to mean that the conversation was over, but there was something about that moment that made me pause. I thought then about what had happened seven years earlier and how it brought us both to this place. How one bad decision – mine, his, it didn't matter – had destroyed an entire life. I sat back down.

"I'm sorry," I told him.

He looked at me. Surprised, I guess.

"I know I never said it before," I said. "But I want you to know that I'm sorry for everything that's happened to you. Or at least for my part in it."

He stared at me. Maybe he was trying to gauge whether I was being serious. Maybe he was still drunk and wasn't sure that he heard me right. Hell, I don't know. I waited for quite some time, but he gave no indication that he was going to respond, so I took that to mean that our conversation was truly over and got up and left without saying another word.

When I got back to my office, I told Vic what Robbins said about Hager and the car. Then I instructed him to call Joe Furth, head of our DPW, and tell him to get over to the elementary school to look for those car keys. Vic reminded me that Joe was in the town band and would be at the band concert until at least ten o'clock.

I told him to get over to the park then and wait for him and take him to the school as soon as the concert was done. He said he would. Then he asked me what I was going to do.

"I'm going up to arrest Yancy Hager," I told him.

HAGER

I finished putting away my clothes, as the deputy had in-structed me to do. I sensed him watching me from the doorway to the bedroom, as I remained standing at my dresser, staring into the open drawer on top. I didn't want to close it just yet, stalling for time.

"Give me your car keys," he said.

I told him they were on the kitchen table and he went out to look for them. After pulling on my windbreaker, I came out of the bedroom. "You were out there, weren't you?" I said. "You were one of them."

"Shut up," he said. He looked annoyed, and I knew I was right.

He picked up the keys from the table and pocketed them. He then took out a pair of handcuffs and instructed me to turn around. He pulled my hands behind my back and put them on. Then he turned me back around to face him and took out a gun that was tucked into the back of his pants, partially covered by his shirt.

"Are you going to shoot me?" I asked, nodding at the gun.

"Only if you make me," he said.

"And how will you explain that to the sheriff?" I asked him.

He smiled. I had no doubt that he'd be able to come up with some kind of story, if the need arose. It didn't really matter. Either way, I would be dead. Even if he were ultimately arrested for killing me, it would bring me no satisfaction from the grave. As I have said, I am a survivor.

"So John told you about me," I said, stalling once more.

"Forget it," he said. "Let's get going."

"Did he tell the others, too?" I asked.

He didn't answer. Instead, he shoved me toward the door and reached around me for the knob.

That was when the knock came.

SAM

When we got home, my father sent me back up to my room. Then he went into their bedroom to tell my mother what happened with Mr. Pickens. I guess he didn't want me to hear what he said because he closed the door.

On the way home I asked him if I was grounded. "Damn right you are," he told me. I asked if it would be alright if we started it tomorrow so that I could go to the band concert that night. "You're in no position to negotiate," he told me. "So get that idea right out of your head."

I couldn't really argue with that. He was right, I suppose. And I would have just taken my punishment, too, except that I promised Sylvia I would meet her at the concert that night. Before I left her on Tuesday, we made a deal that while everyone was at the park that night, we would go down to see the sheriff and tell him everything. She said she felt bad enough about her brother being dead because of her. The only thing she could do about it now was to help the cops find out who killed him. With what I saw that Saturday night, she said they ought to have a pretty good chance of doing that. I told her I didn't think Mr. Hager had anything to do with killing Mikey, but she said she didn't care. If he didn't do it, then he probably knew who did.

I knew I was probably taking a chance of ending up in military school instead of that boarding school, but I couldn't let her think I was backing out on her. I didn't want her to go to see the sheriff by herself. I had to be the one to tell it. Besides, if Mr. Pickens was right about me not being in trouble for keeping quiet before, I was pretty sure I would be if I let Sylvia tell the sheriff all that stuff instead of me. So that's why I decided to sneak out.

I went out into the hall to see if their door was still closed, then went back in my room and closed mine. I turned off all the lights and stuffed a bunch of dirty clothes in my bed to make it look like I was sleeping, in case my father came in. You see that in the movies all the time, and it always seems to work. But when I looked at it, I could tell right away that there wasn't a person in there, so I took the clothes back out again and just left the bed empty. I figured the sheriff would have to tell them I was down there anyway, so I was going to get caught one way or another.

Just like on Sunday, I went out the window and hopped down into the side yard. I made a little noise when I hit the ground and looked up to see if anyone heard me. There was no one looking out my parents' window, so I figured I was safe and took off running toward the park.

I went down Landsford Street, even though it wasn't the shortest way there. Thinking back on it, I suppose I did that on purpose. I guess I knew that if I just went and told the sheriff everything, he was going to have to arrest Mr. Hager right away. Just because I thought he didn't do anything wrong didn't mean that the sheriff would feel the same way. Maybe I knew all along that I was going to warn Mr. Hager. I don't know. It's hard to say looking back now. All I know is that's what I was planning to do when I was standing outside his house.

There were a couple of lights on upstairs where I knew his apartment was, and I could see a shadow behind the curtain, so I figured he was home. I went around the back then and up the stairs, like I always do when I'm collecting for the paper. When I got up to the second floor, it was quiet and kind of spooky. Usually, I can hear the people in the other apartments watching TV or cooking or making some other kind of noise, but not that night. For a minute, I thought about changing my mind and just going on ahead to the park, but then I figured if I came that far I may as well go through with it.

So I walked up to the door and knocked.

MIGGS

I was parked out in front of the station and had just opened the door to my squad car when I spotted my daughter Kimberly running down the street in my direction. I knew it was her right away, of course, but it was both odd and unsettling to see her alone on the street again at that time of night. I had expected her to be at the band concert like everyone else in town. I shut the door and waited for her to reach me. I was just about to ask what she was doing when she threw herself into my arms and started sobbing.

"What's the matter?" I asked, unable to keep the panic out of my voice. "Is everyone alright?"

She kept on crying and didn't answer, so I let go of her and held her out in front of me so I could see her face. She wouldn't look me in the eye and that frightened me even more.

"Tell me what's wrong," I said, a little too emphatically.

"I'm sorry," was all she said.

"Sorry for what?" I asked. "What do you have to be sorry for?"

She buried her head in my chest again and my mind started to race. I thought that maybe someone had gotten hurt at home or that maybe she had even hurt someone herself in some way. I asked her again to tell me what was wrong. Finally, she pulled away and looked at me.

"Will you promise not to be mad at me?" she asked, her words coming between sobs.

"I can't promise that if I don't know what it is," I told her.

She immediately started to cry again, so I told her that I promised not to overreact. I told her that was the best I could do. I guess maybe that was enough to satisfy her.

"It's about Mikey," she told me.

Don't ask me why, but I knew she was going to say those words about a second before they came out of her mouth. Maybe it was my police instincts. Or maybe my parental ones. Probably a combination of both. I asked her what she was talking about.

She wiped her eyes and looked at me for a couple of seconds, then she told me that she just saw Sylvia Vogel over at the band concert and that she told her she was supposed to meet Sam Fisher there and that they were coming down to see me to tell me something important. "Except Sam never showed up," she told me. "She said he promised he'd be there."

Something about the way she said that put me on high alert, even though on the surface there didn't seem to be anything sinister about those words. I asked her what that had to do with Mikey, not entirely sure that I was ready for her answer.

As it turned out, I wasn't.

HAGER

The deputy froze, surprised I'm sure that someone else was at my door. Then he turned to look at me and started to put his finger up to his lips to indicate that I shouldn't say anything, except I knew that's what he was going to do.

"Who's there?" I said, loudly.

He gave me an angry look, but I knew there was nothing he could do about it. If he shot me, whoever was on the other side of the door would be a witness of sorts. Unless he killed them as well, which would only make matters more complicated for him and that was too chancy for him to ignore. For the briefest of moments, I saw this as an opportunity to disrupt whatever it was that the deputy had planned.

"It's me, Mr. Hager," said a boy's voice. "Sam Fisher." There was a brief pause, then he added, "Your paper boy."

Brisby had his finger to his lip now and gave me a serious stare. He pointed his gun at me as a threat, although we both knew he wasn't about to shoot me. Not with a child on the other side of the door. Instead, he leaned in and whispered, "Tell him to go."

If it had been anyone else, I might have opened the door and taken my chances. However, I liked Sam and had no desire to put him in harm's way. It wouldn't be right, even if doing so were to somehow save my life. So I did what the deputy asked and told the boy it was a bad time and to come back later. I held my breath as I waited to hear his footsteps retreating down the hall, but they did not come.

"I have to talk to you about something," the boy said then. "It's important." There was something urgent in his voice.

The deputy leaned in and whispered to me to tell the boy that whatever it was it could wait until morning. So I did as he said, and again, I waited to hear the boy leave. Again, he did not.

"It's about Saturday night," the boy said. "I saw what happened with you and that other man. Out in the woods above Vorelyn Park."

The deputy looked at me then, his head cocked.

"I came here to warn you," the boy said. "I'm on my way down to tell the sheriff what I saw."

He had barely uttered that last word when Brisby yanked opened the door.

SAM

I could tell something wasn't right as soon as I saw that Brisby guy standing there wearing his regular clothes. Then I saw the gun in his hand, and I knew I had made a big mistake. Before I could do anything, he grabbed me by the arm and pulled me inside and closed the door real fast.

Mr. Hager was standing there just a few feet away. When he moved to make room for me, I could see that his hands were behind his back and that he had handcuffs on. I was still staring at them when Brisby turned me around to make me look at him.

"Did anybody else come here with you?" he asked. He sounded real nervous and kind of worked up.

I shook my head, but didn't say anything.

"Did you tell anyone you were coming here?" he wanted to know.

I told him no. He looked at me for what seemed like a long time, but it was probably only a couple seconds really, then he seemed to relax a little bit.

"Alright then," he said. "You better come with us."

"Where?" I asked.

"To see the sheriff," he said. "I'm taking him in."

"Don't listen to him," Mr. Hager started to say, but Brisby hit him in his stomach with the butt of his gun. Mr. Hager bent over and moaned.

"You don't talk unless I say so," Brisby told him. Then he told me to open the door and go out in the hall.

I knew he wasn't arresting him, even without Mr. Hager saying anything. If he was going to arrest him, he would have been wearing his uniform and the sheriff would have been there with him. But I didn't know what else to do, so I did what he said.

He had me go down the stairs first. Mr. Hager was behind me and he was bringing up the rear.

When we got to the bottom, he told me not to say anything if we saw anyone outside. He said I should just keep walking until he told me to stop. But I already decided I would say something if I saw someone out there. I was thinking it might be my only chance to stop him from doing whatever he was planning to do, but it turned out no one was there, just like when I came. I thought about yelling for help anyway, but no one would have heard me. The street was dead. Everyone was at the band concert.

When we got to the end of the driveway, Brisby pushed Mr. Hager in front of me toward a car parked on the street. I didn't notice it when I first got there. If I did, I probably would have thought it was just another car in the street. I didn't know whose it was, but it definitely wasn't a police car.

He shoved Mr. Hager into the front seat and closed the door. Then he turned around and told me to get in the back.

I didn't move right away. He just stared at me, waiting to see what I was going to do I guess. Looking back on it, that's probably when I should have made a run for it. I don't think he really would have shot me. I was just a kid, after all, and if he chased me, Mr. Hager could have gotten away. Maybe both of us would have. But that was looking back on it. When somebody has a gun pointed at you and tells you to do something, you don't think. You just do it.

So I got in the back like he said, and he got in the front and we took off.

MIGGS

There was no one in the station, so I didn't want to leave her there. I had called Brisby to have him come down and stay with her, but there was no one answering at his house. I assumed he was probably at the concert, like everyone else, so I had no choice but to drop her off at home where I knew nobody was. She had told me the short-hand version of what she had witnessed with those boys on Saturday night. From what she said, I knew the two men out there had to have been Hager and Irwin, and only one of them was still alive, and he was the one who I was on my way to arrest. I wasn't quite sure how it all fit together, but I didn't have time to work it all out. I was only concerned that she might also be in danger and felt that my home was probably the safest spot for her.

She had stayed home alone before, although not often. Usually it was just for an hour or so, and never under any circumstances like the ones we were facing that night. I went in with her and looked around quickly, trying not to frighten her, but at the same time making sure it was safe to leave her there. I told her to lock all the doors as soon as I left and not to open them again unless it was her mother or me on the other side. She looked scared as hell, but she nodded. Then she hugged me and I kissed her on the top of her head. "It's going to be alright," I told her. "I promise."

"You're not mad at me?" she asked.

"No," I told her, although that wasn't entirely true. What she had told me was certainly troubling and out of character, at least for the daughter I thought I knew, but I was going to have to sort that all out later. "Right now I have to go do something." I told her, as if she could read my thoughts.

She let me go, and I waited on the porch for her to close the door and lock it. Then I hurried back to my car and took off for Hager's.

It appeared that I was wrong about the man. He seemed capable of more than I had thought. According to my own daughter, Irwin was dead at his hand, and that only reinforced what I had concluded after speaking with Robbins just moments before. Given the circumstances, I considered calling someone to accompany me. However, if news of Irwin's body being recovered had leaked out beyond Robbins, it was possible that Hager would flee, and so I went alone, so as not to waste any more time.

When I got there, I parked the car out front, blocking the driveway, just in case. Then I walked around the back, near where Hager had burned the suitcase. I gave the empty barrel a quick glance before I entered the back door.

I tried to be as quiet as I could going up the stairs. I wanted to catch Hager off-guard. I realized that I had hoped the same thing each of the two previous times I visited him, but had clearly failed.

When I reached his door, I put my ear to it to listen for movement inside, but heard nothing except for the hum of the fan I had seen in there on my previous two meetings with him. I listened for a few seconds longer without hearing another sound, then finally gave up and rapped hard on the door.

I put my hand on the butt of my service revolver as I waited for him to answer. More seconds passed, but no one came. I put my ear to the door once more, and again there was no sound from inside. I thought that he might possibly be asleep, even though it was still pretty early and the music from the band concert could be heard pretty clearly, so I knocked again, this time even louder, and called out his name. If he was in there, he would have had to have heard me.

I waited and listened and finally determined that he was either not at home or was refusing to answer. Either way, I knew I couldn't just enter the apartment without a warrant or Hager's permission, not unless it were an emergency of some sort, such as someone's life being in danger. I suppose I was risking not only the entire case but my own career, but I thought that if I were to enter and later got asked in court why I did so, I would just say that, based upon what my daughter had told me, someone had to be in danger, and that was good enough for me. I was about to go find Abernathy to have him use his key let me in, when I thought to check the door first.

I took a deep breath and unsnapped the flap on my holster and removed the revolver. Then I reached for the knob and turned it. When I pushed in, the door gave way.

So I entered.

HAGER

Brisby drove by the street where anyone would turn if they were going down to the police station.

"Where are we going?" the boy asked him, as we went through the intersection.

"We're meeting the sheriff somewhere else," the deputy said. "He's not at the station." The boy said nothing. I think he had to know that Brisby was lying. He had always seemed like a bright young man to me.

We drove on in silence for awhile. Then I asked Brisby how many people knew about me and what I had done. I was referring to putting the other boy in the pool, although the boy in the back seat couldn't have known that.

"It doesn't matter," Brisby said. "Not now."

I didn't like the sound of that.

"You picked up the boy that day," I said to him. Actually, I didn't know that, but it had suddenly occurred to me that it must have happened that way.

He looked over at me. "I don't know what you're talking about," he said.

"Did you and John arrange it the night before?"

He turned to look in the rear view mirror at the boy, as if he was concerned about what he might be hearing.

"Smart," I said. "A policeman in a police car. He'd feel safe. But you couldn't risk having someone see you near the pool.

Where did you have him meet you?"

"Shut up," he said, "Or I'll make you." I realized then that he was talking for the benefit of the boy as well. How odd, I thought, that we were both worried about what this boy might think, even though there was little doubt that both the boy and I were about to die.

"How did you happen to see me Saturday night?" I asked, turning to look at the boy.

It took him a second or two to realize that I was talking to him.

"My friend knew about the hole in the ground," he told me. "She wanted to show us."

"Who's 'she'?" the deputy asked him.

The boy didn't say anything.

"Who?" the deputy asked again. There was an edge to his voice.

"Nobody," the boy said. "Just a girl I know."

"And that's when we showed up?" I asked the boy.

"Yeah," he said. "I guess."

"You saw what happened?" Brisby asked the boy. Of course, Brisby couldn't have known what happened to John, other than that he was dead. He had to know that or he wouldn't have come to see me.

The boy didn't answer him right away.

"You saw him kill that man?" he asked the boy, obviously referring to me.

"It was self-defense," the boy said, confidently. "That other guy was going to kill him."

"Well," said Brisby. "We'll have to let the law decide all that."

The boy got quiet again. I noticed then that we had left town and were out on route two heading toward the farm near the railroad tracks. I turned around to look at the boy.

"First chance you get, you need to run," I told him. "He's

going to kill us."

As I turned back, Brisby struck hard and fast, catching me on the cheekbone with the butt of his gun.

SAM

I knew where we were going even before he turned onto the tractor road. I knew why, too, even before Mr. Hager said anything. I just didn't want to believe it. When this whole thing started I didn't think anyone would be able to protect me, not even the cops. I just didn't think a cop would be the one who was going to kill me.

That Brisby guy must have been out there before because he drove us someplace I didn't see either time I was there. It was way past where Gehring's farm land ends. Some sort of a parking spot in the woods. It looked like somebody cut the grass and bushes to make it like that. When he parked the car, you could tell it would be hard to find if you didn't know it was there.

He turned off the car and looked over at Mr. Hager who was holding his cheek after getting hit pretty hard by Brisby. I could see the blood coming out between his fingers. Brisby then got out and opened my door and yanked me out. I lost my balance and fell, but I got right back up before he could grab me again.

"Don't even think about doing what he said," he warned me. "I'll shoot you before you get ten feet away and no one will hear. Now put both hands on the car and stay put."

I did what he said. Like I said before, when somebody has a gun pointed at you, you listen. He went around to the other side of the car and opened up the other door and dragged Mr. Hager out and let him fall on the ground. Mr. Hager rolled over and Brisby picked him up and pushed him up against the car. I could see the cut on the side of his face then, and I remember thinking he might need stitches. Then I remembered what we were doing out there and that stitches wouldn't really matter.

After that, Brisby pulled Mr. Hager around to my side of the car. There was a path that started right in front of the car, and he reached down in the weeds and picked up a big flashlight that somebody must have left out there. He turned it on and shone it on us. He looked at both of us for a little bit, like he was thinking about something.

"Put both your hands on the chain there," he told me. He pointed at the handcuffs behind Mr. Hager's back.

There was hardly room for both my hands, but I did what he said.

"Keep them there and let's go," he said. Then he got behind both of us and shined the flashlight on the path in front of us and we started walking.

"You planned this all out, didn't you?" Mr. Hager asked him after a minute or so. I guess he was talking about the flashlight. Probably the car, too. I already figured out that the car must have belonged to Mr. Hager. It only made sense. Brisby wouldn't want to use his own car if he was going to kill somebody.

"Let's just say I know what I'm doing," he said.

"But you couldn't have planned for the boy showing up," Mr. Hager said.

"No," he said. "That was unexpected."

"How are you going to explain it all then?" Mr. Hager asked him.

"I'm not," he told him. "You are."

For a second, I thought that maybe he wasn't really going to kill us, but that didn't last for long.

"You're going to commit suicide," he told Mr. Hager. "Out of guilt. Blow your brains out over your final criminal act, which will involve this boy."

"You really think that's going to work?" Mr. Hager asked him.

"There won't be any other explanation," he said. It sounded to me like he might be right.

The woods were pretty thick on either side of the path and I didn't know where I was exactly. My heart was beating pretty fast then, and I was thinking about what Mr. Hager said to me. All I knew was I didn't want to keep going wherever Brisby was taking us. Even though he sounded pretty serious when he said he'd shoot me, it seemed like my only chance to get away was to do what Mr. Hager said.

So that's what I decided to do.

MIGGS

The house was empty and everything seemed to be in order. I checked every room and didn't see anything that raised any suspicion. I did notice a duffel bag sitting on the floor in the bedroom. I didn't know what to make of that, but there wasn't anything particularly incriminating about it either. I had looked in his closet and it was full, as was his chest of drawers. In the bathroom, I found both his razor and toothbrush sitting on the sink. He may have been thinking of leaving, but it appeared that he hadn't done so yet.

I came back around to the entryway, satisfied that I hadn't missed anything. In my two previous times there, I wondered what I might find had I been allowed to look around. It turned out to be rather disappointing. Fritz had been right. There was no doubt that a search would reveal nothing to incriminate Hager. That didn't mean that he hadn't killed the boy, only that there was no proof of it in those four rooms.

It also didn't mean that the Fisher boy wasn't in danger. Based on what both Robbins and my daughter had just told me, the person most likely to be the source of that danger was the person whose apartment I was in and he wasn't home and I didn't know where the boy was. That's all I needed to know, so I went to the telephone on the small table near the door and dialed the Fishers. I figured that a phone call would be faster than me driving over there.

George Fisher answered on the sixth ring. I told him who it was and apologized for calling so late. I asked him if he knew where his son was.

"Up in his room," he told me.

"So he didn't go to the band concert tonight?" I asked, momentarily relieved at hearing that.

"No," George said. "He stayed home tonight." For some reason, he sounded nervous to me when he said that. Defensive almost.

I suppose that's what prompted me to ask him why Sam stayed home when every other kid in town was going to be at the concert. Fisher took some time before he answered. "Can I ask you what this is all about?" he said.

I debated whether I should tell him what Kimberly had told me, but then I thought it would only alarm him, so instead, I asked if he would mind putting Sam on the phone so that I could speak to him for a minute. It was deceitful I admit, but necessary in light of what was going on.

Again, Fisher hesitated. "Should I be calling Zachariah Pickens again?" he asked me.

"I don't think that'll be necessary," I told him. "I just want to ask Sam a question. You can listen in if you'd like. If you think for any reason he shouldn't answer, then that will be fine. I'll hang up and you can call Zachariah." Of course, I wasn't actually planning on asking the boy anything. I just wanted to hear his voice and satisfy myself that he was truly safe before I hung up, and I didn't know any other way to confirm it.

Fisher said OK, but he still sounded wary. I heard the phone being set down on the table and waited, thinking of what I was going to say when the boy came to the phone.

Probably thirty seconds later, I heard Fisher returning. His footsteps sounded much louder than when he left. When he got back on the line, his voice was frantic.

"He's not up there," he said. "What the hell is going on?"

I told him to stay right there and that I would send someone over right away.

HAGER

We were about fifty yards down the path when I felt the boy's hands come off the handcuffs. In response, I slowed my pace so that the distance between us would close, making it harder for the deputy to see what the boy had done. I knew in that instant what the boy had in mind and that is why I did what I did next.

Without warning, I stopped and took a big step backward, with considerable force. My intention was to startle both the boy and the deputy. Which I did. The boy bumped into Brisby who, in turn, dropped the flashlight. Fortunately, his gun didn't discharge. In that second or so of confusion, I took off between the trees on my right.

My original plan had been to work my way back to the car. I kept a spare key hidden in the front under the passenger side floor mat. I thought if I could reach it before the deputy and somehow get my hands around in front of me, I might be able to get the car started and get out of there.

Please don't misunderstand. I wasn't planning to leave the boy alone out there with the deputy. That was not my intent at all. I simply reasoned that the boy would run off as soon as he saw me do so, and that I would be able to lure the deputy away from him. After all, he was going to have to choose between coming after me or the boy, and I was the greater risk to him, so I believed he would choose me. The sound of someone following close behind as I picked my way through the trees told me I was correct.

The woods at that point were quite thick, making it hard to find a path to follow. On the positive side, with the trees so densely packed, it was equally difficult for the deputy to see me. He had to rely mostly on sound, which he must have been able to do because I could hear him keeping a somewhat steady pace behind me.

"You're only going to make this worse," he shouted at one point.

I didn't respond, of course. However, with him so close behind, I realized that I wasn't going to be able to get back to the car with enough time to free my hands and then find the key and start the car. I probably wouldn't even be able to get the door open before he was on me. Therefore, I changed both my plan and direction.

I curled back around, wide of where we had come from, and stopped and crouched next to a large tree. I heard Brisby keep going for awhile and then he too stopped. I watched from not far away as he swung the flashlight around, first in the direction I had been running, then in a full circle. Fortunately, I was far enough away so that when he shone it in my direction, there wasn't enough light to reveal me, even if I had been standing out away from the tree. It was clear that he didn't know where I had gone.

As quietly as I could, I then swung around back toward the path, so that I could go try to find the boy.

SAM

At first, I didn't realize what Mr. Hager was doing. Then when the flashlight fell out of Brisby's hands and Mr. Hager took off, I knew he was trying to help me. I guess you could say he was trying to help himself, too, but I really felt like he was doing it more for me than him.

Brisby got ahold of the flashlight again and looked over at where Mr. Hager went and then back at me. "You stay right here," he told me. Then he ran into the woods after Mr. Hager.

He must have thought I was pretty stupid or maybe so scared that I would do whatever he wanted, but when he was gone and I didn't have that gun pointed at me anymore, I took off down the path.

I didn't really think about what I was going to do after that. I guess I just wanted to get away from him, so I just kept running down the path, away from where we came in. It didn't take long till I got to the old hobo camp. When I did, I stopped and looked around for a minute and knew right away I couldn't stay there. There wasn't any place to hide. I'd be out in the open and too easy for him to find. So I looked for the path that leads to the back of the houses on West Main. That was how I came there the night I saw Mikey. I went through the backyard of a house next door to Sylvia's. I figured I could go back the same way, and then when I got to the street, I could knock on some doors until I found somebody home and tell them what happened and ask them to call the police. If I had to, I might even go to Sylvia's house. Of course, I hoped I wouldn't have to do that.

There was only about a quarter moon out that night, so it was kind of dark out on that path without a flashlight. I guess that's why I didn't see it. It was probably from a fox or a possum. Maybe a woodchuck. I was running about as fast as I could when I felt my foot sink into the hole and heard something snap.

MIGGS

I was acting solely on gut and not proper police procedure when I called Vic on the squawk-box and told him to forget about Joe Furth and those car keys. Instead, I told him to get over to the Fishers right away and stay there.

Vic knows me well enough not to ask too many questions when I tell him to do something. Nevertheless, he would have been derelict in his duty if he hadn't asked me why he was going over there and what he was supposed to say when he got there.

I told him what my daughter had said about the Fisher boy and just enough of what she had told me about Hager and Irwin so that he would get the idea and realize that it was urgent. I told him not to tell the Fishers any of that and just to say that he was there as a precaution and that we were pretty sure that Sam wasn't in any danger. I didn't see the point in getting them alarmed. After all, there was always the possibility, slight though it may have been, that the boy had snuck out to the band concert or gone to one of his friend's houses. I knew that if I was wrong, I would have to pay dearly, but that was my call.

Before I signed off, I told Vic to find out where the hell Brisby was and to have him get up to the swimming pool to keep an eye out for Hager and the boy up there. It seemed like a logical place to go, if Hager had killing on his mind.

When I was done with Vic, I called the state police and, fortunately, ended up speaking with the same detective I had spoken with the day before. I repeated the same story to him, only this time I emphasized that it sure looked like Hager had killed their man Irwin. I told him I knew it wasn't really their investigation yet, but that I was shorthanded and could use their help. He didn't even hesitate and asked me what they could do. I told him to send someone up to Vorelyn Park and somebody else up to the turnoff road for Kitchiwa Lake, giving him the same instructions about watching for Hager and the boy. I told him that Hager was missing and could be anywhere. I only picked those spots because they had some previous connection to the investigation.

Before I hung up, the statie asked me where I was going to be. I told him I was already on my way out to the old hobo camp beyond the railroad tracks out by Gehring's farm. I told him that if he had any extra men on duty that night, he should send them out there to give me a hand with the search. He said he would see what he could do.

HAGER

My decision to change course allowed me to put some distance between myself and the deputy. I was also becoming more adept at finding my way through the trees. Using the sky as a reference, I selected a direction that I hoped would bring me toward the clearing where we had met those two times and where the deputy had obviously planned to take us. I hoped that it would be the last place he would look for me.

A short time later, I came to a path, which I assumed to be the one we were on before. I turned onto it and quickened my pace, hoping that it would bring me to that clearing. Although there wasn't a great deal of light, I could immediately see that the path was pretty well worn, as if used by a lot of people. I recalled also that the place where the deputy had parked, although secluded, had space for several more cars. Perhaps my mind should have been focused only on finding the boy and escaping from my pursuer, but I couldn't help but think that the worn path and the parking area were what the others must have used on those two nights we met out there. The instructions John gave me for where to park and which path to follow were different, only confirming what I had suspected in recent days about the others perhaps knowing about me but me not knowing about any of them. He must have felt that until he could fully trust me, he would keep me on an island, ready to cut loose at the first sign of trouble. It was probably also the reason why he chose me to dispose of the boy's body. It

was naive of me to believe it was because I'd be the one the authorities would have least reason to suspect. I was a fool to ever get
involved with him and an even bigger fool to rely on anything he
ever said. But I suppose sex makes fools of us all at some time in
our lives.

When I reached the clearing, it almost looked unfamiliar to me.
First of all, I had come upon it from a different angle. Second, the
feeling I had upon arriving that night was obviously different than
on those other two nights. I quickly walked the perimeter, but
didn't see any sign of the boy. I wondered if he might have stayed
in the woods, hoping to hide from the deputy. Or perhaps he got
turned around and was heading back toward the car, where he
would no doubt encounter him.

I knew then I had a decision to make. I could find my way to
the railroad tracks and follow them back to where I had parked
when I had come out there those other times, as well as on the
night I ran into those three boys. In the alternative, I could head
back on the same path that brought me there, to see if Brisby had
re-captured the boy. Finally, I could take the path that appeared in
the opposite corner and which had to lead somewhere, although I
did not know where.

I decided to follow that third path, hoping it would take me into town. Again, I wish to make it clear that I wasn't abandoning
the boy. I simply reasoned that Brisby could not kill the boy without also killing me. If he did, I would be able to tell the authorities
what had happened earlier that night and his story would not hold
up. After all, I was still wearing his handcuffs. He needed me dead
in order for his plan to succeed. Therefore, I determined that I
would try to reach town and look for help. Whatever consequences
that action might bring, I was prepared to endure.

I was probably no more than fifty feet down the path when I
spotted the boy laying on the ground. My first thought was that the
deputy had indeed killed him, even though I could not recall hear-

ing a shot. However, as I approached, the boy sat up quickly to face me, causing me to think that luck may have intervened once more and that we might get away after all.

The tear tracks running down his dirt-stained face told me instantly that I was wrong.

SAM

I couldn't walk. I couldn't even stand up. I tried once, but it hurt too much, so I had to lay back down. I was sure that guy Brisby was going to show up any second and I was mad as hell because I wasn't going to be able to put up much of a fight if he did.

When I heard somebody coming down the path a few minutes later, I was sure it was him and that it was all over. Lucky for me, it turned out to be Mr. Hager. At first, I was embarrassed that he saw me crying, but then I realized that being ashamed was the least of my worries. Besides, he didn't say anything about it. He just came over and crouched down next to me and asked me what happened.

"Let me take a look," he said, after I told him. He sounded real calm and that made me feel better right away. When I pulled up my pant leg, he let out a weird sound. So I looked down to see what made him do that, and it was like I was looking at somebody else's leg. A big piece of bone was sticking out where my shin was supposed to be. It was really white next to all the blood. For some reason, I didn't feel any pain and just kept staring at it for a few seconds. Then I leaned over and threw up. Mr. Hager rubbed my back while I did and told me that everything was going to be OK. For a minute there, I almost believed him.

When I was done, I asked him if he knew where Brisby went. He said he didn't, but that we had to get going. "Do you know where this leads?" he asked me. He was pointing down the path.

I told him about West Main Street and the back of the houses.

He nodded and said that's where we should go and that we'd be safe once we got there. I asked him how we were going to do that with my leg, and he asked if it would be OK for him to carry me. I told him I thought so.

He sat down on the ground then and tried to get his arms from behind his back to the front. He's a pretty skinny guy, so he was able to wriggle his arms around his hips and rear end, even with the handcuffs on. Then he pulled his legs through, one at a time. I think he might have hurt his shoulder doing it, because I heard him curse once, but he did it. When he stood up again, he held his arms out in front of him to make a kind of cradle. Then he got down on one knee and told me to lay back against him with my leg out to one side.

Because of the handcuffs, there wasn't any other way for him to carry me, so I did what he said. I'm not as big as Richie or Keith even. I only weigh about eighty five pounds, but like I said, he's pretty skinny and didn't look that strong to me. I guess he must have been strong enough though, because he managed to get back to his feet. I asked him if he was OK and he smiled and said he was fine.

Then he turned around and started to carry me down the path toward town.

MIGGS

I decided to park on West Main and work my way through the woods behind those houses. To my way of thinking, it was the fastest way to get there. I was a teenager the last time I walked that path, but I was certain that it couldn't have changed much since then. It's a fairly long way out because the camp is on the other side of the railroad tracks and they run pretty far south of town. Still, it was better than driving all the way out to Gehring's farm and working my way back from there, like I did just a few days before. I estimated that I'd be saving at least ten minutes, which could mean the difference between life and death.

As I pulled up to the curb, Vic called me on the squawk box.

"The Fishers are going crazy," he told me. "They want to know where their son is."

"Tell them I got it covered," I said, even though that was far from the truth.

He didn't answer right away, and I knew then there had to be something else.

"What is it, Vic?" I asked him.

"Zachariah Pickens is here," he said. "He's on the phone with the state police."

Of course, we both knew what he meant by that. I was disappointed to hear it, but hardly surprised. Hell, maybe I deserved it. Maybe I had screwed this whole thing up, just like before. "I already talked to them," I told Vic. "They're already assisting."

"Right," he said. I couldn't tell if he was relieved, although I suspected he might be. I couldn't be sure. Over the last seven years, I have often wondered what my men really thought of me, what they said to one another when I wasn't around.

"What about you?" I asked him, unable to leave it at that.

"What do you mean?" he asked.

"Am I as big a fool as they all seem to think?"

There was a short period of silence on the other end that left me wondering if I should have just kept my mouth shut. "There's nobody I'd rather work for, Daryl" he said finally. "You ought to know that by now."

I am not an emotional man, but I had trouble speaking for a second. I wanted to thank him right then, but it didn't seem appropriate.

"What about Brisby?" I asked instead. "Did you get a hold of him yet?"

He told me no one was answering the phone at his house and that he didn't take a squad car home when he left that day.

"Where the hell is he?" I asked.

"Probably at the park with everyone else," he said.

"Well then, keep calling," I told him and signed off.

Then I grabbed the twelve-gauge from the gun rack, along with a flashlight, and got out of the car and ran down the driveway belonging to the Vogels. I slipped through a gate in the fence in their backyard and then began making my way through the tall grass toward the woods and the camp somewhere beyond.

HAGER

It was nearly impossible to make up any ground carrying the boy the way I was. I had to stop every few feet to avoid falling and injuring him any further. I was experiencing considerable discomfort in my right shoulder, which I had hurt getting the handcuffs from behind me around to the front, but I was determined to keep going.

"Maybe you should leave me and go get help," he said, at one point.

"No, I just need a minute to rest," I told him.

"Really," he said. "I'll be OK."

The irony of the situation was almost too much for me to bear. Three weeks to the day had passed and here I was with another boy in my arms, only this one was alive, and I was resolved to do everything in my power to keep it that way. I set him down to give my arms a rest for a bit.

"I put that boy in the pool," I said then.

In the silence after I uttered those words, I could hear what seemed like a cacophony of birds and crickets and other assorted night life. I hadn't heard them before or maybe I just wasn't listening. Why I felt the need to confess at that particular moment remains a mystery to me. Perhaps I sensed what was about to happen. Perhaps I just needed to unburden myself. Whatever the reason, it just seemed important to me that I tell him what I did and why. So I did, leaving out the more lurid details of what we had been doing out there the night the Vogel boy came upon us. I tried to gloss it over, saying that we were simply doing "adult" things. Things that would embarrass us if the boy ever told anyone.

"You didn't kill him, though, right?" he asked, when I was done.

I assured him that I hadn't.

"Who did then?" he wanted to know.

"That deputy, I think," I told him. "It might have been that man you saw me with on Saturday. It was one or the other. I can't really be sure."

Once again, he was quiet for a time, and I thought perhaps I may have frightened him.

"So you were one of those people with the masks and the paint and all of that?" he asked.

I was taken aback by the question, as those were some of the very same details I had just left out. I asked him how he could possibly know about all that.

"I was there," he said.

It took me a moment to process that. I certainly hadn't seen him, nor had anyone else to my knowledge. It seemed impossible that someone else could have stumbled upon us that very same night. But then why would he lie about something like that? I asked him what he was doing there.

He told me that he was supposed to meet the boy's sister there that night. "We were going to sleep out together," he said, as innocently as could be. "Just me and her." I knew he meant "sleep together" literally, not the way most of us refer to sex. My heart almost broke when he said it. "She sent her brother out to tell me she couldn't come," he said. "I saw all of you. And him. And I ran away. I'm the reason he's dead. It's all my fault." The sorrow in his voice was truly affecting.

I assured him that he wasn't in any way at fault. I pointed out that if his friend had been able to meet him out there, her brother might still be alive, but both of them would probably be dead. He looked at me like he hadn't thought of that. Then he asked me why we were out there in the first place, doing what it was that we were doing. I thought of how best to answer him, of how I could possibly explain. However, I soon realized that anything I said would make little sense to a boy his age. Or anyone for that matter. "I don't know," I told him. "I wish I could tell you, but I really can't."

He nodded, and it seemed to me that he accepted that. "We should get moving," I said finally.

I had just managed to secure him in my arms and get back to my feet, when I saw the glow of a flashlight.

SAM

Brisby must have been able to catch up with us because of what happened with my leg. I didn't see him until Mr. Hager turned around with me in his arms. When he saw my leg sticking out, he asked me what happened, like it was just any other day, in any other place. Not in the dark, in the middle of the woods, with him holding a gun on us.

I told him I fell trying to run away.

"Serves you right," he said. "I told you to stay put." I didn't really see how it served me right to get my leg broken when he was planning on killing me anyway, but I didn't say anything.

"What are you going to do now?" Mr. Hager asked him.

"I'm still thinking about that," Brisby said.

"If you let us live, I'll tell the sheriff that I killed the boy," Mr. Hager told him. "I won't say a word about you."

"Nice try," he said. "Even if I trusted you, it wouldn't work."

"It has to be better than whatever you have planned," Mr. Hager said. "At least my way you wouldn't be committing two more murders."

"Three's no worse than one," Brisby said.

Mr. Hager started to set me down again, but Brisby stopped him. "No, let's go," he said. "We're going to finish this." And so we headed back the way we came.

I was starting to feel kind of lightheaded around then. The doctor said later it was because of breaking my leg and losing all that blood. All kinds of things were going through my head at that point. I remember thinking that I wasn't ever going to see my sister or my parents again and wondered what Richie and Keith would say when they found out what happened to me. I figured I might even be in the paper. Two more people dead after Mikey and that guy up in the woods above Vorelyn Park would be big news. Even bigger than Mikey. What really bothered me was that Brisby was probably going to get away with it. He was a cop. He was supposed to protect people, not kill them.

When we got to the clearing, Brisby told Mr. Hager to take me over by the spring at the other end of the clearing. He did what he said and then set me down next to the water, but he stayed between me and Brisby.

"Is this where you killed him?" Mr. Hager asked him. I guess he meant Mikey.

"Shut up and put him in the water there," he said.

"Are you going to drown him, too?" Mr. Hager asked.

Brisby smiled. "No. You are."

"How are you going to explain his leg?" Mr. Hager asked.

"I'm not," he said. "That'll be up to the sheriff. And the DA. I'll just put the pieces in place for them."

He waved his gun at him and told him to put me in the water again.

"No," Mr. Hager told him. "You're going to have to do it yourself. I won't help you."

I tried to make myself stay alert and be ready for whatever was going to happen next. No matter who put me in there, I was going to fight back. Or try to anyway. Brisby didn't say anything right away. You could tell he was trying to figure out what to do. Personally, I didn't see how he could make Mr. Hager drown me if he didn't want to. He'd have to threaten to kill him, but he already told him he was going to do that.

Mr. Hager must have thought the same thing because he took

a couple steps away from me.

"Stay where you are," Brisby warned him.

Mr. Hager shook his head and took another step away.

That's when Brisby raised his gun.

MIGGS

I was pretty far down the path when I heard the shot. I stopped and looked around to try to get my bearings. It sounded like it came from where I was heading, so I slipped the shotgun strap over my shoulder and took off in that direction.

The beam from the flashlight was bouncing all over the place as I ran, creating a disturbing strobe-like effect that actually made it more difficult to see where I was going. So I tossed it aside and continued on, until I heard what I thought was another shot, only louder this time.

I stopped once more to listen, and then suddenly the sky above me seemed to explode.

The town has a pyrotechnic display twice every year. Once on the Fourth, the second time at the end of the summer, after the last of the band concerts. I had forgotten about it with all that had taken place already that night and cursed that fact as I started racing down the path again.

What I heard the first time wasn't fireworks. It was a gun shot. I was sure of that. But I also knew that if there were going to be any more, they would likely be disguised by what was taking place above me.

As I neared the opening in the trees where I knew the old hobo camp to be, it occurred to me that I might be entering a situation that I wasn't fully prepared for.

At the same time, I hoped that all the noise from the fireworks might also camouflage my approach.

As it turned out, I was right on both counts.

HAGER

The shot went by near enough that I could actually feel it as it passed by. I even put my hand up to my ear to see if I was bleeding. I was not.

Based on what the deputy had told me, I assumed that he was planning on making it look like I shot myself, after killing the boy, which would mean that he would have to get close enough to put the gun to my head. He must have only fired the weapon to startle me. If he shot me from any distance, it couldn't be ruled a suicide. The authorities would know a third person had to be involved. Meaning that the investigation would still go on. His suicide scenario was meant to wrap up everything nicely, with all the blame pointing in my direction. As long as I kept some distance from him, I realized, he couldn't execute his plan. From the look on his face, it was apparent that he was coming to understand that as well.

For that reason, I expected him to charge after me and I was prepared to run into the woods once again, but he surprised me and walked over to the boy, pointing the gun at him as he did.

"Change of plans," he said. "Take another step and I'll just shoot him instead."

He might have done so too, had the fireworks not started. He froze at the first sound, then looked up and behind him to see the flickering lights suspended above. After a second or two, he turned around to face me again. If he hadn't done so, I'm sure he would have seen someone step out of the woods some twenty feet behind him.

That the someone was Daryl Miggs. I tried hard not to change my expression, so as not to alert Brisby to the sheriff's presence. Instead, I raised my hands and took a step toward him and the boy.

I could see that Miggs was trying to say something as he approached the deputy from behind, but the noise from the fireworks was too loud to allow any of us to hear him.

Brisby aimed his pistol at me once more, still unaware that Miggs was right behind him. Just then, there was a pause between the explosions, not a long one, but enough so that the sheriff's yelling caused Brisby to spin toward the sound.

SAM

When Brisby fired the gun, I remember thinking that he must have shot Mr. Hager. Except he didn't fall or grunt or make any kind of noise or anything. He just stood there and put his hand up to his ear, but I didn't see any blood or anything.

Then Brisby came over and pointed the gun at me again and said something to Mr. Hager about killing me. The fireworks started right around then and that made me look up. Like I said, I was feeling sort of fuzzy then and I suppose that's why I just kept watching the fireworks for awhile, at least until I thought I heard somebody else's voice coming from somewhere. That's when I turned around to see Sheriff Miggs standing right there, as if he came out of nowhere. He was facing Brisby, and they had their guns pointed at each other, just like something out of a John Wayne movie. Except it was real and happening right in front of me.

"What are you doing out here Pat?" the sheriff asked him. He sounded pretty calm, like he was down at the coffee shop asking him to pass the sugar.

Brisby stood there looking at the sheriff and didn't say anything at first. Then he looked back at Mr. Hager and smiled. "I had a hunch about this son of a bitch right from the beginning," he said. I guess he was talking about Mr. Hager.

"You didn't answer my question," the sheriff said.

"Right," Brisby said, lowering his gun. "Like I said, I had a hunch, so I went by his place tonight and saw him getting in the car with the boy there. So I followed them. Good thing I did, too. I think he was about to kill him."

For a second, the sheriff looked like he was buying his story and lowered his gun, too.

That's when I decided I better do something.

MIGGS

Brisby showed some quick thinking, I must say. When he said the thing about suspecting Hager and following them out there, it did give me pause. As did the handcuffs that Hager was wearing. At the same time, I could see that his gun wasn't his department issued Smith and Wesson. It was an old Colt .38, something we haven't used in years. I was trying to think of why he might have such a weapon when the boy shouted that he was lying, and I leveled the shotgun on him again. I was a split second too late.

Brisby had the .38 pointed at the Fisher boy then. "Put it down or I'll kill him," he yelled.

I didn't move. I wasn't sure what I was going to do at that point, but I definitely wasn't ready to give up my weapon.

Brisby jammed the barrel of the gun hard up against the boy's head. "Think about it, Daryl," he shouted. "You don't want to lose another one, do you?"

The question was probably meant to rattle me and, to be honest, it did. However, I tried like hell not to show it. I told him if he harmed the boy in any way I'd have to kill him.

"But he'd still be dead," he said. "And you'd have to explain another one."

I tried to calculate what I might do next. Out of the corner of my eye, I could see Hager watching us, frozen. At that point, I had no idea what his part was in this whole thing, but I saw the blood on his face and it was obvious that he had been beaten, most likely by my own deputy. Still, a part of me was hoping that he might be of some help, but he just looked small and afraid. Plus, there were those handcuffs.

"What's your plan here?" I asked Brisby, hoping to stall for time.

"I'm still working on that," he said, looking more and more desperate.

"Well, I don't know what you've done, but it can't be worth the boy's life."

"It's worth mine, though," he said. "Now throw the shotgun in there." He gestured to the stream on my left. "Your sidearm too."

Once again, I wasn't ready to give up my weapon, but I could read the terror in the boy's eyes. I think he may have pissed himself. I could smell it, along with the cordite from Brisby's earlier shot. I briefly wondered if I might be able to pull the trigger on the twelve gauge and hit Brisby but not the boy. I didn't like the odds I came up with, so I reached into my holster and slowly removed my service revolver and threw it in the water. Again, I was only trying to buy time.

"Good," he said. "Now the shotgun."

The boy was staring at me then, I'm sure hoping that I had some sort of plan, but Brisby was right. I couldn't just stand there and let him kill the boy. And I believed him when he said he would.

"On one condition," I told him. "You let the boy go. You can do anything you want to me after."

I doubted that I could trust him, but it was all that I had. He couldn't go back to his old life after whatever he did next. He wouldn't have time to cover his tracks out there, meaning his only option was to go on the run, in which case a live witness wouldn't matter much. I tried to convince him of that anyway.

"OK fine," he said. "Let's go. Do it."

In light of all the mistakes I'd made, it did seem a fair bargain: my life for the boy's. Don't get me wrong, I didn't want to leave my wife a widow or my children without a father, but there was an undeniable justice to it, an outcome I probably deserved. So I did what Brisby asked and tossed my shotgun in the stream. Then I watched as he turned the gun from the boy toward me.

As if to punctuate the moment, the fireworks went into their finale then, lighting up the whole sky like it was daytime.

That's when I saw Hager take a step forward and raise his hands.

HAGER

Despite all his otherwise careful planning that night, I guess the deputy never considered that I might have John's gun. Which was a mistake on his part, since I had obviously survived and John was dead. Maybe he thought that I had disposed of it, as I had originally thought to. Or maybe he wasn't aware of John's choice of weapon and, therefore, never aware of its existence. Whatever the reason, he most certainly overlooked the possibility that I might have it.

When he had me put my clothes away back at the apartment, it was obvious that he didn't want the sheriff to come in after I was found dead and see a packed bag. That wouldn't make any sense if I was planning to kill myself. However, by doing so, he gave me an opportunity to open the top drawer of my dresser, which is where I had placed the snub-nose revolver when I returned home that night. I had decided to keep it as a bit of protection. It was a risky thing to do, you might think, but I reasoned that if the police were to ever come search my house, they would do so only after having found John's body and, if I played my cards right, I would already be gone, and with me the gun.

While Brisby was retrieving my car keys from the table in the kitchen, I pulled it out from under a pile of underwear and slipped it into the front pocket of my khakis. I then put on my windbreaker to cover it. I know what you must be thinking. I would have used it sooner, back there at the apartment, but in the short time I had to consider it, I couldn't think of how I might possibly explain a dead deputy in my home. And, of course, then he put those handcuffs on me.

However, those were no longer behind my back and I could reach into my pocket quite easily while he was distracted with the sheriff.

It was the first time in my life that I fired a gun. Under the circumstances, it felt good.

SAM

I closed my eyes when the sheriff threw his shotgun away, thinking I was about to die. And at first, I thought I did. The sound was really loud and close by and made my ears hurt. Except I didn't feel anything. I remember thinking that if this is what it feels like to die, it's not so bad.

Then I remembered the fireworks and opened my eyes and saw Brisby laying on the ground right in front of me. At first, I figured the sheriff must have shot him somehow, but he was just standing there empty handed, looking behind me. So I turned to look too, and there was Mr. Hager holding a gun. It was smaller than the one the sheriff threw in the water. I recognized it right away, though. It was the only one I had ever seen before that night. Of course, I knew where he got it.

That's the last thing I can remember before I passed out.

MIGGS

I didn't know where Hager had gotten the gun or how he could have kept Brisby from finding it, but I was surely grateful that he had. At first.

After watching Brisby crumple to the ground, I looked back at Hager who was still holding it, except now it was pointed in my direction.

I gave a quick glance over at Brisby's .38 laying on the ground next to him. It didn't take much in the way of calculations to determine that Hager would have easily been able to shoot me before I could get to it.

The boy had passed out around then, leaving me to conclude also that there would be no witnesses if he chose to do so. He would probably be able to make a clean getaway, too, if he was quick about it. I wondered if that was to be my fate. To die at the hand of Yancey Hager, the most unlikely of men.

"I didn't kill him," he told me, pulling me out of that thought.

At first, I assumed that he was referring to the Fisher boy and was confused by the statement since he had only fired one shot.

"OK," was all I said. And all I could think of to say.

"It's important to me that everyone knows that," he added. That's when it occurred to me that he must have been talking about Mikey Vogel.

Seeing it as a chance to buy some more time, I told him that I might be able to help him with that if he let me.

He shook his head. "I don't want to go back to prison," he said. "You must know what happens to men like me in prison."

I did. I had heard a number of disturbing stories, and what I didn't know I could easily imagine. I told him that we could sort all that out, but that we should probably do it somewhere else.

He didn't respond. He just kept looking at me, the gun still aimed in my direction, and I tried to think of what else I could say to convince him not to use it a second time. That's when I noticed the blood on the leg of the boy's jeans.

"Was that from the shot I heard?" I asked, nodding in the boy's direction. Really, it wasn't part of any kind of plan or psychological play on my part. Again, I was only hoping to buy some time.

"No," he said, looking over at the boy. "He fell. It's a compound fracture. A bad one."

"He's going to need to get to a hospital then," I told him. "He must be in shock. That's why he passed out. He could die if he doesn't get treated soon." All of which was true, whether he chose to believe me or not.

I wasn't sure he heard me at first. He was still staring at the boy. There was something peculiar about his expression as he did. I'm not quite sure how to describe it. Guilt. Regret. Sorrow. Maybe a mixture of all three.

The moment seemed to go on for a long time, the only sound coming from the wind rustling the trees. Then he let out a deep and audible sigh that sounded almost like he was in pain. In retrospect, he may have been. Whether that was from what he had already done or what he was thinking of doing, I can't say. All I know is that I was more than a little relieved when he simply walked over and handed me the gun, with the grip extended toward me.

"You're doing the right thing," I managed to utter. But he ignored me and went over to check on the boy.

I went over to do the same with Brisby, picking up his flash-light and kneeling next to him to get a closer look at his wound.

The bullet had struck him in the back, and I could see that he was losing a lot of blood. I rolled him over and his eyes opened, telling me that he might still have a chance to survive. It would be slim, but possible, if help arrived soon. He didn't speak. Instead, his eyes went to the gun in my hand. Then he looked up at me. I knew what he was asking.

"No," I told him. "I won't make it that easy for you."

Hager came over then, and I was about to ask him what the hell happened to bring them all out there, when two state troopers entered the clearing and ordered me to drop my weapon.

HAGER

There are only two cells in the basement of the town hall. That's one of those things where you can live in a town forever and never have any idea. If you're lucky. Which I was not. I was placed in one of them that night. They removed a fellow from the other one right after they brought me in. He looked like a bit of a desperate character and reeked of alcohol and other odors I couldn't readily identify. He stared at me as one of the sheriff's men, one I didn't know, opened the door to let him out. The two cells are adjoining, with just bars in between, and I suppose they didn't want me talking to anyone. At least not before they could talk to me.

That opportunity came the next morning. The district attorney was sitting in that other cell, along with the sheriff and a court stenographer who was there to take down everything I said. The door to their cell was open. Mine was not. I knew that it wasn't likely to be for a long time.

They began by asking me if I wanted an attorney present and I said no. I told them I just wanted to get everything off my chest. They exchanged a look, and then the district attorney asked me if I understood that I would likely be going to prison and that my conviction would be based, in large part, upon what I was telling them. I told them that I understood that perfectly well and that they needn't worry that I might change my mind. The whole time the stenographer took down what we were saying on some sort of device with keys that sounded like a typewriter, only softer.

They started by asking me some basic questions, but I stopped them and told them I wanted to tell the story my way, from the start, otherwise I wouldn't say anything. I said that they could ask me any questions they wanted to after I was finished.

That seemed to satisfy them and so I told them the whole thing, or at least all the parts I knew. They appeared to accept most of what I said, other than the part about not knowing who those other people were who were out at that abandoned hobo camp, as I came to learn it was called. I told them that except for John and Brisby, I didn't know any of them. I said that I wasn't even sure about the deputy, but had to believe that he was among them, given his intention to kill me and the boy. Then I told them the story John gave me of why no one could know anyone else and how I later came to think that I had been set up when things went badly with the Vogel boy. I watched the sheriff and the district attorney exchange another look after I said that. The district attorney told me he wasn't sure he believed me.

"I'm the only one here, aren't I?" I said.

"Maybe you're protecting someone," the sheriff suggested.

"And what reason would I have for doing that?" I asked.

"I don't know," he said. "Why don't you tell me?"

"The only one I wanted to protect was that boy Sam," I told him. "I think I did that quite well, wouldn't you agree?"

He looked somewhat chastened and didn't answer. Instead, the district attorney asked me why I thought none of the others had come forward to confirm what I was telling them about John and the deputy. "Surely they can't all have been in favor of killing that boy."

I told him that since I didn't know who any of them were, I couldn't really answer his question. "But I imagine they might feel that they have something to lose," I added. "Even if they didn't want the boy dead."

"What're you talking about?" he asked.

"Do you really expect them to come in and be interrogated by you?" I asked back.

"If they didn't do anything wrong, they shouldn't have anything to worry about," he said.

"In a town like this?" I asked. "What do you think their lives would be like after that? Even if you didn't charge them with anything?"

Neither one replied. It was hard for me to believe that they hadn't thought that through.

"Do you really think they could just go back to their jobs like nothing ever happened?" I asked. "Attend church every Sunday? Volunteer over at the grade school? After everyone finds out what they were up to out there? Why do you think those two men killed that boy in the first place?"

They just looked at me without saying anything, as if it was the first time they had ever considered any of that. Meanwhile, the stenographer just sat there with her hands poised above the keys, staring straight ahead. I wondered if she understood it any better than they did.

The district attorney changed the subject then and asked how I got the boy in the pool.

"I was told that the gate in back would be unlocked," I said.

"And was it?" he asked.

I told him it was. He asked me who unlocked it.

I told him I didn't know. I just said that John had assured me that it would be unlocked when I got there and it was. I told them also that the pool area was empty and there were no lights on when I arrived. After placing the boy in the water and putting his clothes back in the locker room, as John had instructed, I left through the same unlocked gate and drove away without seeing anyone for several blocks.

They seemed awfully interested in the fact that it was my idea to put the boy in the pool. I told them my reasoning behind it, but I don't know whether they believed that either. Again, they just stared at me when I finished. Even the stenographer was staring at me then.

Since they seemed to have run out of questions for the moment, I asked them what I was going to be charged with. The DA seemed surprised by that. "What do you think you should be charged with?" he asked.

I laughed, even though there was nothing funny about the situation. "Stupidity," I told him.

Once again, they exchanged a look, as if they had never encountered anyone like me, which I am fairly certain they hadn't. "Well, there's nothing in the criminal code regarding that," the DA said. "But I'm quite certain we can come up with something to indict you for."

I assured him then that whatever it was, it would be a lesser charge and one that I would happily accept.

SAM

I had my own TV in the room at the hospital and there was a button on a thing attached to a wire that let me turn it on and off and change the channel right from the bed. They had to operate on my leg right after they brought me in, so I didn't get to watch anything until the next day. Still, it was pretty cool.

My mother and father were already at the hospital when they brought me in that night. I had woken up in the ambulance on the way there. My mother was pretty upset when she saw me and my father had a few choice words for the sheriff who came in along with the ambulance guys. The sheriff didn't say anything right away. He just let my father go on. Finally, when it looked like he might go too far, Mr. Pickens showed up and got a hold of him and took him away.

I got my chance to talk to the sheriff the next afternoon. I was still tired from the operation, but I was thinking OK. Mr. Pickens was there again, but the district attorney told him before we started that I wasn't going to be charged with anything. Mr. Pickens said he was still going to stay and listen. I was glad he did. Like I said, the sheriff was there too, but my mother made my father wait down in the cafeteria with her.

I told them everything I knew, starting from the beginning. Believe it or not, the hardest part was telling the sheriff about Kimberly. He didn't even flinch when I said it. You would have thought I was talking about some kid he didn't even know. In a way, maybe I was. I did make sure to tell him I didn't think of Kimberly that way and that I never was with her. He nodded, but he didn't smile or anything.

The district attorney asked me a ton of questions about when Mr. Hager killed that guy in the woods. I didn't know until right then that the guy was a state trooper. I was afraid that might make a difference, but Mr. Pickens told me later that it didn't and that he'd "bet the ranch" that Mr. Hager wouldn't be charged with killing him. Especially if Keith and Richie and Kimberly all said the same stuff as me. It was still self-defense, he said. Just like we thought.

They asked me a lot about who else I saw the night I saw Mikey out at the old hobo camp. I told them that I couldn't tell who any of them were and that I was pretty sure Mikey couldn't have either. They asked if I heard any voices and I said maybe, but that I couldn't be sure. Besides, I told them, I took off running almost as soon as I saw what they were up to.

The thing they were most interested in was why I didn't come forward right away. I went through the whole thing about not knowing who killed Mikey and being scared that they might do the same to me. I think they understood. If they didn't, there wasn't anything they could do about it. I didn't say anything about being pissed at my father. I thought that was a private thing, between me and him, and so I didn't see the point.

The doctor came in around then and said I was probably pretty tired, which was true. The sheriff and the district attorney thanked me and said they might have some more questions for me later. Mr. Pickens told them to contact him first if they did. They said they would.

Before they left, I asked them what was going to happen to Mr. Hager. The sheriff told me that he would be going to prison for awhile. I told him that I hoped he wouldn't have to be in there for too long. He looked surprised that I said that and asked me why I felt that way. I told him what Mr. Hager said to me out at the clearing about putting Mikey in the pool so that his family wouldn't have to worry about him being missing and not knowing where his body was. Like with me not coming forward right away, it might have been the wrong thing to do, but in the end it worked out alright. If either of us did anything different, then Mr. Hager would probably be dead and no one would know who really killed Mikey.

They all stared at me. Even Mr. Pickens. I don't know why. I mean, it was true.

Richie and Keith came by to see me later that same night after dinner. They said they both had to go down to the station and talk to the sheriff and the district attorney earlier that day. Richie's father was pretty pissed about it, but Richie said the sheriff warned his father not to lay a glove on him. He told him he would know if he did and that he'd make him pay. Richie said he wasn't ready to start liking the sheriff or anything, but he was coming around a little.

Keith said he told the sheriff everything that happened, including how we lied to him after the meeting at the town hall that night. He told him that the guy we saw Mr. Hager stab out in the woods on Saturday was the same guy who was with him at the Custard Cup. The sheriff told him he already figured that out. I guess that would make sense.

They asked me how long I was going to be in the hospital, and I told them I wasn't sure but that the doctor said I was going to miss at least a month of school. They said that sounded pretty cool. I told them yeah, but that my mother wasn't too thrilled. She said she wanted them to come by the house every day to cheer me up and drop off my homework.

They both looked at me funny, like I had amnesia or something. "How are we supposed to do that?" Keith asked. "We don't go to that school."

So I told them the big news. I wasn't either. My father had changed his mind. He didn't want to at first, but my mother told him that this was how it was going to be and that he wasn't going to get his way on this one. It was a minor miracle. Richie and Keith started shouting and jumping around then and one of the nurses came in and told them to shut up and made them leave before they woke up the whole ward.

Before they did, Richie gave me a letter Sylvia asked him to give to me. It was in an envelope and sealed and he promised that he didn't steam it open and read it. It's funny he said that because it looked like that was exactly what he did. It was such a Richie thing to do, but I didn't care. I just wanted them to go so I could see what it said.

She said she wanted to come see me but her parents wouldn't let her. She told them the whole story about how we were going out to the old hobo camp that night and how Mikey ended up there. They weren't too happy about that and forbid her from ever seeing me again. She told me again that she didn't blame me and hoped they would get over it in time. I didn't really think they would, but I was happy she said it. She also said she hoped we could stay in touch while I was away at that school. She didn't know that I would be back at the junior high once my leg healed. It was going to be weird to see her again after all that went on, but I've already decided that we can still be friends and maybe someday it will all work out. I hope so anyway.

Later that night, after everyone was gone, another doctor came in to see me. I hadn't seen him before and he didn't want to look at my leg. He said he just wanted to talk. I told him I was pretty sick of talking and he said he understood, but that he'd be available if I ever changed my mind. He said that in the mean time it looked like I would be spending a lot of time in bed with nothing to do and maybe I should think about writing down everything that happened to me in the last three weeks. He said it might be a good way to sort things out. I told him that sounded too much like home-work. He laughed and said that nobody would be grading it and that I should give it a try. I said maybe and then he just gave me a pat on the back and left.

The next morning, the nurse came in and gave me a huge thing of paper and some pencils that the doctor left for me the night before. I didn't touch them for the rest of the time I was in the hospital, but I did bring them home with me, just in case.

It turned out he was right. I did get bored, so the other day I started to do what he said. It wasn't as hard as I thought it would be. It all just kind of poured out once I got going. And I do think it's helped a little. I still have bad dreams some nights, but the doc-tor told me they should go away over time. I sure hope he's right about that, too.

Anyway, what you have just read is what I wrote and as much as I know.

MIGGS

Brisby died in the ambulance on the way to the hospital, which certainly made things more complicated. I suppose it doesn't really matter in the end, but I'm still bothered by not knowing who actually drowned the boy. Even though both of the likely killers are dead, I would have liked to have known, if only for my own conscience. That Brisby could work for me as long as he did and keep the kind of secrets he kept makes me wonder how many other people in town I really don't know.

I feel particularly bad for Brisby's family. I'm told that his wife is moving back to Rochester to be near her parents and get the children as far away from this mess as she can. Unfortunately, I don't think they'll ever be able to go far enough, but I don't blame her for trying.

Yancey Hager was surprisingly helpful in providing us with the details of what happened, at least as much as he claimed to know. He insisted that he didn't kill the boy or know that he was going to be killed, and I have to say that he was pretty convincing on that. He admitted that he didn't know exactly what happened with Mikey and Irwin and Brisby, but he had his theory. He told us that he believes that Irwin had arranged for Brisby to pick up Mikey somewhere away from the pool that afternoon. He believes that Irwin then had Brisby bring him back out to the old hobo camp. Once they got him there, he believes that one of them drowned him in the stream. Maybe both. He said Irwin never told him who actually did it. I still don't know if I believe him completely, but it does seem to fit the evidence.

I asked Hager why Brisby and Irwin would wait a day to kill Mikey when they could have done so the night before when he first appeared out there. He felt that perhaps they didn't want to do anything in front of all those other people, figuring the less they knew the better. He said they might have also been afraid that the boy could have told someone where he was going that night. He said they probably figured that if no one came out there to look around that night, then their secret was safe. They simply made sure of it the next day. I wondered aloud why they would trust the boy not to say anything. Hager said that Irwin could be quite persuasive and must have felt that he could convince the boy to keep quiet for one night. He thought they may have offered him money. They may have even told him that the police needed his help to solve a crime. Given Brisby's involvement, the latter sounded like a pretty plausible theory and would certainly explain why the boy never said anything to anyone.

Hager insisted that he only became involved when he received a call from Irwin asking him to meet him out at that camp the night the boy was drowned. He claimed he wasn't told why and that it was only when he got there that he learned that the boy had been killed. He said Irwin told him that as the newest member of their group, it was his responsibility to dispose of the body. Hager believed that Irwin set him up as the killer from the start. Given what I came to learn later, that made some sense as well.

Hager said that when he arrived out there, Irwin was alone and the boy's body was already wrapped in a blanket. I asked him what he knew about the sneaker Vic found out there later. He said that when he put the boy in the trunk of his car, he noticed that he only had one shoe. He thought the other must have fallen while he was carrying the body back to the car. After he put the boy in the pool, he said he put the only shoe he had in the locker room, along with his other clothes, where we found them that night. We never released any information about finding the clothes or the other shoe in the locker room, except to the family, so that part of his story seemed to hold up also.

The day after we talked to him I sent the coroner out to the old hobo camp to take some water samples to compare to what he found in Mikey's lungs. He confirmed to me later that the organisms he discovered in those samples were "absolutely consistent" with those that he found in the autopsy, so it seems that part of Hager's statement holds up, too.

Hager's role in the whole affair remains the most perplexing part of the case to me and will probably continue to haunt me for a long time. He readily admitted to putting the boy in the pool and having taken part in those activities out in that clearing on two occasions. However, he could have just as easily clammed up, and we probably would have had a very difficult time proving that he had anything to do with killing Mikey. In the end, if you took away everything he said to us and the Fisher boy, all we'd be left with was a mask, a burnt suitcase and an intoxicated Cyrus Robbins saying that he saw Hager driving Irwin's car into the school lot. And the latter was only evidence that Hager might have killed Irwin, not the boy.

The day after our fateful night out at the hobo camp, the front page of the local paper featured a photograph of me carrying the Fisher boy out of the woods behind West Main Street. Someone must have notified the press that night or maybe they heard something on the scanner. Fritz tells me I'm lucky they did. He says that photo alone ought to assure my re-election. He's probably right, but I'm not sure I deserve it.

Both that photo and the accompanying story were picked up by the UPI and appeared in a number of newspapers across the state, as well as others up and down the eastern seaboard. That got the attention of both the governor and the attorney general down in Albany, with both of them putting pressure on Fritz to obtain a murder indictment against Hager for killing the Vogel boy. With Irwin and Brisby both dead, I guess they wanted someone's scalp.

As always, though, Fritz went his own way. Citing the lack of evidence against Hager and the muddy waters created by the disturbing behavior of those two law enforcement officers, for which there was plenty of proof, he refused.

In the end, based almost entirely upon him admitting to putting the boy in the pool, Hager agreed to accept the DA's offer to enter a guilty plea to accessory after the fact, putting the matter to rest, much to the consternation of those two politicians down in Albany.

I've thought a great deal about what Hager said about why none of the other participants have come forward, and I think he may be right. Their lives would become hell. As soon as one came forward, the others would be exposed. They'd all be ostracized then and the town likely divided. Even those who had no interest in the boy being killed would forever be suspected. I imagine that Irwin and Brisby weren't the only ones in favor of making sure the Vogel boy kept quiet, but from what we can conclude, those two were the only ones who had acted on it. Wanting someone dead and killing them are two different things. Besides, I would guess that they'll all suffer every bit as much as Yancey Hager, only not behind bars. So maybe it's best we don't ever find out who they are and just let sleeping dogs lie. That's not easy for me to say as sheriff, but there it is.

I have to admit that I've spent a lot of time looking at people and wondering if they might have been part of that group out there. Anytime anyone avoids eye contact with me, I can't help but suspect them. It's certainly not enough to formally question them, but I do wonder. So far, no one has incriminated themselves. Donna Wisnewski has come closest. She resigned her position at the pool and announced that she's moving out to Las Vegas. I thought that was odd, especially considering the timing of it. I visited her the day after we talked to Hager and asked if there was any chance that she had left the gate open at the pool the night Mikey was found. She looked surprised that I would ask such a thing and swore she didn't. I'm still not sure whether I believe her. I asked her who else had a key besides her, and she said that there was only one other one that she knew of and that the town parks department had it. I went back to town hall afterward and found it in the top drawer of the only desk in their office. Since the parks department is empty on most days and the door to their office is almost always open between nine and five, anyone could have walked in and gotten it and returned it the next day without being seen, Brisby being right at the top of that list. I sent the key down to the state crime lab to test for fingerprints, but it came back inconclusive. I guess we'll never really know about Donna's possible involvement, unless she decides to confess someday, and I'm not holding my breath on that.

I'd be less than honest if I didn't admit that my relationship with my daughter has suffered some in the wake of all this. I'm far less concerned about her activities with those boys prior to Mikey's death. She probably didn't do anything that I didn't do at the same age. I was far more hurt that she felt that she couldn't come to me after seeing those people out at that abandoned camp, and even more troubled that she didn't tell me what happened with Hager and Irwin out in the woods that other night. Her mother tells me to let the dust settle and give her some time to process what happened. She reminds me that she's only thirteen and predicts that eventually our relationship will become even stronger than it was before this all happened. I hope she's right.

Not surprisingly, given my previous history, I've spent many sleepless nights wondering if I made a mistake by not calling in the state police right away. Would the killers have been found any sooner? Would anything have changed? In the end, just like with

Hager and the Fisher boy, my decision may have been wrong, but it seems to have worked out for the best. I've spent the last seven years of my life thinking that wrong is always wrong. I still believe that, but it would be foolish to dismiss the notion that there may be other forces at work that might make such an absolute not so easy to cling to.

I can't help but feel also that my survival means that I am supposed to learn some lesson from all this, although I've struggled to figure out what that is. I've always strived to be a decent man and a good husband and father, and to be fair and just while still doing my job. That hasn't changed any. About the only thing I've come to realize is that we're all flawed and have to pay for our sins in some fashion. And that maybe, if we're lucky and decent enough, time and circumstances might allow us to repair some of the damage we've done. I hope that I might have been so fortunate, but only time and the next election will tell.

I have never lived anywhere else, so I don't know what it's like to live in a big city where things like this probably go on all the time. I think that in a place this small, the bad often seems worse and the good often better than it truly is. I also think that the reality of everyone living practically on top of one another can have a positive effect to go along with the negative. I suppose that only makes sense. Why else would we choose to live here? I've always told my wife that I hoped that our kids would get a good education so that they can move somewhere else and have a better life than ours. You'd think after all this, I'd feel even more strongly that way, but I'm not so sure anymore.

I asked Fritz the other day if I needed to make out some sort of report about the case, even though Hager was going to plead guilty. He said he heard from someone down in Albany that they might convene a judicial inquest to examine all aspects of the investigation, seeing as there isn't ever going to be a trial. I guess they're still looking for that scalp. In any event, he said I would no doubt be called as a witness and that it might be a good idea to put my thoughts down in writing while they're still fresh. Even if the inquest never takes place, he said, it might help bring me some peace of mind. As always with Fritz, I thought that was pretty good advice, so here it is, in my own words.

Whether I ever manage to find that peace remains one of the many questions this case leaves behind.

HAGER

The sheriff came to see me again two days after I spoke with him and the district attorney. He was alone this time and wanted to know if I had anything else I wanted to tell him. I told him that I had already given them everything I knew. He then pulled up a chair and sat down across from me. I was thinking that perhaps he was going to ask me some more questions anyway, but he just sat there for awhile, staring.

"What's on your mind?" I asked finally.

He took a piece of paper out of a folder he had been carrying with him and handed it to me between the bars. I felt my face flush. He must have seen.

It was a criminal record with the name prominently displayed at the top, but the picture was missing. The name almost looked foreign to me, since I hadn't used it in so long. "Is that you?" he asked, indicating the name I was staring at.

I nodded. I didn't see the point in denying it any more. Not from where I was sitting. "That incident did not involve a child," I told him. "The boy was seventeen. I was twenty one."

"I know," the sheriff said. "I spoke with the detective yesterday."

I handed him the paper back through the bars. "I would never harm a child," I told him.

"No," he said. "I don't believe you would. But you were right."

"About what?" I asked.

He then explained that John had given him that report a couple of weeks after the Vogel boy was killed. He believed that John had indeed arranged it so that I would be blamed for the boy's death. After I was dead, of course. He would later claim to have found the photo and would bring it to him to wrap things up. I guess John had been able to discover my real identity based on certain things I had told him about my past.

"He was going to bury me out in those woods, though," I reminded him.

"I think he probably felt it would be better if we were looking for you somewhere, rather than to have a dead body to examine. Making a murder look like a suicide isn't easy. If he failed, it would only keep the matter open longer."

I nodded. That sounded like John. He was thorough that way.

"So why here?" he asked me.

"This cell?" I asked, confused by his question.

He said no, the town. He wanted to know why I had chosen to settle here with my new identity.

I told him that it seemed like a fine place to make a life.

"For someone like you?" he asked.

Now I would be lying if I said that question didn't hurt my feelings. I didn't tell him that, of course. Instead, I told him that I probably enjoyed some of the very same things that made him choose to settle here. He nodded, although he hardly looked convinced.

He then asked me some specifics about what we were doing out in that clearing on those two nights. I'm afraid I disappointed him when I refused to go into any great detail. I thought that might end that line of questioning, but it didn't.

"Did you actually enjoy it?" he wanted to know. It didn't sound like he was asking as sheriff, and I was surprised by that.

"At the time I thought so," I told him.

"Not so much now?" he asked.

"It all seems rather foolish, looking back on it," I admitted.

"I suppose that's the lesson," he said.

I didn't reply to that. Instead, I asked him if he had ever strayed outside his marriage. It was rather bold of me, I admit, and I would not have been surprised if he had stormed out.

Surprisingly, he didn't react badly at all. He said that he had been faithful to his wife for their entire marriage. "That doesn't mean I haven't had thoughts," he added.

"Thoughts rarely have consequences," I told him. "It's only our actions we have to pay for."

He said he couldn't argue with that. He then asked me about John, "Irwin" as he called him, and whether he had the same "predilections" as me. I was frank with him and said that he most certainly did, along with some others I didn't share.

"Brisby too?" he asked.

I told him I was less certain about him, since I couldn't be sure that he was even out there, although I had to believe he had been part of the group. I added that even if I had known he was there, I couldn't quite tell who was partnering with who. He didn't press me any further on it. I'm not sure he really wanted to know.

I then asked him about that boy Sam and whether he was doing alright. He told me that he was fine and recovering at the hospital and would be home soon, although he was going to have to miss the start of school. I told him I was sorry about that. He told me that the boy had insisted that I had saved his life and wanted him to be sure to thank me.

I told him that I wished I could have done the same for the other boy.

"So do I," he said.

He then stood up and moved the chair back to where it was. I thought that meant our conversation was over, but he turned back around and fixed his gaze upon me.

"I suppose I owe you some thanks as well," he said.

I imagine he was talking about my saving his life too, although I sensed that there may have been something more to his statement than a simple thanks. However, he didn't elaborate, so I didn't ask. I have come to believe that Daryl Miggs is the kind of man who has trouble expressing his feelings, even after something as life-altering as we all went through. "You're welcome," is all I said, sparing him once more.

He told me then that they would be transferring me to the county facility in a couple of days, as soon as some space opened up over there. He asked if there was anything he could get me before they did.

After giving it some thought, I told him there were two things. The first was a notebook with a lot of blank pages and a couple of pens. He told me that it was no problem and that he would have them for me in the morning. I think he knew that this was what I was intending and perhaps that was why he said yes so readily. Maybe he was hoping to read it someday. If so, I hope he does.

The second thing was a change of clothes from home. I specified the pants and shirt I wanted and, once again, he said that was acceptable and that he would go over to my apartment to get them himself. True to his word, he delivered them the next morning, along with the notebook and pens.

I said at the start of this that Sheriff Daryl Miggs is no fool, and yet he never questioned why I would refuse an attorney and confess as freely as I did. Then again, he may have been even smarter than I've given him credit for. Perhaps he knew that the built-in belt in those trousers would come out easily and prove more than adequate for the job. I know he refused Brisby's request to end his suffering out at the clearing that night, but perhaps he wanted to honor mine and I offered him a way to do so without looking like anything more than an innocent mistake on his part. If that's the case, I'm glad he did.

My only regret is that I'll never know what it would have been like to live out my life in this town until my heart gave out or the cancer found me. It would have been nice to see what that boy Sam might become. Perhaps a doctor. Or a lawyer. Someone important. With a life he could be proud of. We might have even become friends. I might have had dinner with him and his family every Christmas. Perhaps I would have sat with them at the band concerts each summer, sharing some popcorn and lemon ice while we took in the music and watched the children chase fireflies.

I think I would have liked that. I think I would have liked that very much.

READING GROUP GUIDE

Questions and topics for discussion

1. How might the story have changed had this taken place in the present day?

2. How might the story have changed had the people at the old hobo camp not been wearing masks?

3. What do you think about Sam's decision not to tell his parents what he witnessed?

4. Do you agree with Sam and the sheriff that doing the "wrong thing" can some times turn out to be the right thing?

5. Do you agree with the sheriff's assessment of why the others who were out at the old hobo camp refused to come forward at the end?

6. Is there a true hero in the story? If so, who is it?

7. Is there a true villain in the story? If so, who is it?

8. What themes do you see expressed in the book?

9. Who do you think knocked on Hager's door on that Sunday morning?

10. Do you think the pool director was one of the group out at the old hobo camp? How about any of the other characters?

11. Do you think justice prevailed in the end?

12. Who do you think killed Mikey Vogel?

ACKNOWLEDGEMENTS

The author would like to thank the following: Gary Tanguay for his keen eye, strong story sense and unfailing support; Kris Meyer for his early read and input; Barbara Hansberry and her reading group in Watertown, Mass. for the "grand experiment"; Chris Castellani of Grub Street for patiently answering my numerous questions; Kate Flora for a terrific edit; John Clark for his professional read; and, especially, all the past and present residents of my hometown where it was my privilege to grow up.

Finally, to Suzanne and Meghan, without whom none of this would have been possible.

ABOUT THE AUTHOR

Drew Yanno grew up in upstate New York and practiced law in Boston before turning to screenwriting and later founding the screenwriting program at Boston College where he taught for eleven years. This is his first novel.

31530402R00201

Made in the USA
Lexington, KY
15 April 2014